FATALISM

a Life. Destiny. Fate. *novel*

The story of Alexa and Vincent.

LK COLLINS

ISBN: 978-0-578-12772-9

Table of Contents

Dedication

To my amazing husband William.
Thank you for pushing me, believing in me, encouraging me, and
never doubting my abilities.

Prologue

Vincent

It had been five days since I saw her. Five grueling, excruciating days, since I held her in my arms. She was like no other woman I'd ever experienced. As I closed my eyes, I could still picture her face; it was perfect and flawless. Thankfully my memory easily took me back to that night; I was reminded of her sweet lips and how they tasted like heaven. What'd I do to have another feel of them. Simply thinking about her made my dick twitch. I guess I really had no one to blame except for myself. I shouldn't have let go. I should've kept her in my arms and pulled my head out of my motherfucking ass before it was too late. Now here I laid, with images of her green eyes flooding my memory; again, it kept me awake. Although I suffered from insomnia, I could normally manage at least a few hours a night. That all changed merely a week ago.

I decided to drag my ass away from my computer

and take a swim. As I walked through the kitchen on my way out back, the clock on the stove read 3:13am. *Fuck, it was late.* I stripped naked and dove in. Thankfully, none of my neighbors lived close enough to see into my backyard. That's one of the reasons I bought this house. Privacy was important to me and I needed it.

Swimming was a great release and a way to clear my mind. I indulged, searching for a little clarity. As I swam lap, after lap, after lap, all I could think about was her – Alexa. What a name, so unique and different. I wondered if she liked to be called Lex. I'd call her what ever she wanted as long as I could hear my name come out of those lips in return. *Focus, fucker! Swim.* I changed my positioning and began doing the back stroke. Staring up at the stars was surreal. They were something else tonight, so bright and fiery, but nothing took my mind off of her. After exhausting myself, I finally felt a bit tired. I wasn't sure if it was from the swim or if my mind was breaking down. Regardless, I hopped out of the pool and grabbed a towel, drying myself off and then contemplating going to bed. Thoughts of sleeping alone depressed me. *God dammit I wanted her.* I settled on relaxing outside on one of my plush lounge chairs. I'm not even sure if these things should've been considered patio furniture due to their comfort. As I laid back, my erection slapped my stomach. I was hard a lot lately more so now than ever. I'd become used to it, I guess. I tried to close my eyes and think of something non sexual, but who was I kidding. I'm a man and a dirty one at that. As soon as my eyes closed, I was rewarded with my Lex. I clutched my cock, gripping hard at the base and working my hand over my length. Mentally, I went back to that night. Her smile, so shy and self conscious, yet she was wickedly appealing. Beauty radiated from her and those eyes, the greenest I'd ever seen. As I worked my shaft, I remembered slamming her against the wall. She smiled when I did it and kissed me like a maniac. I should've taken her into the bathroom and fucked her against the wall. Made her scream my name until she lost it. But a girl like Alexa deserves better. She needs to be loved and cherished. I could do that if I was given that chance. I'd still spank her, but I have a feeling she would want it. *Hmm…Oh fuck!* Thinking about her like that, got me so close. I jerked myself and could've come at any moment, but I was enjoying this. I was so close to her again. Maybe one day, fate would intervene and cross our paths. The thought of ever seeing her in person again, hit me hard and I exploded. As I came, I moaned and grunted letting out a violent blow. As the trembles in my body stopped, I threw my towel off of me and rested my arms behind my head. Regardless of how shitty the situation was, I still had the memory of her and the kisses we shared. No one could *ever* take that away from me.

Chapter 1

Birthday

As I drove home after work, the sun was setting on the skyline of the Rocky Mountains. I loved the weather this time of year, especially because I could put the top down on my car and just drive. It was still eighty degrees outside at almost six o'clock at night. The warm evenings were few and far between with Colorado's erratic weather, but I enjoyed them while they were here.

Normally I dreaded the highway traffic congestion, but I didn't mind it tonight as I needed some alone time to unwind. I was a senior paralegal at Smith and Brown; having worked for years to move my way up from being a peon to doing my dream job. Finally I was there, working hard every day and loving it.

I turned up the song playing through my sound system. Gotye was singing 'Somebody That I Used To Know'. I threw on my sunglasses and rested my arm on the open window. I was excited to get home and hang out with my roommate, Cara. Some take-out and relaxing was definitely in order.

With the weekend ahead, there was no work, alarm clock, or attorneys to answer to. I pulled off the highway and took the exit towards our condo. I turned into Tipsy's, the local liquor store, to grab a bottle of wine. Sadly, I was a regular there.

Jay, the skinny emo kid behind the counter, was playing a video game.

"Hey, Alexa," he said without taking his eyes off the game.

"Hi, Jay. Did you get my Riesling in?"

"Yup, it's on the bottom shelf. If anyone asks, I tell them we are all sold out."

I laughed to myself. He was sweet. "Ah thanks, Jay. But really, if you run out again, it'll probably be better for me."

Jay finally took his eyes off the game as I walked around to the cooler.

"What are you talking about?"

I looked at him with a small smile on my face. "I just meant the extra calories."

Jay laughed and rolled his eyes. I grabbed a six-pack of beer for Cara and three bottles of lime juice to go with it. That girl would drink any beer as long as it was half lime juice. She smuggled those little bottles into wherever she was drinking to ensure her beer tasted disgusting.

I paid Jay, deciding to ignore his earlier laugh; I

really didn't feel like probing into what he meant. I knew I wasn't overweight, but I wasn't in the best of shape of my life. My mother always told me I needed to keep an eye on my weight if I ever wanted to find a man that would stick around longer than my father had.

I brushed aside the horrid thoughts and pulled into the gated community where our Tuscan-style condo laid nestled in the heart of the Cherry Creek District, a suburb outside of Denver. There's so much to do around the condo, and with Colorado's beautiful weather, we have over three hundred days of sunshine a year. Most days, when I ventured out, I would walk. I loved to shop the little boutiques that lined First Avenue. The grocery store and Starbucks were around the corner as well as one of the best shopping malls around.

My Grandfather came across the condo a few years back and purchased it as a rental property. Tenants were in and out as the years passed. Unfortunately he recently passed away, but being the generous soul he was, he left it to me. He knew I'd loved the condo since the day he bought it.

I unlocked the front door and yelled for Cara; normally, she was lounging on the couch watching TV or playing on with her iPad. Cara was a nurse and worked earlier than me, which usually ensured she made it home first.

I set my bags on the counter, put the alcohol in the fridge, and grabbed us two beers, squeezing lime juice in

Cara's before making my way up the stairs to the second floor.

I could hear Cara's music as I approached her room. No wonder she didn't hear me yell when I came in. I opened the door to her modern all-white room. This was her zen; a place where she could relax and unwind away from the hospital.

Cara was in her closet and I plopped down on her bed. I took a drink of my beer as I sat hers on the nightstand. *Yuck. Why didn't I just open my wine?* Cara came out of her closet holding two tiny dresses, one in silver and one in teal.

She saw me and smiled, "Hey, I didn't hear you come in."

"Maybe it's because you have that God awful music on so loud."

She laughed, "It's not God awful Alexa, it's vintage Madonna."

"Mmm-kay, whatever you say. Here, I got you your favorite and put lime juice in it. Wanna cheers?"

I handed her the beer and could see the confusion on her face.

"Cheers to what?"

I smirked at her. "Hmm, how 'bout a relaxing weekend?"

Cara laughed at me, and I glared at her. Finally stopping, she looked at me again with a serious expression.

"Relaxing? Really Lex? If that's what you want to call tomorrow, because after tonight, all you'll be doing is nursing your hangover and sleeping till Monday."

What was she talking about?

"Oh my God. Don't tell me you forgot?"

Now who had the confused look on their face?

"Forgot about what? And will you please stop saying 'oh my God,' like you're from the South?"

"Alexa Lauren Schaefer! Do not tell me you forgot about Bridgette's birthday party tonight!"

Sonofabitch!

I did forget. How could I have forgotten my own sister's birthday?

"Shit, I didn't even call her today. I don't have a gift or anything."

Cara sat next to me and said, "Don't worry. I sent her flowers from both of us."

Cara always had my back no matter what. That was one of the things I loved about her, that and her brutal honesty.

"Come on Lex, it'll be okay. We'll go to dinner and celebrate, she'll never know about this."

I gave her a small smile.

"Don't stress, okay? Now, will you please help me pick a dress and then go get yourself ready? Like, really fast?"

I couldn't help but laugh at her sudden subject change. How had I gotten so lucky to find a friend like her? She had been there for me through so much. She was there when I stopped talking to Vivian, my mother, and when my grandfather passed. I couldn't have made it through those times without her. I looked over at her flawless complexion, long blonde hair, and aqua eyes. I couldn't help the tears of gratitude that overcame me when I thought of her.

"Oh no, Lex. Please don't cry. I told you Bridgette doesn't even know."

"I know, thank you. I love you, I mean I really love you. I'm so lucky you're my best friend. I don't mean to get upset, but I always feel like I've failed Bridgette."

Cara pulled me into a hug, embracing me for a few moments. "You're a great sister, stop being so hard on yourself. You always do this, and there is no reason for it."

She always made me smile, and had a way of making me feel better. "Thank you," I said as I got off of the bed.

"You better?" Cara asked.

I nodded my head and she grabbed both dresses. "What dress? Silver or teal?"

"Teal, definitely teal. With your eyes, that'll make the guys go crazy."

I walked downstairs to my room, which was on the main floor. I grabbed my cell phone on the way and checked it. I had a missed text from Bridgette.

Haven't seen you in forever. I'm so ready to get to party for my birthday. Love you.

Quickly I texted her back.

I can't wait. Just finishing up getting ready now.

I ran into my bathroom and stared at my reflection in the mirror. My skin was blotchy and my green eyes were red from crying. *Crap. Okay, this was not going to work.* I put on as much powder as I could and added a clean line of eyeliner.

One thing about me getting ready was I could improvise well, and I could do so quickly. I put on more mascara and a thick coating of nude lip-gloss. I pulled my chocolate brown hair over to one shoulder and did my best to tame it all together, then I braided it down my right shoulder.

There that was better.

I walked into my massive closet. I loved to shop, for shoes and purses, but clothes, not so much. I didn't like the way anything seemed to fit. Tonight, I knew I was going to wear something dark, not only to match my eyeliner, but to make myself feel more comfortable with my body. I searched feverously through my clothes; they all seemed so bland, I needed to add color. I found a pair of gold high-waisted shorts and a long, black lacey tank. I put the clothes on with a pair of gold and black wedge sandals; I grabbed my black clutch and popped my cell phone and lip-gloss into it.

As I glanced at my reflection in the full-length mirror, I stopped and noticed how good I looked. Yes, I was a little curvy, but this outfit complimented my features. The wide cuffed shorts and wedge shoes made my legs look long and lean, not to mention the long black lacey tank elongated my torso.

I needed to remind myself of that more often; I was beautiful, no matter what my mother had said about me. I grabbed my I.D. and cash from my wallet and put them into my clutch.

Cara came down the stairs in that teal piece of fabric she called a dress. Her long legs, nude peep toe patent leather pumps, and messy hair made her look like a rock star. I mean, the girlfriend of a rock star.

"Damn, you look amazing. I don't think you'll be paying for a drink all night."

She twirled around. "Right back at cha, friend. You look sexy as hell."

"Thanks. That was the look I was going for."

Chapter 2

Vincent

We hopped from bar to bar, paying ridiculous amounts of money each time for cover. We were wandering around, looking for our next spot to hit, when I spotted a place called 9th Door. I'd heard some of the people at work talking about it and thought what the hell, it's gotta be better than the places we've been.

The night started out exciting, with my sister getting spanked at this random piano bar and since then, things went downhill from there. The last place we were at was called Wicked Garden. It was in an underground basement with stripper poles for the patrons, hardcore rap music, and far too many people than safe for fire code.

"Hey, girls. Let's check this place out," I said and batted my lashes. Cara laughed at me, I guess because I was definitely feeling a bit tipsy. Bridgette grabbed my arm and stumbled a step. She was well on her way to being wasted. "Sure thing, sis, but you're buying since I never get to see you."

I loved my sister, I really did, but spending time with her was hard. My job had become my life and was one of the only places I felt at peace. Burying myself in my work was a release. Hanging out with Bridgette brought up a lot of the past issues from our childhood, as well as the fact that I hadn't spoken to our mother in three years. Plus, Bridgette went to school in Fort Collins, which is almost two hours away. That made it difficult to see one another.

As kids we were so close, especially after my father left. I remember the morning he walked out, I was eight and Bridgette was two. After that, Vivian was there, if that's what you could call it, but she struggled with depression and therefore left Bridgette and I to fend for ourselves most of the time. The best memories I have are from the summers we spent with our grandparents.

"This place is beautiful," Riley said as we walked into 9th Door.

The décor was modern, warm, and all different shades of red. To the right was a long row of plush red booths that lined the wall with a view of the dance floor. To the left was a long bar. The floors were a dark wood and red curtains hung throughout. The music was eclectic and funky, which I totally loved.

"Let's order some drinks and grab a table. I heard they have the best Sangrias here," I said.

I'd danced so much I felt like my feet were going to fall off. I yelled to Cara, who was dancing with her typical tattoo-covered douche bag.

"I'm going to take a break and grab a drink. You need anything?"

She smiled from ear to ear and pointed at herself. "Who me? Need anything? Nah, I'm good."

I laughed and made my way out the front door. I needed to sit, and fast. I found a bench right out the front doors. I pulled out my cell phone and checked my texts. There were no new messages.

I could see the girls inside the open walls of the club. They all looked so happy and carefree. I wished that could be me, I wanted to just let go and have fun with no stress. I did love to let go as long as I had a few drinks in me. The liquid courage made the bar scene tolerable. I rested my head on the rough wooden bench looking up into the clear night sky. *Jesus, the stars were bright tonight.*

After to much time outside I went back in. The girls were still on the dance floor I smiled at their silliness as I headed to the bathroom.

Just as I rounded the corner I rolled my ankle. *Damn shoes.* I was about to fall to the floor before a pair of large hands caught me. I yelped in surprise when his hands kept me steady from falling.

I looked up into his eyes. "Shit, I'm so sorry. I…I don't know what happened, but this…I'll never wear these shoes again."

He smirked down at me with a smile spread across his face. As soon as our eyes connected I was lost. He had the brightest hazel I'd ever seen. The world around me began to spin as I stood paralyzed in his hold, under his gaze.

"Don't be sorry," he said in a deep seductive voice. "I'm glad I caught you. Are you all right?"

I nodded my head. "Yeah...I'm...I'm fine. Just a little tired from dancing."

I looked down at his hands as he still held onto me and ran his fingers down the backs of my arms. I shivered with pleasure.

Hmm, that felt good!

I smiled and squeezed past him. What was I doing? I didn't let men touch me in public regardless of how good it felt. I was a one-night stand girl. No PDA, it was something I didn't do. Once I was in the bathroom and a safe distance away from that smile, his piercing eyes, and those strong hands, I braced myself on the sink. *What was happening to me?* I stood there in a strangers arms feeling completely awestruck. I'm sure he thought there was something wrong with me. I barely spoke and when I did, I stuttered. I took way to much time before I left the stall. As I washed my hands, I told myself to pull it together. My reflection stared back at me, with flushed cheeks and messy hair. *Damn I need a drink.* I walked out of the bathroom on a mission, but was immediately stopped. He was there. His back was to me as he glanced down at his blackberry. The bright light illuminated his face, damn it he was perfect.

He was tall, so tall. His hair was dark brown, almost black; it was longer on top and cut close around the sides. He wore it in a disheveled mess, and I itched to run my fingers through it. His jeans were dark and hugged his perfect ass. As my eyes traveled up his body, a gray button up dress shirt with the sleeves rolled up, topped him off. His clothing made me imagine myself removing it with my teeth.

What was going on with me? I didn't let men control my thoughts. I forced myself to start walking, but he must have sensed I was behind him. The instant I started to move, he turned around. He smiled at me and *again* I lost my words.

"Glad to see you made it out okay. I was getting worried. Thought maybe I'd have to send in a search party."

I looked down at the floor and shook my head.

Pull your shit together, Alexa!

I took in a deep breath before meeting his stare.

"No search party required. I…Uh. I needed to rest my feet. I'm surprised to see you still out here. I'm sure you have other things you'd rather be doing with your time."

He stepped closer to me and was mere inches away from my face. His sweet breath washed over my skin. *God, he smells good.*

"How would you know what I'd rather be doing with my time?"

My breathing increased, it became rapid.

"Just a guess. I mean, waiting outside the bathroom for some girl who can't even walk, doesn't seem like it would be on the top of anybody's list."

He shook his head and rubbed the back of his neck with one hand. "First of all, you're not a girl, you're a woman, and secondly—"

I lunged at him. I couldn't stop myself. My mouth was on his before he could finish his sentence. As he wrapped his arms tightly around me, I could feel the smile on his face. I was blazing with need and on fire from his touch. I moved my lips over his with hunger and need. A growl escaped his throat when I moved, and his tongue parted my lips. He explored my mouth, getting to know my abilities. The feeling was bliss, my body raged for more. It had been so long since I'd been with a man. I needed to feel this again, I began sucking and caressing his tongue. My hands reached for the back of his hair, as a small moan escaped my lips. He pressed me against the wall and showed me what I did to him. His erection dug in to my pelvis, and I pushed back against him.

As we kissed I thought about his seductive voice and him calling me a woman. Quickly I felt myself losing control. I wanted to wrap my legs around him. However, I knew I couldn't. I had to stop myself. *What am I doing? I'm in public. I don't even know his name.*

I slowed the kiss, and he protested by lustfully nibbling on my bottom lip. Finally I stopped. I had to. I pulled my tongue away and tried to control my breathing. He continued to peck my lips, as if he couldn't stop. I rested my forehead against his chin, and when I opened my eyes, I looked up into his stare. He looked at me with so much wantonness and kept me tightly tucked in his arms.

I took a deep breath before speaking. "Hi, I'm Alexa."

He smiled down at me and shook his head. Everything within me yearned for him, the effect he had on my body was like nothing else. However, I apparently had the same effect on him because I could still feel his erection pinning me against the wall.

"Hi, I'm Vincent."

I looked at him with infatuation. "It's nice to meet you, Vincent."

He kissed me again. "And the same to you, Alexa."

"Alexa, oh my God! Are you okay?"

Oh Cara, perfect timing. "Yeah, I'm fine. Why?"

She looked from me to Vincent and back again with a confused expression written on her face. I felt the need to erase the confusion and introduce the two.

"Cara this is Vincent. Vincent, this is my best friend, Cara."

He gave her a slight nod, and smiled. "It's a pleasure to meet you, Cara."

She scowled at him, I guess because I was wrapped up in his arms.

"Cara, Vincent was…eh. He helped me out, I rolled my ankle in these wedges and he caught my fall."

Cara wasn't buying it as she crossed her arms and smirked at us.

"Well, thank God for Vincent. Are you ready Lex? Bridgette is hammered, so I called cabs to get us all out of here."

I didn't want to go, I felt so comfortable and at peace in his arms. Something I never *allowed* myself to feel when I was with a man.

"Yeah, sure."

At that moment, Cara pulled me out of Vincent's arms. I was being dragged away before I could do anything else. I looked back to Vincent as he ran his hands through his hair clearly frustrated. Our eyes stayed connected, and I gave him a small wave. I kept walking because it felt better to leave than face my fear of heartache. I couldn't have just a one-night stand with him and I knew that. I wasn't about to break my number one rule for a stranger. He was too much for me to have only once.

Chapter 3

Fate

"Oh my God. My head is throbbing."

I struggled to wake and gather my bearings on where I was as well as the events that had taken place the night before. I rolled over to find Cara face down in bed next to me.

"Cara, what the hell are you doing in here?"

She spoke into the pillow, "I couldn't make it upstairs last night; it would've been unsafe for my health."

I slapped her arm and she screeched.

"Hey, what was that for?"

"Sleeping in my bed uninvited and saying 'oh my God' in that damn Southern accent."

Cara snorted and her hand flew to slap me.

"You better knock it off, or I'll kick your ass out of here. Better yet, why don't you go and get us some Starbucks?" I said.

Cara rolled over and propped herself up on her elbows. I looked at her with one eye open. "Not until you tell me what really happened between you and that Vincent guy last night. It didn't look like you rolled your ankle to me."

I closed my eyes and thought about last night, especially Vincent. I missed the way it felt to be in his arms, the security, his smile, and those lips. I thought about what I wanted him to do to me with those lips.

"I don't know what you're talking about, Cara. I rolled my ankle as I turned the corner, he was there and, thankfully, caught me before I fell."

Cara narrowed her eyes at me. "You honestly expect me to believe that you rolled your ankle and he caught you? End of story? You two were inches apart and wrapped up in each other's arms. I've never seen you with a guy before. Then when you introduced us. he didn't budge. Don't you find it strange that he didn't shake my hand? He held onto you like his next breath depended on it. I mean, I know I was drunk, but I saw what I saw, and there was no denying the lust between the two of you."

I sighed in frustration, she was right. Something was different with Vincent and as much as I wanted to avoid the topic and sweep it under the rug to mull over on another day, I needed to talk to her about what had happened not only with Vincent, but the feelings I was currently experiencing.

"All right, there is more to the story, but I need coffee first. Can we go get breakfast and talk things over there?"

"Sure thing, but you're buying."

"Fine. Let's get dressed and go."

It took us all of five minutes to throw on some sweats and leave the house. The food here was always delicious; Café Lux was my all-time favorite breakfast place in Colorado and the coffee was to die for, literally. As I sipped on mine, I looked at the surroundings. We were seated outside on the garden patio made up of natural stones and wrought iron tables looking out onto First Avenue. The people were flowing all around; most were going in and out of the shops with a leisurely pace. Some were capturing pictures of the far off mountains while others were biking down the river.

I started to pick at my croissant, contemplating how to bring up the feelings I was experiencing without sounding crazy.

"Do you believe in fate? I mean do you believe that no matter what you do in life your destiny is already planned?" I asked.

She looked at me with an ambiguous expression on her face, thinking about what I said.

"I guess so. You mean, kind of like karma? You steal something, then the next thing you know you can't find something else and spend days on end searching but it never shows up?"

I thought about her statement. Fate was kind of like karma.

"Yeah, I guess like that too. I just mean, maybe I was supposed to meet Vincent, and that is why I felt so connected to him. It was like there was a tether pulling us towards one another. Maybe it was fate."

Although that sounded crazy considering I'd just met him, it was how I felt.

"I can see where you're coming from, but it's a little extreme to feel so connected to someone you don't know."

"I did kiss him, and the minute our lips touched it was as if everything felt right."

Her mouth dropped open. "You did what? You kissed him? You kissed Vincent in public?"

I nodded my head. "I couldn't stop myself. Honestly, I rolled my ankle, and he caught me. I went into the bathroom a complete and utter mess of hormones. Everything inside of me wanted him. Cara, I've never wanted a man the way I wanted him, and it scared the shit out of me. You know me, I don't do PDA. Normally, I would've hooked up with him and then ended it. But I couldn't, the attraction was too strong for one hook-up and that's not like me."

She stared off into the distance not making eye contact. My words had clearly floored her.

"I'm speechless. I don't even know what to say. You've always made it clear that you don't date, and now here you are, after meeting a guy one time, you're off in la-la land, dreaming of a relationship. Do you have any idea how crazy that sounds coming from your mouth? You have *never* dated anyone."

I took a deep cleansing breath and put my face in my hands. "I know it sounds crazy, and the shitty part about all of this is, none of it matters. I don't know who he is; I don't know his last name or anything about him. And I'm never going to see him again."

"Good Morning Sunshine."

I moaned into my pillow. Damn it, I forgot Cara and I were going to work out at Red Rocks this morning. I really wanted to sleep in, but there was no way Cara was going to let me. Red Rocks was a tradition for us. We loved going to the world-renowned amphitheater that has held some of the biggest names in music. During the daytime it was a popular place to run the massive stairs that acted as the seating and was nestled in between large Red Rock formations.

"Uhh, what time is it?"

She laughed at me. "It's five am, you asked me to wake you up remember? If you continue to bitch we're not going to see the sunrise."

She was right, as much as I was not an early bird, I

wanted to see the sunrise. There was something about watching the sun move that always started my day off right.

I hurried out of bed and threw on some yoga pants, a hoodie, and my running shoes. Cara was waiting for me at the front door before we loaded into my car and headed off into the early morning darkness.

As I pulled into the empty dirt lot you could smell the fresh mountain air. It was still dark outside, but I've been there so many times I could find my way around even if the moon wasn't out.

I liked to park in the lower lot because it made for a more strenuous workout. Exercising her was brutal, not only was the air thinner up here, but you had to hike up almost one hundred stairs to get into the amphitheater. Once inside, there were sixty-nine rows of wooden benches expanding the length of the inside of the amphitheater. That was the real challenge; it was almost like doing lunges up the side of a mountain.

Cara smacked my ass. "You ready to head up, girl?"

I winked at her. We always raced from the car inside the amphitheater.

"Loser buys breakfast," she said.

"As always, that will be you," I teased.

She put her hands on her hips and gave me a dirty look as I blew her a kiss. With that, we were both off sprinting across the dirt parking lot and up the long curved, paved road to the bottom of the stairs. The stairs were wide and had multiple railings running up and down the middles of them.

Cara tackled them by grabbing the bar and taking two at a time. I on the other hand, took one at a time but with ferocious speed, my tiny steps always got me the win. Cara was ahead of me but quickly lost her momentum. I kept my short strides intact and didn't look back.

When I got to the top of the stairs, I looked down at my friend and she gave me the finger. I laughed so hard I had to bend over. Once I caught my breath and stood up, she was still glaring at me.

"Oh, come on, Cara. I told you last time to change up your strategy." She reached the top of the stairs and spoke inches from my face. "You better not want to eat anywhere expensive. I can't afford it."

I laughed again, I think this time I really pissed her off. Cara lived with me rent-free so she could definitely afford to splurge on breakfast.

"You better believe you're going to take me somewhere expensive."

She chuckled and elbowed me, "Oh fine, Lex. Expensive it is." I squealed, and we started to head up the stairs.

Once we reached the top, the sun was just peaking over the horizon. It was incredible. This was by far the most beautiful place to watch the sunrise. It was worth waking up at five am. I stood there and looked at the sky that was a menagerie of pinks, oranges, and red. I suddenly saw hazel. Thoughts of Vincent began to creep into my mind and I couldn't help but picture myself back in his arms.

Chapter 4

Kane

The week seemed to fly by. It was already Thursday when I finally got to sit down and watch my DVR. I sank into the plush couch, nuzzled into my soft throw, and got lost in one of my favorite TV shows. I'd spent the week preparing for the arrival of Kane, my new boss and partner at the firm. It was nice, knowing we would have a full team again especially with the Albertson case going to trial soon. Cara flew down the stairs and sat next to me.

"Are you hungry?" I asked without looking at her as I was too consumed in my show.

"Yeah, a little. Do you want to go out?"

Is she crazy? There was no way I was leaving this house or my couch. This was the first night I didn't work late. I paused the DVR and sat up. "Why in the world would you ask me if I wanted to go out?"

She shrugged her shoulders like it was no big deal. "Uhh. I want to celebrate."

I rolled my eyes at her. "And what do you want to celebrate?"

She turned towards me. "Do you remember that guy I was dancing with at 9th Door? We've been texting, and he asked if I wanted to go to dinner next week."

I plastered the best smile I could on my face.

"I'm happy he called, but you know your track record with guys like that."

She sighed and slouched back into the couch. "I knew you were going to say that, but he seems different. He really does. We had a great time dancing, and he didn't try to take me home. He gave me his number, and I've got to know him better this week. He's really genuine; you can't judge him just because he has tattoos."

She was right. I was the last person to be judging anyone, especially to judge someone because they had tattoos.

"Fine, if you like him and really believe he has good intentions, I'll give him the benefit of the doubt. But no going out tonight. Let's order in and open a bottle of wine. Then we can discuss a game plan to keep your heart safe."

She smiled at me and hopped up off of the couch. I got up after her and grabbed my favorite wine from the fridge. I poured us each a glass while Cara ordered dinner. She knew me so well; she didn't even have to ask what I wanted to eat. We'd been friends for years, and every detail about each other came as second nature. I felt like being bad tonight and the normal order of brown rice and steamed veggies was not going to satisfy my craving.

I yelled up to her, "Will you add some egg rolls and crab rangoons, please?"

She laughed and said, "Yeah, sure thing."

She came downstairs and snatched the wine out of my hand. We retreated back to the couch, and both of us sat down to discuss her date as we waited for dinner.

"So, tell me what his name is," I said.

She took a deep breath, and leaned into the couch. "His name is Jon. He's a real estate agent and just moved here from Florida."

Hmm, a real estate agent with tattoos, now that was a first. But possible, I needed to stop judging and give him a chance.

"Okay, where is Jon, the real estate agent, taking you for dinner?"

"He said I could pick anywhere since he's new to town. The first place I thought of was Elway's."

Elway's was a nice restaurant owned by John Elway of the Denver Broncos.

"Okay, I like Elway's. So just dinner?"

She shrugged her shoulders at me. "Yeah, I think so. If it goes well maybe we will go out for a drink afterwards."

I hope that's all that happens. Cara was known for falling fast and falling hard. If she drank too much then there would definitely be sex involved, and as soon as she slept with someone, she was *in love*.

"Well, good. I'm happy for you. But if he so much as harms a hair on your head or even thinks about making you cry... I'll cut his balls off."

Laughing, she hopped off the couch to get the doorbell, which had just rang. She ignored my comment. She was good at avoiding things like I was.

Dinner was delicious and after some more girl talk, Cara and I parted ways for the night. As I laid in my bed restless, it was odd for me because sleep normally came easily. But tonight it didn't, not even with the few glasses of wine I'd consumed. My mind was racing as images of Vincent's face flashed before my closed eyes. God my body yearned for him. I needed to know him; to see if what I was feeling was real. But I knew I would never see him again; I should have slept with him that night. Now all I would ever have was the one kiss that we shared.

I stared at the ceiling in my bedroom and sighed heavily, trying to let the exhaustion take over. I turned on my side and closed my eyes for the last time that night. *I must fall asleep. I must asleep. I must fall asleep.* I repeated in my head over and over.

Suddenly, I was interrupted by a warm hand resting on my hip. I knew who the touch belonged to without needing to look. Slowly he grabbed me across my stomach pulling me against his body.

Heat radiated off of him and every detail of his body entangled with mine felt so familiar. He was immense and smelt delicious. His presence immediately comforted. Gently he brushed the hair off my neck, with his smooth fingers and kissed behind my ear.

Whispering into my skin he said, "You're so beautiful, Alexa." Leaving a trail of sweet kisses down my neck, sucking and nipping along my shoulder, and pushing his bulging erection into me. I moaned in pleasure, rolling onto my back, wanting to touch his face and have his hair knotted in my fingers; swiftly he moved to cover me.

Pressing his full body into mine, we fit like a puzzle, all of our body parts locking together like they were made for each other. I stared into his alluring eyes, and his mouth curved into a mischievous grin.

"How did you find me?" I asked.

He rubbed my cheek with the back of his hand. "Shh, that's not important now. Close your eyes, beautiful."

I did as he asked as if I had a choice. I leaned up into him with my mouth, feeling his breath on my skin. It was sweet and hot, a heady combination.

The moment our lips touched, the spark was instant. I felt electricity move through my entire body, the desire I felt for him was unlike anything I'd ever experienced. I was sure he felt it too, as he intensified the kiss, a growl from deep within his throat escaped.

Sweat radiated off of his ample body, and he pressed me into the mattress. Slowly, he moved one of his hands clenching my breast firmly in his grip. My body bowed beneath him, pushing into his touch as his fingers teased my raised nipple. Greedily I moved my hands into his hair and gripped the satin strands while he moved his mouth from my lips to my nipple. He sucked and flicked the hard peak, back and forth in his mouth. I moaned with lust and wrapped my legs around him, encouraging him to enter me. I needed him inside of me.

My alarm clock went off; I smacked the top and read the time, 6:00 am.

I turned back to Vincent, but he was gone. *What the hell?* Where did he go; he was just here? I mean, he was here, wasn't he? I could still feel his touch and smell his scent. My mind raced back through the events that had just taken place, and now I laid there confused and pissed off.

I drove to work still heated and angry. Why was I dreaming about someone I didn't even know? I had to pull myself together. It was especially important that I do so today.

With Kane starting today, I wanted to make a good impression. Since I got word he had joined the team, we had been in constant contact via email, and thankfully, he seems really great. He didn't ask a lot of me, unlike the last attorney who I worked for Kane sent over a simple request of supplies to have for his office. I had to order stationary and business cards along with getting the IT team out to ensure his office was all set up with his laptop, computer, and blackberry.

He offered to get me Starbucks this morning, which was a shock to me since Trent, the last attorney I worked for, made me go every day, twice a day to get it for him. And if it didn't taste right, I had to take it back and get him another one.

I pulled into the parking lot and parked in my normal spot. I made my way into the office building that was home to Smith and Brown. The firm was now staffed at capacity, and I hoped things would run smoothly going forward. With all the buzz going around about Kane's track record that he had never lost a case, I think we were in for smooth sailing.

The office building was in the heart of the Denver Tech Center just south of downtown Denver. It was thirty stories high, and I worked on the twenty-ninth floor. I moved through the lobby, which was marble and gold, with large pillars throughout, and made my way to the bank of elevators.

I caught the elevator with Portia, one of the other paralegals on my team. I put my best smile on, considering I was still in a foul mood.

"Morning, Portia. How are you today?"

She smiled back at me, she was beautiful. She was Latino with perfectly tanned skin, long dark hair, and the bluest of eyes. She hit the jackpot on the gene pool.

"Hey, Alexa. I'm great, thanks for asking. How are you doing? Are you excited for Kane to start today?"

I leaned my head to the side, contemplating the question. "Yeah, he seems great."

She scooted closer to me and whispered in a low voice. "I talked to a friend in Phoenix last night who knows of him. She said Kane is not only a gentleman, but he's extremely easy on the eyes."

Well, good thing for me, I had rules. One of those rules was that I didn't date attorneys, but I didn't mind a little office flirting now and then. I needed a distraction, and hopefully Kane would be just that. He seemed nice enough through our emails this week, and if he was as good-looking as Portia says, then I'm sure I wouldn't think about Vincent again.

"Well I am sure he won't be any worse than Trent, so it's a win-win for me."

She winked at me, and I laughed. Portia was very outgoing and didn't hold much back. Her mouth didn't come with a filter, but I liked that about her.

The elevator opened and we walked in sync down the hall to our desks. Our desks were cubicles that lined the east side of the wall. Portia and I shared a cubicle wall, which was fun. I was glad to have her on the other side, and I thankfully had an end cubicle so no one was on the other side of me.

On the corresponding side from our desks, and with a spectacular mountain view, were the offices of our Attorney's: C.J Smith and Liam Brown. They had the two end offices and Kane, my new boss, would take over the middle one.

I booted up my computer and checked my voicemail in the meantime. We had an eight o'clock staff meeting, and I didn't want to be late, so I grabbed my iPad and headed into the conference room. I was in desperate need of coffee, but didn't want to offend Kane and his offer to bring me some today. So I opted for a bottle of water from the mini fridge as I waited for my Starbucks and to meet Kane.

Portia came in and sat down next to me, "Have you seen him yet?"

I shook my head no. He must have just gotten here.

"Well to say he is easy on the eyes is an understatement; he's drop-dead fucking gorgeous."

I smacked her arm. "Will you keep your voice down?"

She laughed, unable to control her non-existent filter was something everyone had become accustomed to. No one looked in our direction as our other co-workers entered the conference room.

"Sorry, but I wish he was going to be my boss," she said.

I rolled my eyes. "Please, C.J. has it bad for you. If you would just give him the time of day, you wouldn't be out looking for a boyfriend. And good thing for you, I don't date attorneys. So now you have your pick."

She laughed again until. C.J. and Liam came into the conference room, quieting her immature fit. We all turned our attention to Liam, who spoke first.

"Good Morning, team. As you all know, Kane, our newest attorney, is joining us today. He just got in from Phoenix, so go easy on him, and please make him feel welcome. Alexa, I expect that you have everything in order for his arrival?"

I nodded my head and gave him a reassuring smile.

"Good. In case you need help, I expect everyone to pull together and assist you in any way possible. We have the Albertson case to get Kane up to speed on."

Just then, he came into the conference room and everyone's attention turned from Liam to the man standing before us.

Holy shit.

C.J. spoke up next. "Kane, welcome. We were just getting started. How about we go around and do introductions before diving into next week's agenda?"

Kane smiled, "Sure, but I have a coffee for Alexa."

He looked right at me and my heart was pounding so hard in my chest I swear the whole room could hear it. C.J. looked from Kane to me and back again.

"I'm sorry. Have you two already met?"

Kane's smiled widened.

FUCK, that smile.

Everything below my waist tightened and I didn't know what to do. Should I leave, or throw my self at him, or yell at him for being here? Before he could speak, I jumped up.

"No, of course not. I'm obviously the only one here without a coffee."

I reached out to take the Starbucks from his hand and forced a smile on my face.

"What can I say, Alexa is the only one without a coffee, enjoy. And it's truly a pleasure to meet you in person, and that goes for all of you. I'm looking forward to being part of the team."

I sat back down and sank into the chair. How was this even possible? I'd been talking to him all week, preparing for his arrival, and filling him on things here. All the while, I'd been having wet dreams about him and having to take cold showers to calm my libido. I was royally screwed and had no idea how I was going to handle this.

I couldn't take my eyes off of him. As he turned to sit Kane ran his tongue across his lower lip, or should I say Vincent.

As the meeting progressed, I was unable to focus on anything Liam or C.J. said. My mind raced through a thousand different scenarios. *How did I end up in this situation?* How was I going get through working so closely with him, when I had a lust for him I...I couldn't control?

My eyes stayed on Vincent, he was three seats next to me; I couldn't seem to focus on anything else. As I watched him my mind drifted back to the dream I had this morning. My fingers itched to touch his hair. He looked so different than he had the night I met him at 9th Door. He was now dressed in a charcoal gray suit with a white shirt and black tie.

The meeting seemed to abruptly come to an end; I hadn't taken notes the entire time. In front of me, my iPad laid untouched and that was not like me. Quickly, the room disbursed and Vincent approached me.

"Alexa, may I see you in my office please? We have a lot to go over, so I would like to get started as soon as possible."

Portia sat frozen next to me, and for the first time, she looked awe-struck.

"Of course, let me run to the restroom, and I'll be right in." I kept my voice calm. I hoped my exterior was as I was portraying, cool and professional. I gathered my things and walked away, leaving Vincent alone with Portia. I'm sure five minutes alone with her would have his mind down a path of Latino love and far away from any thoughts he may have had of me. I sat my things on my desk and headed to the restroom.

On the way, I ran into C.J.

Crap.

"Hey, Alexa. Are you okay today? You seemed rather quiet this morning."

I rubbed my neck. "Yeah, I'm alright. Thanks for asking. I had a long weekend, and I think I may be getting sick, that's all."

He frowned with concern. "Oh, I'm sorry. Well,

please let myself or Kane know if it gets worse and you need to leave early."

That was my out, I should tell him I had to go now. That way I wouldn't have to face Kane and hear his bullshit excuse for why he lied to me when we met. Why he didn't tell me his real name. I'm sure all week, when we were talking, he knew it was me.

And here I am, so consumed with thoughts of him that I am unable to close my eyes without seeing his face. When he can't even be honest with me and tell me his real name. No, I wasn't going to leave, not yet anyways. I was going to call him out on his bullshit game.

"Thanks C.J. I'll let you know if I start to feel worse, but hopefully I can fight through this today and get some rest this weekend."

He smiled at me, and I walked past him continuing onto the restroom. I opened the door, and thankfully it was empty. I opted for a stall rather than stand and stare at myself in the mirror.

I leaned up against the cold tile wall and immediately sank to the floor. I hadn't had feelings for a man in years, and the one time I do, the one time I let myself, he ends up being a liar and my boss.

I'd avoided these kinds of situations for years and for this reason. I didn't like the feeling I had in the pit of my stomach. I needed control. I needed to know where we stood. With him I didn't know anything. I had to handle the situation with Kane. He was my new boss, and

I *did not* date attorneys - end of story.

With that thought, was there really a point in talking to him to find out why he lied about his name, or if he had known it was me he was talking to all week? I thought the best plan was to keep it professional and act as though he and the kiss we shared meant nothing to me. I had to hide my feelings for him and eventually they would disappear. *Wouldn't they?*

Plus he was probably interested in someone like Portia anyways. She was gorgeous: skinny, tan, and her long dark hair reminded me of a super model. She was an exotic package compared to me, which was just plain.

I'm sure the only reason he even kissed me was because I threw myself at him like a drunken fool. I pulled myself off of the bathroom floor. I had a game plan; I was going to keep things strictly professional.

I left the bathroom and went back to my desk. I started to go through my emails, when an instant message popped up from Kane.

Kane Mileski: Alexa, may I please see you in my office?

Shit, that didn't last long. I was hoping he had forgotten that he asked me to go in there. *Hah, yeah right.*

Alexa Schaefer: I'm not sure what to call you, but I'm sure whatever you need, I can handle from out here. Just email me a list and I'll get it done.

Kane Mileski: *My legal name is Kane Vincent Mileski. At work I go by Kane, and outside of work I go by Vincent. I prefer to keep the two separate due to the high profile cases I handle. This ensures the safety of those close to me. Now, I assure you that you cannot handle my requests from your desk. Please don't make me come out there.*

Ahh, this man was exasperating, to say the least. I did feel better knowing that he didn't give me a false name and had a valid excuse. Against my better judgment, I gathered my iPad and went to his office.

Walking up to the door the sight of him instantly took my breath away. He had taken his suit coat off and was sitting behind his large desk with his white shirt, grey vest and black tie. I wanted to climb into his lap and wrap my arms around him.

His eyes immediately met mine and there was that panty-dropping smile.

Did he have this effect on everyone, or was it just me?

"Why, thank you Alexa. Please come in and close door."

I did as he asked and went over to the expansive windows overlooking the amazing view of the Rocky Mountains. I had always taken the beauty of the landscape for granted. I stood and stared out at the snow-covered peaks unsure of what to say He came and stood beside me crossing his arms across his massive chest.

"It's beautiful, isn't it?" I asked.

He smiled down at me and reached to touch my face. "It is, but not as breathtakingly beautiful as you are, Lex."

I pulled away from his hand "Don't call me Lex," I snapped. "Vincent, you don't even know me. I didn't come in here for this."

I walked across the room and sat in one of the chairs opposite his desk. Glancing up at him he looked hurt. I could see the pain in his hazel eyes, it was the same look when I was pulled out of his arms the other night. He ran both of his hands through his hair and sat across from me.

"I'm sorry, Alexa. I can't control myself when I'm around you. You're all I have thought about for the past week."

I put my hand up to stop him from continuing.

"Please don't. We can't do this. You're my boss. The other night…it was a mistake. That wasn't me. I shouldn't have acted like I did. I had far too much to drink and reacted in a way that sent the wrong message. I thought I would never see you again."

He creased his brows and leaned forward as he spoke.

"You think the other night was a mistake?"

It pained me to say it, much less to hear him repeat it back to me, but it was the only way. I had to lie to him; I had to tell him that I didn't feel anything for him. I swallowed hard, to ensure I spoke clearly.

"Yes."

His jaw clenched and he shot up from his chair. He paced the room, then said, "Bullshit, you're lying. I can see it in your eyes now, and when I walked into the meeting today, I felt something between us. I know you did too."

I took a few deep breaths before I spoke, I needed to be strong and end this before it started.

"Vincent, we have a job to do. If you would like to proceed with work, then please, let's do so. I cannot repeat myself again, the kiss we shared was a mistake, and I'm sorry if you felt something. I didn't mean to lead you on."

The sound of my own voice pained me, and I had to fight back the tears. I was lying to myself and it hurt even more than I thought was possible. In the next moment, Vincent was kneeling in front of me, between my legs. I couldn't look at him. I kept my gaze down as a tear escaped my eye and rolled down my cheek. He wiped it away and ran his thumb over my lips.

"Look at me, Alexa."

I couldn't. I knew what would happened if I allowed myself to get lost in his eyes. As much as I wanted to, I had made it this far and caused this much pain to both of us, there was no going back.

"I'm sorry, I…I can't. I have to go."

I bolted out of his office before he could respond. I walked by my desk and snatched up my cell phone as I then left. Thankfully I didn't have to wait for the elevator and slid in with the UPS guy. He didn't notice me as I leaned onto the elevator wall. He was oblivious to what was going on around him as he focused on his hand scanner showing his next stops and listened to some hardcore rock music way too loudly.

As the elevator descended the twenty-nine floors, it seemed to take forever. Once we were on the ground level, I went outside to the seating area. Normally it was crowded with people eating their lunch and enjoying the sun. However, it was still early, so no one was outside. I sat on one of the benches and pulled out my cell phone to call the one and only person who could tell me what to do.

"Lex, what's up, girl?" as silence came across the line, I heard panic in her voice when she spoke. "Alexa, you there? Is everything okay?"

"I'm here. Cara, I need your advice. Everything's so complicated. I don't even know where to start."

"The beginning would be nice."

I huffed into the phone. "We don't have enough time for all that. He's here Cara. Vincent is here."

"Whoa, excuse me? How did he find you?"

I let out a long sigh. "He's my new boss."

"Are you serious? How did that happen? I thought you said your new boss's name was Kane?"

"It is. I mean, that is his name."

"So he lied to you? I'm on my way down there right

now, and I'm going to kill him."

I couldn't help myself from laughing. "Calm yourself down. You know you're not going to do a thing. That's what I thought at first, but he has a good excuse. His name is Kane Vincent Mileski. He goes by Kane at work and Vincent outside of work. He takes on a lot of high profile cases, so he uses the two separate names."

"Well, that does explain a lot. Did he know you worked there?"

"I haven't asked him, but I will. Right now, I really need your advice on how to handle him. You know I don't get involved with attorneys, no ifs, ands, or buts about it. I love my job, and I've worked a really long time to get where I'm at, so I'm going to have to learn to work with him. I told him the kiss the other night was a mistake, and I didn't have feelings for him."

"You did what? Lex, that was a bad move. Now you're just adding fuel to the fire. You can't kiss a guy one minute then say you're not interested the next. It's only going to make him want you even more."

"Uh Cara, you're not helping!"

She laughed. "Okay, sorry. Game plan time: you could tell him you have a boyfriend?"

"Hah, yeah right. He would call me out on it. He'll ask me why I threw myself at him."

She snorted into the phone. "Fine, keep it cool, strictly business. That's really your only other option. Be an awesome employee, tell him that you're there to do a job and that's it."

I didn't want to create some elaborate lie. I already told him the kiss was a mistake. I had hurt both of us enough maybe we could learn to be friends or something. Who was I kidding? I could barely breathe when he was around. If we tried to be friends then it would give him time to work through me and push my feelings to the surface. I needed to push him away, strictly business. I could do that. I was strong enough, hell I had been through worse in my life.

"Okay, strictly business it is. Wish me luck. Thank you, Cara."

"Of course. Be strong, girl. I know you can do it."

We hung up the phone, and I sat in silence, staring out at the lake. I hoped I could have the will power the fight through this; in the end it was best for both of us.

Chapter 5

Avoidance

Since going back inside from my phone conversation with Cara, the rest of the morning flew by. I hadn't heard a peep from Vincent or seen him. I ate my lunch at my desk, the small amount I could stomach down. I guess one good thing about this situation was, I would lose the extra nagging pounds I'd been carrying around with me for far too long. I stayed busy on my computer and going back and forth to and from the file room. I did my best to not look in the direction of his office. I knew he was in there, and I also knew what would happen if we locked eyes.

When it was five o'clock, I gathered my belongings and snuck out of the office. I knew I wanted Vincent, and the desire that burned inside of me was undeniable. I just wished there was a way to make things work for us. God it would feel so good to have his hands on me again and kiss his sweet lips, just one more time.

On the drive home I stopped by Tipsy's. Once inside, I noticed Jay wasn't working. He must have the night off. I enjoyed our fun bantering and wished he were there to laugh with. I grabbed a bottle of my favorite Riesling and a six-pack for Cara. Heading out to my car, my stomach rumbled. I knew I needed to eat a good meal since I hadn't eaten much today, and with it being Friday, there was no better time to veg out.

After putting the liquor in my car, I decided to walk next door to Whole Foods. It was slow inside. There were no customers in sight, and the clerks were taking advantage of the down time by standing around gossiping. I grabbed a cart and skipped right past the fruit and veggies section. There was nothing there of interest to me.

After an hour in the market and poking around in just about every aisle, my cart was overflowing. Checkout was quick, and as I exited the store, I noticed a small chill in the air. I loaded the car quickly, thinking about Cara's reaction when I got home with all of this food. Since she was a nurse, she always preached the benefits of eating your six daily food groups. In my opinion an oatmeal raisin cookie was part of the fruit and grain food group, and that was two of your daily servings.

The neighborhood was quiet, like it always was. That's one of the things I loved most about living here. I pulled into the driveway, hoping I could sneak the food in. I grabbed an armful of groceries and when I opened the door, Cara was on the phone. She rolled her eyes at me and followed me back outside to help me bring in the rest of the bags. Then she retreated to her bedroom, still on the phone. Immediately, I started to put the groceries away. I couldn't tell who she was talking to, but I figured it was her sister; they normally talked in the evenings.

I opened my wine and poured myself a glass. My mind was clouded with thoughts of Vincent as I stood in the middle of the kitchen. I felt dumb for throwing myself at him. I'm sure that's not the first time a woman has done that, though.

Normally I would have just hooked up with him and called it a day. That was my MO; I'd get my fill and never have to see the guy again. With him, there was something different that stopped me from doing just that. I walked away with the feeling that he was too important to just hook up with. Thinking about it now there was no way I could ever trust him. Not with the stories I've heard. There's a reason he's a prodigy in the field of law and has never lost a case. He's a criminal defense attorney, and they are known to be ruthless. I couldn't be with someone like that; God knows how much trust means to me.

Cara strolled downstairs, looking a little glum.

"What's wrong? Are you okay?" I asked.

"Yeah, that was Amber. She got laid off today, so she's a bit down. I feel bad for her. I wished she lived here so I could help."

"Oh, no. I'm so sorry. What happened?"

"They are closing the agency and let everyone go."

"I'm sure with her degree she'll find something quickly, plus she has the best sister in the world to support her."

She smiled at me and opened the fridge. "Holy crap! What in God's name caused you to buy all this junk food?"

"It's not junk food. I bought it from Whole Foods, so everything is all natural and kind of healthy."

She turned to me with a package of cookie dough in her hand. "Really? You think this is healthy? I don't care where it came from, this stuff is loaded with sugar, and it's not good for you to eat. What has gotten into you anyways? You normally swear this stuff off."

I hopped up on the counter. "I don't know. I stopped by the liquor store after work and realized I was hungry. I didn't eat much today, so I went next door to grab dinner, and this is what I left with."

"I get that you were hungry and went to buy dinner, but when was the last time you bought cookie dough?"

"I didn't buy it for me. It's for you."

"Hah, yeah right. You know I can't eat this with my gluten allergy. Spill the beans. What's really up?"

I rolled my eyes and grabbed a candy bar from the cabinet next to me. I peeled the gold foil wrapper off, breaking off a small piece and indulged before I spoke.

"It's Vincent; I don't know what else to say. I know

there are tons of guys out there, but I can't get him out of my head no matter what. With him I feel something different There is this crave inside of me for him that's so strong. It's like, if I have him once, I'll never have enough. And that scares me because you know I don't date. Then there is the fact that he's my boss and is a ruthless attorney. There is no way I could ever trust him. I'm sure he wouldn't think twice about lying right to my face."

"Geez Lex, I wish I could say something to make this easier on you, but I don't think there is anything that can be said. You're strong enough to fight through these feelings though. I know you can do it. You have a good plan with keeping things strictly business, and with time, the feelings will fade away."

I had nodded off to sleep at my computer, not once, but twice. The weekend was miserable and that was putting it lightly. My mind was consumed with Vincent. I couldn't sleep or relax, which just agitated me. All I thought about was seeing him again. Not that it mattered, but it didn't stop me from imaging him walking in here and bending me over my desk.

My stomach was uneasy as I kept staring into his

office and watching the elevators, waiting to see him again. When I heard the elevator ping, I knew he'd arrived without needing to look. Sensing his strength and authority, I acted like I was busy on my computer. And then he was in front on me. He was dressed in a black suit with a lavender shirt and a dark purple tie. Damn, the man wore purple. I smiled at him, reminding myself to keep it cool.

"Morning, Kane. How was your weekend?" I asked.

"Boring, to say the least. How was yours?" He extended a Starbucks to me, and I danced on the inside - he remembered what I liked to drink. As I took the drink out of his hand, our fingers touched, sending a bolt of electricity through my body. I played it off like I hadn't noticed.

"Mine was the same. I didn't do much of anything."

He walked around my desk and leaned his large frame against it, sitting almost on top of it. He looked deep into my eyes, and I had to focus on keeping my breathing even.

We sat silent for a few moments just staring, then he said, "We should've spent the weekend together. It would've been more fun for both of us."

Oh my God. Did he really just say that to me, with Portia on the other side of my wall? He really had some nerve and clearly was not used to being told no.

"Really, Kane. Is that how you talk to women, including your employees? Do you really think I would be interested in some womanizing prick like you?"

He put a hand over his heart and shook his head. "Ouch, Alexa. That really hurt. Is that what you think of me?"

"I don't know what to think of you." I got up and walked away. I needed to clear my mind. I thought this whole 'keeping things strictly business' thing would be a hell of a lot easier. I never imagined he would blatantly pursue me.

I wasted as much time as I could away from my desk, knowing if I sat there, I was in his direct line of sight. When I got back, there was an e-mail from him waiting for me.

To: Alexa Schaefer

From: Kane Mileski

That was a low blow earlier. Do you really think I'm some womanizing prick?

I didn't know how to respond to his comment. The truth was, I didn't know him at all. If I imagined him on the weekends, I could see him with a different woman every day, lying to them and breaking their hearts. I was sure that I wouldn't let myself get tangled into his illusive persuasion.

To: Kane Mileski

From: Alexa Schaefer

I'm sorry, but I don't know what to think of you. I know your reputation doesn't do you any justice.

To: Alexa Schaefer

From: Kane Mileski

Why don't you give me a chance and get to know who I really am?

To: Kane Mileski

From: Alexa Schaefer

I'm sorry, but you're my boss, and that is a line I will not cross. It's hard enough for me being a woman in this business. I'm not about to be accused of sleeping my way to the top.

To: Alexa Schaefer

From: Kane Mileski

Who said anything about sleeping together? I asked you to get to know me better. If you think I'm just going to give up on you then you're dead wrong.

It was lunchtime, and I decided to head out. I had spent long enough contemplating how to respond to Vincent's last e-mail. The weather was beautiful today, so I decided to walk around the lake. Finding a bench, I sat and I stared at the glass-like water letting the sun warm my body. I couldn't stomach any food, and I wasn't about to sit at my desk making eye contact with mister determined.

I hoped explaining to him that I was not willing to cross the line of him being my boss would make him let up. As much as I wanted to give in, and believe me I did, I couldn't.

On my way back from lunch, I'd spent way too much time gossiping with Max, Liam's paralegal. I loved Max. He was as gay as they came and proudly shined every color of the rainbow. He was a little heavy set, with red spiky hair. He normally styled it in a faux hawk and loved to wear bowties, fake glasses, and vests.

When we arrived on our floor and came around the corner to my desk, there was an enormous bouquet of white roses in a massive crystal vase with a lace bow tied around it. *Jesus, he was relentless.*

"Oh, girl. Who are those from? They're beautiful." Max said.

I snatched the card from the bouquet and opened it quickly. As much as I wanted to throw the flowers at him, I was excited. No one ever sent me flowers.

If you think I'm an asshole, I'm here to prove you wrong. V

What the hell? Did he have split personalities? When he was at work in Kane mode he was an asshole; out to lie, scam, and cheat to get what he wanted. But when he was Vincent, he was Mr. Romantic. I was totally confused.

"So, who are they from?"

"My… My sister. She wanted to thank me for her birthday party and present."

"Ah, well, that's sweet of her. She must have spent an arm and a leg on these."

"She works at a flower shop part-time." I lied. I didn't know what else to say, but I needed Max to drop it. I could feel Vincent's eyes on me.

Max sauntered off to his cubicle in the most graceful fashion, turning back to wink at me. I don't know if he bought it, but I did my best.

I walked over to Vincent's office and knocked lightly. "May I come in, please?"

He gestured for me to sit across from him, "By all means."

I didn't know what to say to him as I stared at him dressed in that purple shirt and tie. He looked mouthwatering. His hair was a mess, like he'd been running his fingers through it. I nervously fidgeted with my fingers and bounced my knee. Part of me wanted to kiss him and let us get lost in each other. The other logical part was starting to panic; work was normally my safe haven. I had control and order when I was here. With Vincent storming in to my career, that was slipping away.

"You came in here for some reason. Are you going to tell me why that is?" he asked.

"Can I have the rest of the week off?" I blurted out. Shit I didn't mean to say that, it just came out. I guess it wasn't such a horrible idea.

"It's a little short notice, don't you think?"

I shrugged my shoulders.

"Is there something in particular that you need to take care of? Maybe we can compromise?" he asked.

"No, I don't have anything to do. I just don't think I can be here with you."

"Why is that?"

I didn't know what to say to him. My mind couldn't think of anything else, and my body tightened at the sight of him. What I wanted to say was that he scared the shit out of me and I needed time to push my feelings away.

"I don't know. The flowers and advances are all a lot for me."

"You lost me. One minute, you treat me like I'm a womanizing prick. Then the next you're telling me you need the week off because I'm a lot to handle? I don't get you Alexa. Obviously there is something between us. Why fight it?"

I chose to avoid answering his question. "Can I have the rest of the week off or not?"

"No, you cannot."

I stood and stormed from his office. I didn't even know what time it was, but I grabbed my purse and left.

Chapter 6

Mistake

I called into work on Tuesday and Wednesday, spending the days on my couch, thoroughly enjoying my mini vacation. I contemplated extending it through Friday. I'd made it this far in life with the power of avoidance, why stop now. The doorbell rang, and I pulled myself from the couch. I was in ratty sweats and my favorite t-shirt. No bra or makeup and my hair was in a ponytail, I hadn't put my contacts in for two days and pushed my glasses up the bridge of my nose as I grabbed the door handle. Lately we had a lot of kids selling stuff in the neighborhood, so I always tried to listen and support them.

When I opened the door, it was not a child standing before me. It was Vincent, fresh from work, looking yummy in another black suit with a white dress shirt unbuttoned and no tie. I panicked and wanted to slam the door in his face but found it odd that he came to my home and that peaked my curiosity enough to step outside. I closed the door behind me.

"What are you doing here?" I asked him.

"I wanted to see if you were all right. You've missed work for two days, and I haven't heard from you because you keep calling C.J."

I felt mortified to be standing in front of him in sweats, with no make-up, glasses and my messy hair. I crossed my arms over my chest to cover my breasts.

"I'm fine Vincent. You didn't need to come here."

"I know I didn't need to. I wanted to."

I turned away from him, unsure of how to respond, when he grabbed my arm and turned me towards him.

"Please don't turn away from me Alexa. These last two days at work have been hard. I needed to see if you were okay. Will you please come into work tomorrow?"

"I can't. I asked you for the time off, but you said 'no.' I gave you a warning that I needed space. You shouldn't have come here," I snapped. Saying the words hurt me, but I had to. My voice was cold and almost unrecognizable.

Stepping back off the porch, he said. "I'm sorry I was concerned for you. I won't make that mistake again."

I watched him walk off and get into his black Mercedes. He didn't look back at me. I had hurt his feelings, and although I intended to, it still made me mad that I had to. I sat on the front stairs of the condo. I didn't mean to sound so cold, but it was best for both of us.

Cara was working a swing shift so I was solo for the night. I went in and ate a piece of cold pizza then retreated back to the couch to get lost in another one of my TV shows. Hours had passed, and I was completely zoned out on some crap reality television. Feeling tired, I decided to head to my room. As I laid in my bed, I tossed and turned, contemplating going into work tomorrow.

I know I should stick to my guns and make a point to keep pushing him away, but I never meant to hurt him. I couldn't get the image of his face out of my head when I snapped at him. I had been really cruel lately and didn't want him to think I was a bitch. I regretted how I acted and I needed to apologize. Since I couldn't do that tonight, I would have to go to work tomorrow.

Sleep was restless, but that had become a habit for me lately. My alarm went off, waking me for the day. Not that I was sleeping soundly anyways. I turned it off and zoned out on the ceiling. Unbeknownst to me, my eyelids became heavy and I drifted off into a peaceful sleep.

"Sweetie, are you staying home again today?" Cara asked.

I awoke in shock to the sound of Cara's voice. "Shit, no. What time is it?"

"Its nine thirty. Why?"

I shot up and out of bed, running into the bathroom. "Because I'm late for work"

She chuckled at me. "Well I'm glad to see you get

out of your sweats and get back in to the swing of things."

I sneered at her and began washing my face. I put on some make-up and twisted my hair into a low bun. I dressed quickly in a light blue dress and was out the door and in my car.

Crap , crap, crap!

I felt horrible for over sleeping; Vincent was going to think I was an even bigger bitch now. I decided I would bring him a peace offering, in hopes that he wouldn't hate me. I pulled into Starbucks and sped to the drive-thru. Then, realizing I didn't know what he drank, I ordered two of my lattes; it was the best I could do.

When I arrived at work, I parked and took a moment to calm my nerves, breathing deeply with my eyes closed and repeating in my head what I planned on saying to him. I checked my reflection in the mirror and applied a thin layer of my favorite coconut lip gloss. As I entered the building, the deserted lobby allowed me to catch the first elevator up. Once I reached the twenty-ninth floor, I headed straight for his office. I halted at his door when I saw Portia perched on his desk. He sat in his chair and immediately looked at me standing there, holding two coffees. I felt the color drain from my face; I must've looked like a fool.

"Hey, good morning. I wasn't expecting you in today," he said.

I mustered up as much strength as I could because I

didn't want to put Portia in the middle of this. She was one of my friends, and after all, I gave her the okay to pursue him.

"I hadn't planned on it, but was feeling better after some rest, so I thought I would give it a shot. I didn't mean to interrupt you two. I just wanted you to know I was here and give you a Starbucks."

"Thanks, but Portia and I just got back from Starbucks. I was filling her in on the Robinson case."

"Okay, I'll give it to Max. I owe him one anyways." I turned and walked away from him, completely mortified and embarrassed, carrying two drinks. *What was I thinking?* I should've just stayed home. Clearly he had moved on. I don't know why that bothered me. I'm the one that had been a bitch to him. Although I cannot believe he had brought Portia up to speed on the Robinson case when *I* was his paralegal.

I could hear the two of them laughing in his office; thankfully Portia had removed herself from his desk and sat in one of the chairs across from him. My blood boiled thinking of her sitting like that.

When she came out, she gave me a wave, and I smiled back. Anxiety took over as I watched and waited for a message from him to come in. Surely he would apologize for not taking the coffee I had bought him, or for Portia being perched on his desk.

The message never came and by 5:30 he walked out of his office, crossing in front of my desk without looking at me or saying a word.

He had never ignored me before and this came as a shock to me. I shook my head to try and understand why he suddenly wasn't interested in me. I gathered my purse and left to go home in desperate need of Cara's advice.

Cara's car was in the garage when I pulled up. I walked inside, noticing the amazing aroma in the house. She was in the kitchen, cooking and listening to music.

"Hey, girl. How was your first day back at work?" she asked.

"It sucked. What about you? Did you do anything fun today?"

"I got a manicure for my date tomorrow night, cleaned, and did laundry. Nothing big. Why did your day suck?"

"I'll tell you later. Dinner smells amazing. What are you cooking?"

"Chicken fettuccini with an antipasto salad and garlic bread."

"Yum, I can't wait. It smells delicious, and I'm starving. I'm going to change real quick and I'll help you finish up and fill you in on my day."

She smiled at me and said, "Sounds great. Take your time."

I went into my bedroom and felt not only emotionally exhausted, but physically exhausted also. I know it was from the lack of sleep and the stress of today. I had waited too long and pushed Vincent so far away that he now wasn't even on speaking terms with me. I wished that I could go back to last night when he showed up at my front door. I should have handled things differently.

I had feelings for him, there was no denying that. The controlling part of me forced those feeling aside because I was scared. I wished there was something more I could do, but considering the fool I made of myself this morning trying to make amends, I knew there wasn't.

I couldn't sulk forever or miss something I never had. I shredded my clothes off and pulled on a pair of yoga pants and a red tank top. Normally I would have opted for sweats, but deep down I hoped Vincent would show up again. I left my bra and make up on and braided my hair over one shoulder.

Cara was setting the table when I left my bedroom. She looked at me, and laid the silverware out next to our plates.

"You look nice tonight," she said.

"Thanks. My sweats are all dirty."

She didn't respond, and part of me felt like she knew what I was up to. I opened the fridge and took out a bottle of wine.

"Do you want a glass of wine?"

"Sure, that would be great."

I poured us each a glass and retreated to the table.

The spread was amazing. We served our plates and as much as the food looked wonderful, my appetite had diminished; I just pushed my food around my plate.

"Okay, spill it. What's going on?" she asked.

"I ruined things with Vincent, and now I feel like a complete and total ass."

"What do you mean you ruined things? There was nothing going on between the two of you as far as I knew, right?"

"Yes. But he has been really sweet to me, and I've been a total bitch and taken him for granted. Last night he came by here to check on me because I had missed work, and I hurt his feelings. I told him he shouldn't have come here."

Cara took a sip of her wine. "As you should have, Lex. He's your boss. What right did he have coming here? If he was worried, he should have called or texted you."

"He doesn't have my number."

"But he has your address? Listen, you're the one that decided you didn't want to pursue anything with him, due to your *rules* and all. Now you're going to have to live with that. Plus, you don't date, so why waste your time? What is it about this guy that has you so wound up anyways?"

"I can't put my finger on what exactly it is about him, but I do need to let it go and just learn to deal with it. He made it clear today he's not interested in me. Going forward, I'll stick to the strictly business plan and hope that this will all blow over."

"Good choice. I think it's a wise decision, and in the

end you'll be happier. Can you please help me now? I need to decide what I'm going to wear on my date tomorrow night."

Cara rambled on for what felt like hours. I managed to get some of my dinner down and drank one too many glasses of wine. We said good night, and although I was exhausted, a bath sounded inviting. I ran the water extra hot, just how I liked. Stripping off my clothes, I looked over my reflection in the mirror. My five foot eight inch frame looked tiny tonight. I was not fat by any means, but years of being told I was, had painted a different picture in my mind. I would say I was average, basically long and lean. Clearly Vincent saw something in me or had seen something in me. Whatever it was, I needed to hold onto that and know I was not perfect, but I was me.

The water stung my skin as I slid deep into the tub. I focused on relaxing my mind and body by just breathing. I must've dozed off, because I felt my head fall to the side, and it woke me up. I was cold and disoriented.

I pulled the drain and climbed out of the water. Grabbing my robe, I went into the kitchen and checked the clock; it was just after midnight. Shit. I *had* fallen asleep in the bath. I took two Tylenol and drank a glass of water, peering out to the dark street surrounding our home. No one was out. It was still and silent. I went back into my room and climbed into my soft warm bed, still wrapped in my plush robe.

I woke before my alarm clock, and I felt like I had

slept a full night's sleep. I went into the kitchen and poured myself a cup of coffee. Cara always made it the night before and set the pot on automatic. It was nice to wake to freshly brewed coffee.

My morning routine was normally quick. However, I was up far too early and had extra time, so I played with my hair and make-up. When I was finished, I had constructed the perfect smoky eye, with thick eyeliner and perfect mascara. My hair was in big beach waves; I scrunched it and sprayed it with hairspray making it look a bit rocker-chic.

I found a cute tweed skirt with a cream sheer blouse. I matched it with stockings and black pumps.

Driving in, I barely hit any traffic, and arrived early. I went up to my desk and started my morning routine, digging into the work I'd left behind. Soon enough, my co-workers started to filter into the office. I hadn't even noticed Vincent arrive, but I saw him sitting at his desk. Cameron, a paralegal from another firm, took me away from staring at Vincent. He approached my desk with a full smile showing his shiny white teeth. Cameron was young and handsome. He sat in one of my chairs without waiting for my permission.

"Morning. How are you today?" he asked.

"I'm great. Thanks for asking. How are you?"

He smirked at me and leaned over, resting his elbows on my desk. "I'm better now that I get to see you. So, are you ever going to let me buy you that drink you promised me five years ago?"

I laughed out loud, "Uh, no, I'm not. You know I don't get involved with attorneys."

"So you've told me. But that's what I keep telling you; I'm not an attorney. I, like you, am a senior paralegal, so we are equals, plus I work for a completely different firm."

As flattering as it was to have him continuously ask me out, I just wasn't into him like that. "Cameron, you know what I mean. I don't mix work with pleasure."

"Fine, like I always say, you'll give in eventually." I laughed again. "Well, I brought this over for you. It was delivered to our office by accident."

He handed me an envelope and winked as he stood and walked away. I shook my head, as many times as he had pulled this, I was always smitten after he left. It was really sweet of him. I noticed Vincent was staring at me, and when I made eye contact, he looked away.

What was that all about? Yesterday he wouldn't even acknowledge me. Then this morning he's staring and playing shy. Men are so confusing. I didn't know how to handle him so I grabbed my things and went into the conference room for our weekly meeting.

He came in a few minutes after me, still not looking in my direction. I could see we were back to our childish games. I powered up my iPad and took more notes than normal to keep myself busy, interjecting and challenging everyone who spoke. Vincent stayed quiet, and when the meeting was done, he bolted.

I knew we would have to talk eventually today, as the Albertson case was going to trial on Monday, and I needed to go over some additional files with him. I could wait until he was out of his office and just leave them on his desk, but I refused to let him run my life here. I was sticking to my plan, and he was going to have to deal with it.

Chapter 7

Rules

I meandered over to the file room. It was filled with rows and rows of client files and one of the only quiet areas in the office. I liked it in here and often would spend too long, enjoying the silence, organizing and filing away.

I searched feverishly for the files I needed to retrieve and later take to Vincent for the Albertson case. I had a plan; I was going to simply place them on his desk and ask if he needed anything else. He could go through them alone and figure it out.

As I moved down to the last row of shelves, he was behind me. Before I could move, he pushed me against the wall.

His breath was warm on my skin, as he whispered in my ear, "Tell me you don't feel anything for me, Alexa. Tell me you feel nothing inside of you for me, and I'll walk away."

My breathing increased at his closeness. He went

from completely ignoring me and avoiding eye contact to now pinning me against the wall. He started to nibble on my neck and slowly kissed behind my ear. My eyes were closed and the proximity of him was overwhelming. His lips felt amazing, as always he was intoxicating, and his strength was clearly visible. I was trapped against the wall, my back to his front. I couldn't move if I wanted to; he wouldn't have let me. He continued to leave sweet kisses down my neck and across my shoulder. I allowed myself to enjoy the feeling for far too long.

Once I finally found my voice, I spoke. "I have rules, I told you."

He nipped my ear. "That's bullshit. I don't care about your rules. I asked you a question. Tell me that you don't have feelings for me, and I'll leave you alone. I've been going crazy trying to ignore you and then I see some asshole flirting with you at your desk this morning. I can't just sit back any longer and act like I don't care."

He was right. I did have feelings for him, but what those feelings were I was unsure. There was a desire drawing me towards him unlike anything I'd ever experienced in my life. As much as I wanted to fight it, I couldn't.

"Tell me Alexa," he demanded.

"I'm sorry. I…I can't."

He laced his fingers in between mine, and pulled our hands above my head. I was so turned on that it took everything inside of me to control myself.

"You can't, or you won't?"

I sighed in exasperation. He was quickly wearing on me, and he knew just how to push my buttons.

"Turn around and look at me."

I did as he requested, and in that moment, I was lost in his eyes. He was beautiful, so handsome. He unlaced our fingers and wrapped me in his arms.

"Don't you get it? I never thought I'd see you again, and here you are. Please answer me."

I closed my eyes and rested my head against the wall behind me.

"I don't know what to say."

What I did know was that I believed in fate. You can't change the course of your life as it is already mapped out. You have to embrace it and learn why you are being dealt the cards you are.

"Fine, if you won't tell me, then have dinner with me. That's all I'll ask of you. We can't keep playing this cat and mouse game, and if you truly don't feel anything for me, then I will leave you alone and learn to accept it."

I knew the answer before the words left my lips. "Okay."

He smiled at me and leaned down, tenderly kissing my lips. I accepted his kiss, gripping his hips and firmly pulling him to me. I realized then how bad I'd missed him.

"See, that wasn't so hard," he said, pressing his pelvis against mine. The feeling of his erection set my libido into overdrive. I moaned as he leaned into my neck, kissing and sucking on my skin. He moved with pure precision, rocking himself against my clit through our clothing,

Taking his time, he kissed his way down my neck and across my collarbone. My eyes were closed, and my breathing erratic. He stopped his assault and kissed my lips again, gently, yet so possessively.

He held our lips together for a moment, until I couldn't control myself any longer. I moved my arms around his neck and slid my tongue into his mouth. He caressed it passionately, like his life depended on it.

He started to grind against me again, and I whimpered. His mouth fit perfectly against mine, as did our bodies. God he was such a good kisser. He slowed the kiss to a stop, and I felt like an errant toddler ready to throw a temper tantrum wanting more. He ran his fingers down my cheek and I didn't open my eyes as he spoke in a soft tone. "Until later, beautiful."

He kissed me again, this time, tenderly. When I opened my eyes he was walking away. The world around me spun. What had just happened? I had broken the rules and now there was no going back. I had to make the decision whether or not to move forward. I had always told myself I would never get involved with an attorney, much less my boss. Plus, I didn't know the first thing about dating.

I grabbed the files I had already retrieved, leaving

the rest behind, and went back to my desk. I sat in my chair, still in a daze as a cloud of scenarios raced through my head. An e-mail pinged on my computer, bringing me back to the present.

To: Alexa Schaefer
From: Kane Mileski

Are you going to bring those files in here or act as if nothing happened and stay hiding at your desk all day? I thought we were done playing games. If you prefer, I can come out there?

To: Kane Mileski
From: Alexa Schaefer

Well considering what you just did to me in the file room, I'm scared to be behind closed doors with you. But I don't doubt that you would do the same to me at my desk, so I'll come to you.

To: Alexa Schaefer
From: Kane Mileski

You have no idea what I would do to you behind closed doors or not, but I'm a patient man. I could've had you in the file room any way I pleased. Do not be scared. Come in here and leave the door open. It's almost time to leave, and then you may want to be scared.

Geez! This man was exhausting and extremely intense. I was supposed to be fighting these feelings. I should just have dinner with him and end this before it went any further.

I walked into his office, and he smiled at me.

"Why, thank you. Now, if you could please not distract me so we can review these files. I have to get out of here soon. I'm taking the most breathtaking woman out to dinner tonight. Do you have any suggestions on where I should take her?" he asked.

So, he wanted to play games. I batted my lashes at him and looked deep in thought. "Hmm, I'm sorry. I can't help you out there. I heard she's hard to please and that you've only got one shot. Good luck."

His mouth curved into a mischievous grin. "Oh, Alexa, you better watch your mouth or we won't make it to dinner."

I would have never thought he had such a playful side to him. He always seemed so serious. Maybe I should give him a chance. I needed someone to bring the fun out from inside of me. I was always so reserved and cautious with my emotions. I needed to be in control of everything all the time, but with Vincent that seemed to wash away as if I didn't have a choice.

By the time we looked at the clock it was 7:15pm.

"Are you ready for dinner?" he asked.

"Absolutely. Where are we going?"

He shrugged his shoulders and cocked his eyebrow. "That's a surprise, but I think you'll like it."

I smiled. "Good, I love surprises."

I went back to my desk and signed off of my

computer, gathering my purse and cell phone. I watched Vincent in his office shrugging on his coat. He really was quite large and had to be well over six feet tall. I could tell he took good care of himself, not to mention the Arizona sun had done wonders to his tan skin. His dark hair was messy tonight, and as always, I wanted to have my fingers in it. As he walked towards me with his usual confidence and authority, it was unlike any man I had been with before.

"Are you ready, beautiful?"

He held his arm out to me, and I looped mine through his as we walked to the elevator. Before the doors were closed, we were in each other's arms. Our mouths instantly locked on one another. I grabbed his hair; it felt so good to have my fingers in it. I deepened the kiss and a growl escaped his throat. He lifted me up, holding onto me by the back of my thighs. I wrapped my legs around his waist and my skirt started to ride up.

Fuck. The elevator stopped, and just as the doors opened, he sat me back on my feet. I adjusted my clothes and had to hold onto the lapels of his coat for balance. An older gentleman, who I hadn't seen before, got in with us. He smiled and turned to face the doors.

Vincent took one of my hands in his and looked down at me with that panty-dropping smile. He brought my hand to his lips, kissing each one of my fingers, stopping only to suck on my pinky finger. He closed his eyes and I watched his warm mouth slowly moved up and down. I swear I could've come from seeing him do that alone. When we reached the lobby, Vincent didn't let go of my hand as we walked out of the building toward our cars.

"Should I follow you there?" I asked.

He pulled me towards him, and his brows creased. How was I ever going to say no to such a beautiful man?

"No, you're coming with me. Leave your car here. We can come back and get it later."

He squeezed my hand and we walked towards the almost empty parking lot. My heart raced, at the thought of him not wanting to drive separately. We walked up to his stealth Porsche Crossover, and I couldn't believe my eyes; in front of me was my dream car.

"Oh my God. I can't believe you drive a Panamera."

He looked at me with desire burning in his eyes. "I'm sorry, I don't think I heard you."

I stared at the beautiful four-door sleek Crossover Porsche in front of me. It was matte black with tinted windows and black wheels. Turning to look at him, I was stunned.

"Did you really just say that?" he asked.

I laughed. "Say that you drive my dream car, a Porsche Panamera Turbo? Yeah, I did. What can I say, I'm a sucker for speed."

He ran his free hand through his hair. "Fuck, do you have any idea what you do to me? Then you go spouting off about cars. I've been walking around at half-mast since the moment I saw you in that skirt this morning. I don't think I can I sit through dinner with you - I need you."

I smiled on the inside. I had never had a man speak so freely to me. I liked that about him.

"Hey there mister, we have a deal. Dinner, and then I make my decision, and you have to live with it. Remember?

He sighed in frustration and leaned down to kiss my cheek. "If you decide to give us a chance, I promise you won't regret it. If you only knew the things I want to do to you, I don't think there is a way you could say no."

He opened the passenger door for me and playfully swatted my backside I yelped in surprise. I watched him as he walked around the front of the car with such ease and grace and slid into the driver's seat. He started the car and then reached over and grabbed my hand. We pulled out of the parking lot and he turned up the song then kissed my knuckles.

We drove in silence just a few blocks away and quickly arrived at a restaurant I'd never heard of before called Lazio's. The valet opened my door and spoke to Vincent by name.

"Good evening, Mr. Mileski. Welcome back to Colorado."

"Thanks, Chad. Take good care of my girl and no joyriding, okay?"

He smiled at Vincent. "You got it."

Vincent came around the car and grabbed my hand.

The inside of the restaurant had old-world charm with dark woods throughout and dim lighting. A long bar expanded to my left with mirrors on the back, reflecting the hundreds of bottles of alcohol, and to the right was the expansive dining area.

"Good Evening, Mr. Mileski. Just the two of you for tonight?"

He squeezed my hand, and I liked the feeling. Surprisingly, I didn't feel the typical anxiety of PDA, like I normally did.

"Yes, and will you let Charlie know I have a guest I'd like him to meet?"

"Absolutely, sir. Right this way." The hostess walked with a sway in her hips, but Vincent didn't seem to notice. He looked down at me with a reassuring smile and led me in front of him through the dining area. How had everyone here known his name?

We were seated at a private booth in the back of the restaurant. Vincent ushered me into the seat, opting to sit next to me rather than across from me. The hostess rambled something off before leaving, but my mind was too busy racing to notice what she'd said. When I opened my menu, Vincent grabbed it from me.

"Don't bother," he said.

I arched my eyebrow at him. "Excuse me, Vincent. What's going on here?"

He looked nervous. "My father owns this place."

Was he serious? He brought me to meet his father after a week of knowing each other? I put my face in my hands. This was crazy. What had I gotten myself into? Had he not been sitting next to me, I would have run out of this place.

"Say something," he said.

I left my face in my hands as I searched for the courage to speak. "You brought me here to meet your father when we are supposed to be getting to know each other better and making a decision on how to proceed. Do you have any idea how crazy that is?"

He shifted nervously in his seat and then turned towards me.

"I know what you're thinking, and it's not like that. I brought you here because they have the best food in town. I grew up in this restaurant, and I figured if you saw how genuine my father is, then maybe it'll help your decision. I know you think I have a bad reputation with work and the cases I handle, but Alexa, everyone deserves a fair trial, and that's what I give my clients. Please don't be upset with me. I want tonight to be perfect. I want you to get to know the real me and give us a chance. If you say no, I don't know how I'm going to handle that."

I turned towards him in the booth and he ran his hands down the front of my thighs. I looked down at his hands and he lifted my face so I was looking into his eyes. I could see the anxiety etched on his face, and I gave him a reassuring smile.

"Vincent, I want to get to know you as well. That's why I'm here. I'm just surprised that you brought me to meet you father."

He grabbed my hand and brought it to his lips kissing the inside of my wrist. "Thank you, for understanding."

"Am I really not allowed to look at the menu?"

He shook his head. "My dad loves it when he has special guests. It gives him a reason to cook rather than manage and oversee the operations of the restaurant. He used to always cook until my mom passed away. After we lost her, he refused to hire someone to help out with the administrative tasks; that is what she did and loved. He rarely sees the inside of the kitchen now."

"I'm sorry you lost your mom."

He nodded his head as if he was deep in thought. "It's okay. We're not here to talk about that; we're here to get to know each other better."

Again, he ran his deft fingers over my thighs as we sat facing each other. The close proximity was intoxicating, and I needed to continue talking to keep myself in control. "I'm assuming your dad is Charlie?"

He smiled. "Yeah, that's him."

"Any siblings?"

"An older brother. His name's Abel."

I couldn't imagine another beast of a man that looked like the God sitting next to me.

"Are you and Abel close?"

"We used to be before I moved to Arizona and he became consumed with work. He is a fire fighter working on becoming a fire chief. I guess you could say we've grown apart. He's part of the reason why I came back to Colorado."

I saw the genuine expression come across his face, and I couldn't stop myself from kissing him. He had so many sides to him; at work he was strong and confident, but this other side was caring, genuine, and funny. How did I end up with him being interested in me: plain, timid, and controlling Alexa?

"Hhm-hhm," a man said as he cleared his throat.

Vincent pulled away from me and stood up. "Dad, it's so good to see you. You look great."

The two men hugged, and I noticed that Vincent resembled Charlie in more ways than one. They were both tall and broad shouldered with the same hazel eyes.

"I'm sorry to have interrupted the two of you, but please, introduce me to this lovely young woman."

He looked down at me with pure interest in his eyes.

"Dad, this is Alexa Schaefer. Alexa, this is my father, Charlie Mileski."

I stood to shake his hand. "It's a pleasure to meet you, Mr. Mileski."

He shook his head. "Please, call me Charlie. It's nice to meet you as well. How did the two of you meet?"

Vincent gestured for us to sit back in the booth. "We met a few weeks ago at 9th Door."

Charlie smiled at me. "So this is the girl you were telling me about?"

He told his dad about me?

"Yeah, this is her. I never thought I would see her again, and when I walked into work, there she was."

Charlie raised his eyebrows. "Wow, well don't let me interrupt you two, especially since you're just getting to know one another. Plus, I have a meal to cook for you two. Alexa, I do hope you like red meat?"

I nodded my head at him as Vincent stretched his arm behind me.

"Good, I'll have a waiter bring over a bottle of wine while I prepare your meal. Alexa, it was a pleasure meeting you."

He reached for my hand, and I gave it to him willingly, he kissed it in the most gentlemanly fashion.

"Thank you, Charlie. It was nice to meet you as well."

As he walked off, Vincent started to rub my thighs again. What was with him and my thighs? I hated them. I turned towards him again, in hopes that he would stop because I was feeling self-conscious.

"Jesus Christ, you're wearing stockings?" he murmured.

His hands grazed the tops of my stockings, and I quivered from the pleasure it sent through my body. He clenched my thighs with his strong hands and held my gaze with his eyes.

"You have no idea how bad I want to peel those off of your legs with my fucking teeth."

Breathe, Alexa. Breathe.

"Maybe I'll let you."

He chuckled. "A man can only hope."

Our meal was delicious; his father was an exceptional cook. It was by far the best beef tenderloin I had ever tasted. It was topped with a blue cheese crumble that was one of my favorites.

Vincent was affectionate, which was something I normally didn't do in public. Had it been another man, I wouldn't have liked it, but with Vincent, I couldn't seem to get enough of his touch.

We laughed and joked like we had earlier in his office. The conversation was effortless, and I noticed the constant smile I had on my face. I learned that he was a Colorado native and went to law school in Arizona.

Come to find out, he went to high school with C.J. and Liam. So when they had an opening at the firm, he was happy to join. That's why I never saw him when they were interviewing applicants. They had wanted him to come work for them, but he was loyal to the firm in Arizona. After lots of soul searching and a visit to Colorado, his mind was made up. He said he was glad he made the decision to leave Arizona; if he hadn't then he would've never met me.

It was crazy to have someone put their feelings out there like that. I had never had anyone be so honest with me, and at the same time, I didn't question his motives. I could feel that he was being genuine, and for that I was grateful. Honesty was the one and only thing I searched for in people, and far too many times, I was lied to.

Chapter 8

Give a Chance

I watched Vincent as we drove away from the restaurant. He had removed his coat and rolled the sleeves of his white dress shirt up. He looked calm and casual. I loved the way his large hands gripped the steering wheel, and I imagined them on my body. On the inside, I was smiling to myself, thinking of how I ended up here. Last night I yearned for him and thought I had messed everything up - now here I was with him.

He glanced over at me and said, "You're staring."

I rolled my eyes. "Maybe I am."

He chuckled softly; I loved the sound of his light laughter.

"Stay the night with me?" he asked.

I wanted nothing more. Rules or no rules, I wanted to be with him. I had to be with him. I leaned over the armrest and kissed his neck. Taking my free hand, I rubbed the front of his pants. He was already hard and moaned from my touch. I continued to rub between his legs kissing his neck and face.

He smiled and said. "I take that as a yes?"

"Mmm-hmm."

Just then he jerked the car off the highway, and I flew back into my seat.

"Sorry, almost missed the exit."

I laughed out loud and the heard my cell phone ring inside my purse.

"Shit. It's my roommate Cara."

"Are you going to answer it?"

I cringed on the inside, thinking of what I was going to say to her. I figured it was better to handle it now rather than later. I couldn't blow her off. It was already after nine o'clock, and she had her date tonight. She was going to be pissed that I didn't help her get ready.

"Hey Cara."

"Where the hell are you?"

"Listen, I'm really sorry, but we all had to stay late for a big case we have coming up on Monday. I should've call earlier, but I lost track of time. I probably won't make it home tonight, so don't wait up for me."

"Ha, that's bullshit. Since when do you work all-nighters?"

"I'm not bullshitting you."

As much as I hated lying to my friend, I didn't want to get into the details of what had happened between Vincent and me right now.

"You're with him aren't you?" I stayed silent, unsure of what to say.

"I'll take your silence as a 'yes' and that is officially a breach of girl code. Thanks for forgetting about me and my date tonight. Good luck with Vincent."

When she hung up on me, I put my phone in my purse and stared out the passenger window.

"She didn't take that well?" he asked.

I shrugged my shoulders.

"I'm sorry, beautiful. You don't deserve to be yelled at. Please don't let her upset you. You're just following your heart; you can't feel bad for that."

I smiled at Vincent, taking his hand in mine. "Thanks for saying that. You really are too sweet."

He gave me a reassuring smile as he pulled into a long circular driveway.

"Well, here we are. Home sweet home. Come on."

His home stood two stories with a four-car garage. It was modern with a mixture of dark stucco and stone. It was illuminated by lights shining up every few feet. It had large pillars on the front and a set of double front doors made of frosted glass and wrought iron. There were vines running up the pillars giving it a lush feel.

He opened the front door, and I stepped inside. It was just as inviting on the inside. There was a mixture of neutral colors, with plush furniture and light wood floors. The floor plan was open and wide, with a large staircase that curved up to the second level. I watched Vincent as he turned on a few lights, and then headed into the kitchen.

"Would you like a glass of wine?" he asked.

"Sure."

"Chardonnay or Riesling?"

I slid my shoes off and walked to the back glass doors. "Riesling please. It's my favorite."

The doors were more of a glass wall, and the view was breathtaking. As I looked outside I couldn't see any homes close by. There was nothing but sprawling open space.

"Wow. You have a pool in Colorado?"

He handed me a glass of wine, and I took a small sip, allowing the crisp flavor to roll down my throat.

"Of course I do. I've lived in Arizona for the past five years. A home with a pool was a must for me." He grabbed my free hand and said, "Let me show you around."

We made our way through the entire house, and it was just what I pictured his home to be: masculine, modern, yet comfortable. The last room we came to was his bedroom. It was clean and organized, just like the rest of the house. He had a gigantic king-sized bed with the comforter and décor being a mixture of creams, browns, and reds.

When I walked farther into the room, I noticed the expansive skylights in the ceiling.

"Those are impressive."

He walked over to me, taking my wine and placing it on the nightstand. "You like them? Those along with the pool are what sold me on the house. I love the stars. In Colorado you can only see them on a clear night, so I wanted to be able to lie in bed and watch them during the few opportunities I had."

He loved the stars just like I did. As we both looked intently up into the night sky; he wrapped his arms around my waist and pulled my body tightly against his. I looked over into his hazel eyes. He didn't look at me as he concentrated on the stars.

"You're staring again," he said.

"I can't help it. You're enticing."

He looked into my eyes and pushed my hair off of my shoulder, nuzzling my neck. "So are you."

I leaned my head to the side to allow him more access as he kissed and sucked my ear and neck. He knew what I wanted without me having to ask.

"You smell incredible, and I love the way your skin tastes. It's so sweet." His hands left my waist, gliding up my body to my breasts. He caressed them through my shirt and my nipples immediately hardened at his touch. I moaned and pushed my chest out to fill his hands.

"I have been dying to touch your body like this. I can't wait to feel it when you're naked."

I whimpered from the pleasure that was building inside of me. He hadn't even touched my skin and I was ready to explode from his touch.

I moved my hands and placed them on his biceps to steady myself. I was a mixture of lust and desire, and I needed to calm myself down. I wanted to enjoy this moment and not rush things. Normally when I got to this point, I ended things as quickly as they started so I could regain control.

I leaned over and kissed him. He greedily accepted my tongue, caressing it over and over. I moved my fingers and slowly started unbuttoning his shirt, sliding it off his shoulders and letting it fall to our feet.

I pulled away from the kiss to see what he looked like half naked. *Damn.* He was a fine specimen of a man. I would compare his body to that of a Greek God. His skin was tan. I touched his chest and beneath my fingers his hard skin tightened, he had no chest hair and his arms and shoulders were immense. The suits did a fine job hiding what was underneath. I moved my hand down his stomach tracing over the ridges of his defined six pack. I reached the V leading into his pants and wanted to lick it. I ran my fingernails along the top and his body shivered from my touch.

The sight of him gazing at me half naked set me on fire, making me want him in every way imaginable. Without hesitation, I dropped to my knees and undid his belt buckle. I looked up at him, and we locked eyes. His jaw was tense as he watched me closely.

I unzipped his pants, showing his erection straining against his black Armani boxer briefs. I slid both down, allowing his large cock to spring free. I looked over his glorious length, observing how large he was. I had never been with a man this big before. In a way, it terrified the hell out of me, but it also made me so hot that I wanted him inside of me now.

I took the tip of his dick and guided it to my lips, taking my time kissing him. Then, I swirled my tongue over the head and slowly, oh so slowly, slid him in my mouth. I sucked continuously, twirling my tongue up and down. He reached down and grabbed my hair, and when I looked up at him, his head was tipped back. He knotted his fingers into my hair and gently thrust his hips in and out of my mouth. He grunted in pleasure, and I picked up my speed.

Abruptly, he stopped, pulled out, and lifted me to my feet.

"Alexa, do you have any idea how amazing you are? I want to savor our first time together. I have been thinking about being inside of you all day. I want to see your perfect body and learn your every curve." I nodded my head, and he grabbed me by my hips, pulling me securely to him. "I can't wait to make you come, but first, let's get you naked."

I smiled shyly up at him and started to unbutton my shirt. He slid it down my arms and allowed it to fall to the floor. My nipples strained against the thin lace of my bra. He saw them peeking through the fabric and smiled with fulfillment. He cupped both of my breasts and ran his fingers over the hardened peaks through the fabric.

He kissed me swiftly and sucked on my bottom lip. When he pulled, away he gestured for me to turn around. Now standing with my back to him, he made quick work of unhooking my bra, slowly sliding it down my shoulders and arms, all the while his fingertips traced my skin. My body trembled from his touch, as he kissed my neck and back, worshipping my body. He didn't waste much time moving to my skirt, unzipping it and allowing it to fall down my legs, joining the rest of our clothes.

I heard his breathing hitch, and he playfully slapped my ass.

"Christ, Alexa. You haven't been wearing underwear all day?" I smiled, knowing this made him crazy, and shook my head. "Damn, I can't believe you."

I shrugged my shoulders like it was no big deal; to me it wasn't. I never wore underwear. They were always uncomfortable, and I loathed the lines they left.

"Turn around, Alexa."

Suddenly I felt nervous; my earlier eagerness had vanished. I was always self-conscious about my body, especially when it came to being naked. I didn't know if I could do this. Before I could second guess myself any longer, he was behind me. I could feel his erection pushing into my backside, and his breath was hot on my skin as he spoke.

"Alexa, don't make me wait any longer. Please, turn around."

I turned around, securing eyes with him. That gave me all the reassurance I needed. His eyes slowly scanned my entire body with an expression of hunger. He grabbed me by my thighs, lifting me so I was in his arms. I wrapped my arms around his neck and my legs around his waist.

"You're so fucking beautiful, Lex. I absolutely love your thighs."

I laughed. "Really? Because I hate my thighs."

He swatted my behind again, causing me to yelp. *What was it with him and spanking me?* He walked us over to the bed.

"If you keep running your mouth like that, putting yourself down, it's going to hurt a lot worse next time. I think your body is perfect, especially your thighs."

Slowly, he lowered us onto the bed and laid above me, holding his weight on his forearms.

"Alexa, tell me what you want?"

"I want you."

He brushed his lips over mine. "Tell me more."

"I need you."

At that moment, I don't think I had ever wanted anything so bad in all my life. The feeling of the head of his cock being nudged against my sex sent my body into extreme mania.

"Tell me you'll give us a chance. Before I'm inside of you and make love to you, I need to know."

I knew that what I should do and would do were two different things. I had come this far and wanted him, plain and simple. "Yes, I'll give us a chance. But I have to warn you, I've never dated or been with anyone more than once so this is all new to me."

"Don't worry. I want you just the way you are." He moved down my body, positioning his head between my legs. His mouth wrapped around my clit, and he started to lick and suck in perfect unison. He didn't waste a minute; his hands were wrapped around my thighs, spreading my legs as far apart as they would go. I bucked off of the bed, pressing myself harder against him. He stopped the constant torture and stuck his tongue inside of me, swirling all around. His skilled mouth caused me to feel the ecstasy building, and before I knew it, the world around me was shattering as my body shuddered in a mind-blowing orgasm. I screamed his name and twisted my hands in his hair.

He didn't stop once I came back to earth, and the feeling of the continued pleasure was so intense, I didn't think I could handle anymore. I looked down with heavy lids and watched as he flicked his tongue back and forth over my sensitive clit. He tightly held my body to him while I fisted the comforter. My body trembled and moved off the bed.

I had never felt a feeling so strong. I didn't know if I would be able to come again, but Vincent reached up and tugged on one of my nipples. It sent me out of this universe. I whimpered as he continued. When my body stopped convulsing, he slowed the constant assault and moved to kiss my thighs, whispering words I couldn't make out against my skin.

"I think it's time we remove these, don't you?" he asked.

I nodded my head, unable to find my voice. He slowly slid each one of the stockings down my legs and tossed them to the floor. I stared up at him kneeling between my legs. A flame burned within me, wanting to feel him inside of me and to pleasure him like he did me.

"Vince I need you inside me, now."

"I know." He chuckled and rolled a condom down his magnificent length as I watched in amazement. He kissed me and then he lowered his body on top of mine.

"Trust me; I can't wait to be inside of your sweet little cunt."

I lifted my hips off of the bed, eager to feel him inside of me. I didn't know if we would fit together, but I wanted him bad enough I was willing to try. He didn't rush and was gentle, slowly easing his way inside of me, inch by inch, and never taking his eyes off of mine. That alone kept me relaxed. Once he was inside, he laid down and held my face in his hands.

"Are you okay, beautiful?"

"Mmm-hmm."

I lifted my lips to kiss him while he allowed me time to acclimate to his size. He held my face and I leaned into his touch. I closed my eyes and squeezed myself around his cock.

"You're so big." I said.

"Hmm. you're so tight."

Slowly he started to move, pulling all the way out of me and then pushing back in. I was amazed his size didn't hurt me; it pleased me in a way I had never experienced. Everything inside burned with endorphins. I lifted my hips to match his movements, needing more from him. He kissed me with urgency and increased the rhythm. I clenched my pussy tightly around him and wrapped his body in my arms and legs. He moved with precision and rubbed that sweet spot no man had ever found before.

Reaching down, he grabbed the back of one of my thighs. The feeling of him rubbing me and gripping my thigh was incredible. It made my entire body tingle; I tilted my head back enjoying the pleasure. I moved my hands, exploring his body, feeling every hard contour. His muscles flexed underneath my touch as he moved inside of me. I couldn't seem to control myself when it came to touching him; I wanted to feel every inch. Thankfully, he was no longer being gentle with me as he picked up speed and roughly crashed inside of me.

"Come with me, beautiful," he commanded.

I didn't think I would be able to come for a third time, but I felt another orgasm building. I nodded my head at him and he leaned back into a kneeling position keeping me close to him. My butt was now raised off the bed and my legs wrapped tightly around him.

I cried out loudly, instantly finding my release. My body trembled as electricity pulsed through me. Vincent growled, thrusting himself inside of me. I could tell he was coming by his expression and noises. As he poured himself inside of me, he gripped my skin tightly. When he was finished, he lowered my hips to the bed and laid his head in between my breasts.

I wrapped my arms around him, thinking of how sweet it was that he was content lying there still inside of me. The men I had been with previously would've already been up and in the bathroom, but not Vincent. He was different in more ways than one. I stroked his wild strands of damp hair, feeling him relax beneath my touch. His breathing evened out as he traced my arm with soft fingers. I could have stayed in that moment forever. He was perfect, and I wanted him to know that.

"You're incredible," I said.

He moved his head to look into my eyes. "You're incredible. The calmness I feel when I'm with you is like nothing I've ever felt before. I love the way your body feels and how it reacts to my touch. Will you shower with me?"

I didn't know what to say. I had never showered with a man before. I met his hazel gaze with my green eyes.

"I'm not sure if I can stand for long, but I'll try."

He ran his nose over mine and took my face in his hands.

"Let's take a bath. That way, you can just relax."

I nodded my head and he slowly eased out of me. I already didn't like the feeling of not having him inside of me.

I sat up and kissed him before he climbed off the bed. "I'll run the water and meet you in the bathroom?"

I watched his body as he sauntered off.

"You're staring," he yelled over his shoulder.

I laughed to myself and fell back against the plush pillow. How could I not stare? He was perfect. His looks were to die for, and his personality was amazing. He really was a good guy, despite my prior concerns. He had all the qualities a girl could want in a man. And then there was the sex; it was mind blowing and that could have been an understatement. I sat up and headed into the bathroom already noticing how sore I was when I walked.

The bathroom was filled with steam and smelled of coconut. In the middle of the room was a large oval shape tub. He appeared in the doorway and made his way towards me. I felt shy standing there naked in front of him.

"I need to use the restroom real quick."

He kissed my forehead. "Okay. I'll be waiting for you."

"Thank you." I kissed his cheek and walked past him into the restroom. My confidence was so up and down around him. He called me beautiful and never gave me a reason to second-guess the way he felt about me, but a part of me wanted to grab a towel and cover myself up. I would have done just that, but I feared another spanking would follow if I did. Maybe he wouldn't be in the bathtub yet, and I could sneak in before him.

I opened the door and there he was in all his glory, fully submerged in the round tub that could've comfortably fit four people. I took a deep breath and kept looking at him. A sexy smirk spread across his face, and he waved his finger at me, gesturing that I come to him. I did as he asked, and he stood completely naked to help me in. We slid down the back of the bathtub so that I was now lying on top of him with my stomach against his.

"Why are you shy around me?"

I stopped looking at him and laid my check against his chest. I shrugged my shoulders, but didn't speak.

"Your body is wickedly appealing. Every contour is perfect. Your face is beautiful. That's what took my breath away the night I met you. Your breasts are amazing, big and voluptuous and fit perfectly in my hands, which lead into your flat stomach. And don't even get me started on your thighs."

I didn't speak for a few moments. I didn't know how to respond to what he had just told me. My mother had been horrible to me. I endured years upon years of abuse from her verbally. I know that's where my self-image issues came from. I just didn't know if I was ready to share that part of my life with him.

He tickled my back, finally saying, "You don't have to explain anything to me. I just want you to know how beautiful I think you are on the inside and out."

He wasn't pushing me, which was what I needed to feel comfortable enough to open up. I found my voice and began speaking without looking at him. "I don't see myself the way you do."

He grabbed my face and turned it to him. "Lex, you have to know that you're stunning. You're absolutely breathtaking. Please don't think less of yourself than what you are. You're perfect. I love you just the way you are, do you understand me?"

I heard what he was saying but comprehending it was hard.

"It's so sweet of you to say—"

He kissed me tenderly cutting off my words. "It's the truth. Please don't forget that, okay?"

I leaned up and kissed him, forgetting about answering him back.

"On another note, since you haven't corrected me yet, does this mean you are going to let me call you Lex?"

I honestly hadn't even noticed he called me Lex. I felt bad for snapping at him the first day he showed up at work. He didn't know why I was sensitive to the name. Considering all things, I guess since I hadn't corrected him, I truly didn't mind.

"My grandfather gave me the nickname Lex, and he recently passed away. I didn't mean to snap at you the other day in your office. It was just hard for me to hear someone new call me that."

He hugged me tightly to his chest.

"It's okay. I don't have to call you that. I just like how it sounds, but I like beautiful as well. It suits you."

I laughed and looked into his eyes. "Well, you can't call me 'beautiful' at work. Lex is fine with me if you like it."

He pressed our lips together letting them linger and stared into my eyes.

"Oh, I like it."

He pushed his pelvis into me, and I could feel his erection. Leaning up, I intensified the kiss by sliding my tongue into his mouth. He grabbed my hips with his large hands and sat us up as I wrapped my arms around his neck.

"I want you," he murmured against my mouth.

I wanted him too. I needed him. This zeal I was feeling was something I wasn't used to, but it was there, and I couldn't fight it.

"Are you on birth control?" he asked.

I nodded my head in between kisses while he rubbed his large shaft against my sex.

"I have never been with anyone without using protection."

We both had that in common. With him I was

breaking all of the rules.

"Neither have I."

That was all the confirmation he needed. Reaching between us he lifted my body and lowered it onto his cock. The feeling was exquisite as water pushed inside me along with him, stretching and filling me; Skin on skin with nothing separating us. I didn't need to acclimate this time; he easily fit inside of me.

"You feel so fucking amazing."

I smiled at him. "I have never wanted anyone the way I want you." I started to move, feeling nothing but sensation, watching the beautiful man beneath me. Vincent helped guide me up and down by holding my hips. He tipped his head back and closed his eyes. I slowed my movements as I already felt an orgasm building. I left a trail of kisses from his lips down to the middle of his chest.

He leaned up and spoke. "Wrap your arms around my neck and don't close your eyes. I want to watch you come."

I did so, and we really started to move. The water was splashing on the floor, but we didn't care. In that second, I couldn't take my eyes from his if I wanted to; my orgasm spiraling out of my system. He sensed what I was feeling and slammed into me. We came together, our eyes locked on one another. Breathing heavily, I rested my forehead against his and he wrapped his arms around me, leaning us back. I loved how he was never in a hurry to get out of me.

I yawned and he kissed the top of my head. "Come on. Let's get to bed."

Climbing into Vincent's warm bed, I was wearing an entirely too large t-shirt. He got in at the same time and scooted to the middle, pulling me in his arms. My back was against his chest. He brushed my hair out of the way and traced my neck with his fingers as exhaustion set in. I reached back to touch him, and he grabbed my wrist kissing the inside of it.

"Sleep well, beautiful."

Chapter 9

Bugatti

Waking up the next morning, I was extremely hot, like I was overheating. I opened my eyes to the blue sky and rolling clouds. This was amazing to wake up to; Vincent was tangled around me, his head on my chest. Sleeping soundly, his breathing was even and calm. I ran my fingers through his hair, causing him to moan and roll onto his back. His arm fell above his head and his body lie stretched across the bed.

I rolled onto my stomach and propped myself up on my elbows, resting my chin in my hands. He was perfect; that was the best way I could describe him. His hair was messy as it hung on his forehead. His eyebrows where thick and smooth, perfectly proportioned for his face, and his long black lashes touched his cheeks when his eyes were closed. His nose was straight, not a bump or crook to it, and his lips were full. His face had morning stubble on it, looking so sexy I wanted to lick him.

I laid there and stared at him, thankful he couldn't see me. I wanted to crawl on top of him and kiss him with everything I had to show him how much he already meant to me. I went against my better judgment when nature called. I slid out of his bed and padded quietly into the restroom, my entire body was sore. When I returned to the bedroom, Vincent was still sound asleep. I watched as slow breaths moved through him.

Finally tearing my eyes away, I was on a mission to make coffee. I rustled as quietly as I could in his kitchen to get the coffee pot started. I waited for it to brew, looking out into the open space surrounding Vincent's home. There really was no one close to his property. The other homes were far off and looked like tiny trinkets. The pool was glistening in the morning sun; a swim sounded perfect.

I wished I had some clothes or things of my own here. I was sure Vincent would swim naked, but I needed a little more courage to do that. While I waited, I wondered around the house, coming upon a door Vincent hadn't taken me into the night before. I opened it, and I searched for the light switch, it was his garage.

Holy shit.

Why hadn't he shown me his car collection last night? He was aware that I had a love for cars. The speed and adrenaline you felt while driving a car fast and pushing its limits around corners did things to me; it turned me on. The garage was a four-car tandem, allowing it to fit at least eight cars. Currently there were five, and the floor was carbon fiber and heated. I could feel the heat on the pads of my feet as I moved around.

The collection was impressive to say the least. As I walked to the back corner, tucked away was clearly his prized possession; a black and red Bugatti Veyron Super Sport. Holy shit, that car was rare and gorgeous.

I stood there in awe. I would kill to drive any one of these. I was brought back to reality by his large hands pulling me back against his body.

"There you are, beautiful. I didn't like waking up without you there." He kissed my neck, and I tilted my head for him.

"You were so peaceful, I didn't want to wake you. After I got my fill of staring, I ventured off to make coffee and found myself in here. Vince, this is quite the collection of cars. Why didn't you show me last night?"

He leaned his chin on my shoulder. "Honestly? I didn't want you to be distracted by this. I wanted you to make your decision based on your feelings for me. Plus, it would have taken all of my control to not have bent you over one of these cars and fucked you seven shades of Sunday."

"Do you really think a car collection would sway my mind?"

He chuckled. "I don't know. I was nervous, and I also didn't think I could control myself with you in here. Like right now for instance, you look so innocent wearing just my t-shirt. I want to fuck you so bad I can't stand it."

I wanted him just as much as he wanted me. I cocked my head to the side and gave him a playful grin.

"Then what's stopping you?"

He grabbed the hem of the shirt I was wearing and lifted it above my head. I stood naked staring at him. He was only wearing a pair of shorts that were barely hanging on his hips. I stepped forward and tugged them down. His erection sprang free and he stepped out of the shorts grabbing me.

"God, you're so fucking sexy."

He leaned down and kissed me, sliding one of his hands down my body. Once he reached my behind, he squeezed my ass and nibbled on my bottom lip. He pulled away, cupping my breast in his other hand. I stood there in his grip, completely turned on, our eyes locked in a stare of desire. I wanted him to fuck me hard; I needed him inside of me.

As he kissed me with urgency, I kissed him back. I couldn't help myself from reaching between us and stroking his hard cock. "I need you inside me. Now."

He walked us backwards to the Bugatti. "Turn around beautiful and put your hands on the car." I shook my head.

Was he crazy? This car cost over a million dollars.

There was no way I was going to dent or scratch it. He leaned into me and nipped my neck.

"Alexa, I will make you turn around. Don't temp me."

I searched for my voice as need pulsed through me. "I don't want to scratch the car. It costs so much."

He chuckled, and then wound my hair around his hand until he had it in a tight grip.

"I don't give a fuck about the cars. Now bend over it." He tugged on my hair causing my head to fall back, and looked deep into my eyes. "Turn around and tell me how much you want me."

I had never had a man speak to me or handle me the way he was in that moment, and it was such a turn on. I didn't know how to respond.

"Tell me how you want me inside you. Hard and fast, or soft and slow?"

I kissed him with everything I had. He had me so wound up. I just needed him any way I could get him. "I need you inside me. I don't care if it's fast or slow. I just need you."

A mischievous grin spread across his face, and without saying a word, he turned me around and gently bent me over the car. I placed my hands on the smooth black and red paint; it felt slick beneath my fingertips. He didn't let go of my hair as he slowly eased his beautiful cock inside of me.

"Fuck. You're wet."

I moaned at his words. I wanted him and the arousal was apparent. The desire I had for him scared the shit out of me, but at that moment, I didn't care. He slid all the way inside of me, and he leaned his body over mine, releasing my hair. He intertwined our fingers and slowly thrust himself in and out of me. I whimpered with pleasure as he immediately rubbed my sweet spot.

"I love how tight your pussy is. I could come already," he panted.

All I could get out was a mumble before I started to whimper. He chuckled again, that low soft laughter I loved. I stood on my toes to lift my ass into him even more. I needed him inside of me as deep as I could get him. I wanted him to speed up; I needed him to.

"Harder, please." He rose off of me and gripped my hips, pulling me firmly against him, causing him to fill me balls deep. I cried out in pleasure at the feeling of him so deep inside of me. He kept a steady firm rhythm as he reached around to touch my clit. His fingers ran in a slow circular movement causing my body to tighten. Everything tingled and his movements had me close to coming.

"Oh, God," I cried.

"Fuck, Lex. Come with me."

I pushed myself against him as his fingers dug into my skin. Listening to his command, I let go, giving into the pleasure and came hard. His body quivered as he moaned long and deep, coming with me.

As usual, he was in no hurry to leave my body. He wrapped his arms around me, resting on top of my back and kissing me all over. As we stayed there, silent and content my body started to cramp from the two hundred pound man on top of me. We were in a precarious position and I wiggled a little under him. He stood up and asked, "Am I hurting you?"

I pushed myself off the car into a standing position, and the cramp went away. "No, I'm fine. Just a little cramp, but it's gone now."

He kissed the top of my shoulder and eased out of me. I turned around to face him.

"You are insatiable. I love being inside of you. I don't think I will ever get enough."

I cupped his face in both of my hands; his scruffiness was sexy as hell. I was unsure what to say to him, so I leaned up and kissed him. His hands gripped my hips, and we were lost in one another.

After a morning swim and breakfast in the sun, I felt like we were living in a nudist colony.

"Do you always hang outside naked?"

He shook his head. "Nah, I don't prefer to do this alone, and I haven't found anyone to share it with until you."

I smiled to myself. "Aren't you worried that your neighbors have binoculars?"

He laughed, "I sure hope not because if anyone else sees you naked, I will go ape shit on them."

"Ape shit? Who says that?"

He pinned me underneath him, pressing my body into the plush lounge chair. "I do when you talk about other people seeing my girlfriend naked. I don't like it."

Shit. Did he just call me his girlfriend?

This was moving too fast, it had only been a day. What were we supposed to tell people at work? I chewed on my bottom lip staring into his eyes. He could read the anxiety on my face and moved off of me to sit at the end of my lounge chair.

As he sat between my legs he said, "Did I say something wrong? I'm sorry, Lex, but I don't want anyone else to see you naked."

When I shook my head, he stood up and walked away from me. He began pacing and ran his hands through his hair.

"There's someone else, isn't there? Is that why you've been fighting me so hard on this whole thing?"

What? No!

What was he talking about? Why would he think that? Instinct took over, and I hopped up, running to him. I stood behind him and wrapped my arms around his waist. I rested my face against his back.

"No, of course not. Why would you think that? Vince, there is only you. I wouldn't have gotten involved with you if I was with someone else." He stood frozen.

"Please look at me." He turned in my arms and looked down at me as I said, "I'm sorry. I got scared when you called me your girlfriend and I panicked. I've never been anyone's girlfriend before. You have to know there isn't anyone else, there never has been."

He closed his eyes and leaned his forehead against mine as his breathing slowed. "I'm sorry. I can be jealous. I've been hurt in the past, and my mind always goes to the worst-case scenario. I haven't dated in a long time. My last relationship didn't end well and it fucked with me. I haven't wanted to until you; you took my breath away and reignited these feelings I'd suppressed. If you hadn't kissed me the night I met you, I don't know what I would've done. As soon as our lips touched, all of that fear went out the window. For you, it's worth the risk."

I didn't know how to respond to his honesty. All I could do was hug him and say I was sorry.

We spent the day outside in the sun by the pool, constantly tangled in each other's arms. Neither of us brought up the earlier situation that had ensued between us. I acted childishly over a statement he made. I made the decision to give him a chance, and with that, came a title. Quite frankly, I wanted to be his girlfriend. I had come this far with him and was enjoying every minute of it. Why stop now?

I was curled up in his arms on the oversized lounge chair while he slept. I couldn't help myself from drinking all his features in. This all felt like a dream that I was going to wake from at any moment. We had sex in the pool and on this lounge chair. I was exhausted and extremely satisfied all at the same time. I was getting hungry and wanted my own clothes. I traced small circles over his chest, around his nipples, and down his stomach. He slowly stirred to life and stretched as I kissed him.

He nuzzled my neck and wrapped his body tighter around mine. I laughed at how cute he was. "Hey, you can't sleep all day."

He mumbled into my skin, "The fuck I can't."

I laughed again. "Well, I'm hungry and need some clothes, so if you want to sleep will you take me home, and then you can rest all weekend?"

He shot up like a fire alarm went off.

"No, you're not leaving. I can't sleep without you."

What was he talking about? He seemed to sleep just fine. He slept all night and had been napping on and off all day.

"Don't be silly. This is new, and I don't want you to get tired of me."

His jaw clenched and he rubbed his face with his large hands. "You should know I suffer from insomnia. I haven't slept like this in years. I don't know what it is about you, but when I'm with you, I can finally rest.

Don't go. I'll take you to your place, and we'll get you whatever you need."

How could I say no to him? I didn't want to leave him either, as much as I should fight it; I was already comfortable being with him. I wanted nothing more than to spend the rest of the weekend together.

"Okay, but I'm starving, so we need to eat."

He smiled at me and kissed the tip of my nose. "Whatever you need, we'll get for you, beautiful."

We dressed quickly and went into the garage instead of out the front door.

"Take your pick, Lex. What shall we drive?"

My mouth hung open. "You mean you actually drive these things?"

He laughed, and pulled me against his body. "Of course I do. That's what they're made for."

I scanned over the impressive collection of cars. My motto was, go big or go home. "I've come to like the Bugatti."

He grabbed the key hanging on a hook. "After you, beautiful."

I walked over to the car, and the earlier images of us together flashed through my mind. He had bent me over this car this morning, and I loved every minute of it. I smiled to myself as everything below my waist tightened and I burned with desire to have him bend me over again. Surprisingly, we hadn't left a scratch or a dent. He opened my door, and I slid into the sleek, bright red, leather interior matching the accents on the body of the car. I had never seen anything like it. The inside was incredibly sleek and modern; a mixture of carbon fiber and leather woven throughout.

Vincent slid his enormous frame behind the wheel. He was dressed extremely casual today wearing red basketball shorts, a black V-neck t-shirt, and black Nike tennis shoes. He had on a backwards Red Sox baseball hat that sat low on his forehead.

Yum!

Staring at him dressed so casual, with his calm and confident demeanor, made me feel like I was going to die in this car right now. I studied the way he gripped the wheel and brought the car to life. The sound of the engine sent a shiver through my body. He maneuvered the car with ease out of the garage and into the August heat. He put the top down and then grabbed my hand.

"Hold on tight, beautiful. I'm going to handle this car like I'll handle you later."

I squirmed in my seat thinking of what he would do to me. The anticipation alone sent my mind racing. We had already done so much together in such a short period of time. I couldn't fathom sex with him being any more incredible, but I knew it would be. We had sex five times in less than twenty-four hours and I still craved for more.

Thankfully he was wearing a hat so I didn't have to stare at his gorgeous threads of hair. I wanted to run my fingers through it and crawl over the armrest, hoping he would turn the car around or just pull over. I settled for conversation instead, I was a lady after all.

"I like your outfit. I wouldn't have guessed you for a shorts and t-shirt kind of guy."

He laughed lightly. "Why? Because I wear suits to work you think I live in them? I played basketball throughout high school and college, so this is what I'm most comfortable in."

He played basketball? I guess I should have thought of that considering how tall he was. "I didn't know you played basketball."

"There are a lot of things you don't know about me. We're just getting to know each other."

That was true. We would learn with time.

Chapter 10

Abel

We pulled into the small driveway of my condo, and he cut the engine. Cara wasn't home as she worked a lot of weekends.

"Do you want to park in the garage?"

"Nah, you won't be that long, will you?"

I shook my head and reached for his hat. I needed to touch his hair, but before I could, he grabbed my wrist and kissed the inside of it.

He walked around and opened my door while I rummaged through my purse for my keys. We walked hand in hand to my front door and when we stepped inside the condo, it was clean. Cara had a habit of rushing out of the house, leaving things a mess.

"Home sweet home," I said.

He looked around as he walked further in. "It's nice. This is just what I pictured the inside to be."

I smiled at him and went into my room. He

followed me and stopped at the doorway. I looked at him, trying to read the expression on his face. His jaw was clenched and he rubbed the back of his neck as I went over to him. He was staring at my bed, and I reached up to touch his face.

"Hey, are you okay? You look like you've seen a ghost."

He leaned into my touch and closed his eyes. I wrapped my other arm around his waist and held onto him. We stood in silence for a few minutes.

He finally spoke. "We should get you a new bed."

What the hell was he talking about?

"Vince, you lost me. I don't need a new bed."

"Yeah, you do. I don't want you sleeping in a bed that another man has been in. I can't even think about someone else being with you in that way."

He was so sweet even when he was being jealous. I couldn't blame him. Thankfully with my previous sexual experiences, I had never wanted to have someone in my bed. I always wanted to be able to leave. I wanted things to be on my terms, and I needed to have control. If I had sex in my bed, I would've been stuck, and that scared me.

"I've never had sex in my bed," I said.

His eyes lit up, and I saw desire burn within them.

"Really? Never?"

I shook my head, and he scooped me in his arms, carrying me to my bed and lowering us down onto the mattress. His lips met mine, and he crushed our mouths together. A moan escaped my throat, provoking his tongue to slide into my mouth. I caressed his tongue with the same passion he showed mine.

I knocked his hat off and finally threaded my fingers into his hair. He bit my lip as I tugged on his soft strands of hair. I pulled away and lifted the t-shirt I was wearing over my head. I then did the same to his. While he had his hands above his head, I pushed him back onto the mattress, and he pulled me down on top of him. I straddled his hips, enjoying the feeling of his growing erection between my legs. He didn't waste a second and thrust his hips, grinding himself against my sex, it sent chills though my body.

I scooted down and removed his shorts, grabbing his cock and guiding him into my mouth. He was so hard and already had a small amount of cum on the tip. I licked it off and sucked him, squeezing hard as his veins bulged. When he stopped me, l smirked at him while I removed my shorts and climbed back on top of him. As our hot skin touched, it sent a sensation of electricity through my entire system. I rubbed my folds up and down his length. I was so wet that the slickness allowed me to glide effortlessly up and down his cock. I was on all fours above him while we rocked our bodies against each other's.

His hands moved from my hips to my breasts. I pushed my chest out, and his mouth wrapped around a nipple. I moved my hips causing the head of him to ease into me. Slowly, I moved, sucking him tightly inside of me.

"Jesus, you feel so fucking amazing," he said.

I stared down at him with need and moaned. I pushed myself up so I was sitting on top of him. He was extremely deep inside of me at this angle and I had to stop my movements. I rested my hands on his chest and looked into his eyes. His hair was a mess, and a thin sheen of sweat already covered his skin. He started to move his hips, and I moved along with him.

He stretched his arms above his head, completely naked below me, allowing me to take full control. He turned his head to the side, closing his eyes and clenching his jaw. I continued to move as I leaned down to kiss him. I was eager to have his tongue in my mouth again.

When I leaned down, he wrapped his arms around me. We moved like this, in the same position, for a while. Both of us enjoyed the pleasure as well as the closeness of our bodies. I could tell from his noises that he was close to coming. I rocked harder, up and down, while caressing his tongue. He grunted violently, sending my body into a spiral. I found my release with him as he gripped my ass, digging his fingers into my skin. It felt like he was pinching me, but it didn't hurt, it only intensified my orgasm as he continued to move me up and down his length.

We slowed our movements, and I laid on top of him, resting my head on his chest. We stayed like that for a long time, not wanting to separate. He stroked my hair and ran his fingers over my body. I loved the peace and calmness I felt when I was with him. I thought of what sparked this escapade and asked him.

"Have you slept with anyone else in your bed?"

He kissed the top of my head. "No, beautiful, I haven't. It's only been you."

A smile extended across my face. I never knew how much a small detail could mean to me. I kissed his chest, and my stomach growled, telling me I needed to eat.

I didn't want to move, but I had to. I needed to pack so we could get to the store and get back to his place to cook. I slid off him and walked into the restroom; he laid there and watched me walk away naked. When I walked back into the room he was already dressed. He helped me pack, and I had everything I needed for the weekend, including my clothes for work on Monday. I needed to stay here on Monday night to work things out with Cara. I felt horrible that I had blown her off last night, when I was supposed to help her get ready for her date.

We loaded the car and drove to the store to grab what we needed for dinner. Arriving in the Bugatti was an experience to say the least. Everyone stared as we pulled in and parked. It didn't stop when we walked into the store.

"Do you ever get tired of people staring at you?" I asked.

"Are people staring?"

I laughed at him and wrapped my arm around his waist. We moved through the store, tossing everything we needed into the cart. Vincent moved with his usual confidence and authority. Even in a t-shirt and shorts, he still caught the attention of everyone around us. So it wasn't just the car that made people stare, it was him.

"Do you want dessert, beautiful?"

He smirked when I nodded my head.

"Do you have any idea how cute you are?"

I nodded my head again. He grabbed my face, turning it up to meet his. He kissed me softly and let our lips linger together. I grew impatient and wrapped my arms around him, sliding my hand underneath the fabric of his t–shirt, stroking his back. I deepened the kiss, and he accepted my tongue.

"Holy shit, Vincent. Is that you?"

I pulled away to look at who was speaking. I was mortified to see a group of guys staring. They had a cart full of groceries, and were all in Denver Fire t-shirts and traditional blue cargo pants. Vincent kept me wrapped in his arm which I was thankful for.

"Abel, how are you? Sorry I haven't called."

They exchanged a brotherly hug.

"Nah, man, it's all good. Dad said you were back. I figured you were busy getting settled. I'm sorry, I didn't mean to interrupt you two."

He smiled politely at me, and it reminded me of how Vincent looked when he smiled. He was shorter, probably just six feet tall, his eyes were the same hazel, and they had the same dark colored hair, except Abel's was shaved. They were strikingly similar, minus the tattoos that covered Abel's arms.

"No, its fine. We were just getting ready to check out. Abel, this is my girlfriend, Alexa. Lex, this is my brother, Abel."

I met his gaze, and he smiled at me, reaching out to shake my hand.

"It's a pleasure to meet you, Alexa."

I smiled back. "It's nice to meet you as well. I've heard a lot of great things about you."

Abel introduced us to his fellow fire fighters. "This is Sam, Danny, and Troy. Guys this is my brother Vincent and his girl, Alexa."

They all nodded and said 'hi,' and we did the same. It gave me the creeps when Sam winked at me, but I just politely smiled.

Vincent immediately pulled me closer against his side.

"It was good seeing you, Abel, but we've got to get going."

Vincent hadn't spoken much on the drive back to his house, so I just looked out of the top of the car at the now night sky. My hand was enveloped in his. I didn't want to push the situation with Abel, but something had clearly happened there. I wondered what had set Vincent off. Sometimes he was hard to read, but I didn't want to ruin the evening, so I wasn't going to pry.

We pulled into the driveway and Vincent backed the Bugatti to the garage with precision. He opened my door, helping me out, and then we grabbed all of the bags.

Heading inside, he said, "Next time, you're driving."

Uh, no way.

"I don't think that's a good idea. What if I hurt the car?"

We sat the bags on the island in the kitchen, and he grabbed my hips pulling my body against his.

"I told you, cars can always be fixed. If it makes you happy to drive them, then drive them."

I leaned my body into his and wrapped my arms around his waist. In the short time I had known him, he had treated me better than anyone had my entire life.

"Okay. Next time I'll drive."

"Good girl," he said, slapping me hard on my ass. I didn't make a noise because all it did was turn me on. I kissed him softly, and he let our lips rest against each other's. When he pulled back, I looked into his eyes and saw anxiety etched across his face as his eyebrows were creased.

"I'm sorry for getting upset at the store. I shouldn't have reacted the way I did."

"No worries. Do you want to talk about what happened?"

He took a deep breath and said, "Remember when I told you that my last relationship didn't end well?" I nodded my head and he continued. "I was engaged. Her name was Angela. She had cheated on me once. It killed me, but I forgave her. Things between us were going well, at least, I thought they were. Then I caught her having sex with someone else in our bed. The worst part was, when I walked in on them, she didn't see me, but the guy did. He winked at me while he kept fucking her. I stood there like an idiot in shock. I should've done something but I was disgusted. When that guy winked at you tonight, it pissed me off. My instincts kicked in, and it took me back to the past. I just wanted to protect you. I'm sorry for overacting today."

I hugged him tightly. "Vince, please don't apologize for that. I'm not her. I would never hurt you. I'm glad you told me though, honesty is everything to me."

"Of course. So we're on the same page?"

I smiled and stood on my toes to kiss his cheek. "Yes. We're on the same page."

He squeezed my ass and smiled down at me. I watched as the expression on his face changed to calmness.

"Come on, let's cook. You need to eat."

Cooking with Vincent was fun. He was extremely playful in the kitchen. We couldn't keep our hands off each other, but surprisingly managed to complete the meal.

After we ate, I laid curled up in his arms out back by the pool. We watched the fire as it crackled in the fire pit.

I thought back to our earlier conversation. I couldn't imagine walking in on someone you loved, and were planning on spending the rest of your life with, to see them cheating on you. I shivered at the thought.

"Are you cold?" he asked as he ran his large hands up and down my arms.

"No. I'm perfect. What do you think about a late night swim?"

In that moment, he stood and scooped me up in his arms. Walking us towards the pool, he didn't hesitate as he headed down the steps.

"We still have our clothes on," I said, but it was too late, we were both fully submerged in the water. I laughed at him and shook my head.

"I'm sorry, I couldn't wait for you to get undressed. Plus, I wanted to see your body through your clothes, especially your nipples."

I was in black tight booty shorts and a white tank top. I wasn't wearing a bra and of course no underwear. Vincent demanded that I wore this while we cooked dinner; he had packed it himself with the items we brought from my house.

I followed his gaze, his eyes were locked on my dark swollen nipples visible through the wet, white fabric.

He pulled my tank top down below my breasts, causing them to swell above the water. His mouth moved and wrapped around one of my sensitive buds. He sucked on the skin and gently tugged on my nipple, and then he moved to the other. I reached for the hem of his shirt and managed to get it off. His hair was now dripping with water, and I took the opportunity to weave my fingers into it.

Tightly, I wrapped my legs around his waist, and he walked us over to the edge. We pressed our mouths together and eagerly kissed one another. A hungry moan escaped his throat, and his hands moved to my shorts. He tugged them down my legs. Once they were off, they floated to surface. Vincent worked his shorts down his legs.

"I can't wait to be inside of you," he said between kisses.

I yearned to have him fill me. My arms and legs were wrapped around him, and he nudged his erection against my sex but didn't push himself inside of me.

"Please. I need you."

He laughed softly against my mouth and continued to enjoy slowly kissing me. He sucked and nibbled on my lips and took his time enjoying my mouth. I wiggled myself against him to find a release. I needed to be fulfilled by him, but he wasn't budging. I stopped kissing him and bit his neck, sucking on his sensitive skin. That was the push he needed. Instantly, he sank deep inside of me. I wrapped myself tighter around him and began to move my hips. He cupped my ass and helped guide me up and down his cock. His rhythm picked up as he indulged himself inside of me.

"Look at me," he demanded.

My eyes met his, and I was tangled in that moment with him. The eagerness from within him was deep in his eyes as he moved faster and faster inside of me.

"Fuck. You feel so good. I love your sweet little cunt," he rasped.

Those words pushed me to the edge. I dug my fingernails into his back and whimpered into his skin. My body was all sensation and I was hanging on by a thread. He grunted as he poured himself deep inside me, causing me to shudder and convulse. I squeezed his cock and came along with him.

Fuck, he was amazing!

I rested my forehead against his with my eyes intently locked on his. This man was truly a blessing. How had I gotten so lucky? If I had known that things between us could've been this good, I never would've fought him. He was honest, caring, and genuine. I couldn't ask for anything more, and because of that there was no doubt as to why I wanted to give this, us, a chance.

I laid with Vincent in bed, tucked tightly in his arms. He fell asleep long ago; his breathing was even and shallow. I was dreading the weekend ending. I didn't want to go back to reality. I wanted to stay in this world forever.

Monday would be here before we knew it, and I didn't know what to say to him about work. I didn't want to tell anyone there that we were dating, not yet anyways. It was so soon. I was nervous of his reaction, but hoped he would understand. I had broken all of my rules for him, and I was only asking that he give us a little time at work before we told anyone. I had made sure throughout my career that I would never be pegged as a person who was given special privileges, and I didn't want that title now. Not only that, but we had a big case going to trial on Monday. I didn't want to take anyone's head out of the game. Vincent would be in court for most of the week, so that would make things easier. Then with time, and with our co-workers seeing how we acted around one another, we could slowly tell everyone we were together.

Chapter II

Work

I woke with a foggy head, unsure of where I was. I opened my eyes to the blue sky and I knew then I was in his bed. I rolled over to snuggle up to Vincent, but he was gone. I sat up and looked around the room, but there was no sign of him. Frustrated, I plopped back against the pillow and threw my arm over my face. I wondered where he was, then work popped in my mind.

Damn it.

How was I going to bring it up to him? Before I could beat myself up any longer, I heard his footsteps pattering towards me.

"Good morning, beautiful." He strolled into the room carrying a tray in his arms, wearing only his shorts. The tray held an array of breakfast items, Starbucks and a white rose.

"Good morning yourself. What's all this for?"

Setting the tray down, he ran his knuckles down my

face and brushed my lips with his thumb.

"For being you, and for giving me the best night's sleep I've had in years. I had to set my alarm to get up and get this ready today."

"Really? I didn't even hear you leave."

He scooted next to me in bed. "I didn't leave. I ordered it yesterday."

How in the world had he gotten Starbucks to deliver?

No one had ever brought me breakfast in bed, much less had it delivered. I shook my head; this man was far beyond any and all of my expectations. I threw myself into his arms and he caught me as if I only weighed ninety pounds. I faced him and looked into his eyes, but my stare didn't hold long as my eyes traveled to his mouth. I kissed him with passion and gratitude. He kissed me back and began rubbing my thighs.

"The food's going to get cold. We should eat," he said.

I rested my forehead against his and pouted. I didn't want food; I wanted him. My body craved him. I turned around in his lap, not wanting to remove myself from my newfound comfort zone. Pulling the tray over to us, I handed him a fork, and we began to take turns feeding each other. Behind me, I felt his growing erection as I moaned and sucked on a strawberry, in hopes he would devour me.

"Fuck breakfast," he growled.

We stood in the garage as Vincent had said it was my choice of what to drive today.

"I think we should take the Mercedes."

He narrowed his eyes at me and placed his hands on his hips. "Fuck no. We're not taking the Mercedes. Besides, you already have one.

"Fine, the Corvette."

He kissed my head and tossed me the key. "Good choice. I haven't had a chance to drive her yet, so you'll have to tell me what you think."

I shook my head. "No way. I don't want to be the first one."

"It's fine, baby."

"Why haven't you driven it yet?"

"I just got it back from Calloway. After I ordered the car, I sent it there for all of the mods. They just delivered it, and I haven't had a chance to drive it because someone has had me a little preoccupied."

He opened the driver's door of the white Corvette Calloway. "In you go."

Oh my God. I can't believe I'm about to drive this.

Vincent slid in next to me. He was patient while walking me through how to start the car and adjust my seat and mirrors. I put the Corvette into gear, starting in second, without having to ask. I knew cars. Slowly I eased this white beauty out of the garage, and Vincent pushed the pre-programmed button to close it.

"So, where to, beautiful?"

I raised my eyebrows at him and then lowered my sunglasses. "It's a surprise." Then I threw his words back at him. "Hold on tight. I'm going to handle this car like I'll handle you later."

He laughed at me like I was joking, and with that, I took off peeling out of the driveway. This car handled like a dream. I knew just where to take him as we started to head into the mountains. I slowed down a little and enjoyed the scenery, not just next to me, but all around me. Vincent was absolutely breathtaking; today he was in a dark pair of jeans that hung off his hips in just the right way, and a tight grey t-shirt. He looked calm and at ease with his hair messy and Cavalli sunglasses.

He rested his hand on my leg and stroked my sensitive thigh. I was in jean shorts because I knew he'd like them, and I wanted to make him happy. He gave me the confidence to feel beautiful in my skin. I matched the shorts with a silver sequined tank top and black sandals.

"Watching you drive this car has my dick so hard. I want to fuck you right now."

I gasped at his words. This man was sure to be the death of me. I looked over and saw his cock straining against his jeans, he wasn't joking. I wanted to pull the car over right now and slowly unzip his pants to free his huge erection. "I think I know a place where we can fulfill your needs," I said.

I sped up the curvy mountain road until I reached our destination. I pulled off of the main street and drove towards a secret spot I had visited often to clear my mind. And for the second time in two days, we had car sex. Only this time, Vincent sat me on the hood and fucked me as he looked into my eyes. Jesus, he was mind blowing.

We ate lunch on the river at one of my favorite spots where they specialized in wine and cheese and have the best desserts. We had explored the tiny shops, and then fed the ducks as we walked along the river. The best part of the day was how well we got along and could just talk. We had more in common than I realized. We both loved cars, basketball, and were suckers for accessory shopping. I found out that Vincent had an extensive watch collection, just like my purse and shoe collection.

I had Vincent drive us home and thought there was no better time to bring up the work situation. I didn't want to spoil a good day, but we were both so relaxed and in a good mental place together. It was now or never.

I turned towards him and tucked my foot underneath me. "I need to talk to you about work," I said.

His eyebrows creased, and I saw his grip on the wheel tighten. "So talk, beautiful."

I took a deep breath. I could do this. If he cared for

me the way he said that he did and had shown me this weekend, he would understand.

"I don't want to tell anyone at work that we're dating. Not yet anyways."

He ran a hand through his hair. "Why not?"

"I love my job and have worked really hard to get to where I am. I've made my rules clear to a few of my co-workers, and I don't want them to feel like, after knowing you for a week, I've changed who I am. I don't want them questioning my character. I'm not saying that I don't want to ever tell anyone, but can we give it a little time?"

He was silent for a few minutes, and I gave him that. I didn't want to push him.

"Fine. I can wait a few weeks. But I'm not ashamed to tell the entire world that you're mine. I get what you are saying, that you've been there longer and don't want others to question your character. But I can't promise that I'll be able to control myself around you."

"I am not ashamed of you. I want you to know that's not what this is about. I'm just scared, but I'm willing to take the risk for you. I just want to ease into this, to give everyone some time to see us together and then slowly they'll see it coming. I don't want to start office gossip. Two weeks. I promise."

"Shit, shit, shit! I cannot believe you let me oversleep."

Vincent was leaning on the doorframe to his bedroom, dressed in a navy blue suit with a cup of coffee in his hand and a grin on his face.

"Don't yell at me. I tried to wake you. You're the one that overslept."

I glared at him and struggled to get my stocking up without snagging it. "How's it going to look if we both walk in late and my car is already there?"

He shrugged his shoulders and sat his coffee on the dresser next to him. "No one is going to notice. Stop worrying."

I rolled my eyes and slid on a pair of underwear, my skirt, and shoes. I bet he did this on purpose so our co-workers would see us arrive together. I stormed past him on a mission to make my point that I was pissed.

He grabbed me by the waist with a frown on his face. "Why did you put underwear on?"

I narrowed my eyes and inched closer to his face. "Because I'm pissed off at you for letting me oversleep, and for that, I don't want you thinking about me not wearing underwear all day. I call this payback, so don't think you'll be getting lucky today."

He laughed out loud. "If you think that wearing underwear is going to stop me, you're dead wrong. I'll tear those off of you in half a second without thinking twice. And yes, I will get lucky today, so you better watch yourself."

He cupped my ass in both of his hands and leaned down to kiss me. I couldn't deny him, so I parted my lips inviting him in. His scent was intoxicating, and that suit did things to me. He stared into my eyes and breathed heavily, squeezing my body.

"Mine," he murmured, biting my bottom lip. "Two can play this game, beautiful." He released me and walked away.

What the hell?

I stood in his room, frozen. I was the one pissed off, and now, here I stood alone, panting, and damp. *Damn him.* I peeled my underwear off and stormed into the kitchen. Yes, two *could* play this game, so game on. Vincent was making us coffee when I approached him. He handed me a travel mug, which smelled delicious, and I threw my underwear at him and stormed into the garage.

We drove in silence, and I pretended to be angry when really I was horny. I wanted him and he teased me; that's what really pissed me off. After he parked the car, I threw my door open and started towards the building.

He yelled to me, "If you don't want to tell anyone about us, it may look weird if I carry your purse into the office."

Shit.

I turned around and kept the glare in my eyes. "Isn't it time for you to go to court?" I snapped.

He pulled me to him. "Court isn't until two. I told you, I can't promise I'll be able to control myself. If you keep running from me with this attitude, I'll be forced to show you what you mean to me."

He kissed me passionately, and I melted in his arms. Wrapping my arms around him, I threaded my fingers into his hair at the nape of his neck. He possessed my mouth the way I loved, and I let him take control. He pulled away and drank me in with his eyes.

"Please try and be good today. I'm already hard."

I looked up at him through heavy lids and nodded my head. I sucked on my bottom lip trying to calm the flame within me. He smacked my ass, and I almost came undone with the desire it brewed.

We took the elevator up, and once we reached our floor, we parted ways. The morning had passed by in the blink of an eye. Vincent had left for court and I had so much work to get done. After he was gone, it was hard to stay on task, in between the bantering back and forth via text messages with him.

Autumn, from reception, approached my desk, hiding behind a huge bouquet of white roses. My heart sped up, causing my stomach to flip with the anticipation of the note. She sat them down, and I noticed there had to have been over four-dozen roses tucked into the large crystal vase.

"Girl, I don't know who sent these to you, but I'm jealous," she ranted.

I smiled and snatched the card. "Thanks, Autumn."

She rolled her eyes and sauntered off. I don't know what more she wanted me to say. We weren't enemies, but we most certainly weren't friends, and there was no way I was going to get into who they were from with her. Quite frankly, I think she was jealous of my position.

The card was white like the roses, and it read:

Beautiful,

Thank you for an amazing weekend. I'm sad I won't sleep tonight. Next time I'm alone with you, I want you naked and covered in white rose petals.

Until later, only yours XOXO, Vincent

I pulled my cell phone out; my fingers didn't seem to move fast enough as I texted him.

The flowers are beautiful. I'm sorry you won't be able to sleep tonight. I have to make things right with Cara. We'll spend tomorrow night together, I promise.

Cara was home before me, and I walked in with my apology in hand. Corona, lime juice, and dinner. She was on the couch playing on her iPad with the TV muted.

I placed everything on the kitchen counter smiling at her. She patted the seat next to her, and without hesitation, I went over and sat down. Tears filled my eyes, and I tried to control them.

I wrapped my arms around her and said, "I'm sorry I let you down."

She pulled away from me, sitting back on the couch. "Don't be sorry. I should be the one apologizing. I shouldn't have reacted the way I did. Jon blew me off, so I was pissed and took it out on you. It wasn't your fault. Clearly things between you and Vincent have progressed, and I haven't been there for you."

I couldn't help the smile that took over my face just thinking about Vincent. "You could definitely say things between us have progressed. He's amazing."

She grinned at me. "I'm so happy for you. I haven't seen you smile like this in years. You have to tell me everything."

"Of course. Let's eat while I fill you in on the weekend."

Dinner was awesome. It felt great to indulge. I told

Cara every detail of the weekend I shared with Vincent. She was extremely interested and I could tell she was genuinely happy for me. I was unsure as to how she was going to react to the news that we were dating, but she was happy. I picked her brain for details of what I was supposed to do and not to do. Most was common sense, thank God.

After hours of talking, we said goodnight. I went into my room and turned the shower on. I stepped in, allowing the hot water to cascade over my body. As I lathered myself, I thought of the text messages I had been exchanging with Vincent all night. He was sweet and feisty all at the same time. He teased me for leaving my underwear with him. I had to laugh at myself; I couldn't believe I had thrown them in his face. A week ago I would have never dreamed of doing something so brazen, but he brought out a confidence within me. It was as if the need I felt for him pushed me to go outside of my comfort zone. Knowing Vincent was mine was all I needed. I turned the shower off and hated thinking of spending the night away from him.

I dried quickly and threw on a pink cami and matching shorts. I walked into my closet and contemplated what to wear to work tomorrow. I wanted to look sexy for Vincent. Court had been postponed, and he would most likely be in the office all day. I held up a sleek blue wrap dress and a cream button up dress with a wide belt. I couldn't decide which one I preferred so I laid them on the bed and went in search for a pair of shoes.

"I like the blue one."

I jumped is shock. *Shit he was here.*

"You scared the crap out of me."

He chuckled with light laughter and sauntered over to me. He was wearing his signature basketball shorts and a t-shirt that hugged his massive frame, showing off his muscles. He wrapped me in his arms.

"I didn't mean to scare you, but I do like the blue one better."

I slapped his arm, but he didn't flinch. "What are you doing here?"

"I'm sorry, but I can't spend the night away from you. Please let me stay, I just want to sleep in your arms. I promise I'll behave. Trust me, I know I'm still in trouble for this morning."

I smiled at him as my heart raced in my chest. I couldn't believe he was here with me and wanted to stay the night. I wanted nothing more, well I did want more. Payback for this morning was in order, and I was going to have fun with him for leaving me standing in his bedroom panting and about to explode.

"How did you get in here?"

He kept me tucked in his arms and spoke softly. "Cara let me in. I think she may even like me. I thought I was going to have to argue and plead my way in, but she was really cool."

Keep your cool, Alexa.

"Yeah, she's adjusting to the thought of us dating. You really want to stay the night and not have sex?"

He swallowed hard and nodded his head.

"Okay. You can stay as long as you behave. Remember, you're still in trouble for letting me oversleep this morning?"

A grin spread across his face, and he leaned in to kiss me. I turned my head and wiggled out of his arms. He stood there, confused and clearly frustrated. I walked into my bathroom and watched in the reflection as he ran his hands through his hair and stared at my ass. He didn't notice I saw him, so I bent over slowly to pick my towel off the floor. He shook his head and fell back onto the bed, throwing an arm over his face. I was having fun with this. He was too easy to mess with.

"Do you need anything before I turn the lights out?"

He didn't speak and was still lying on top of the covers. His forearm covered his face, and without speaking, he shook his head.

"Are you going to get under the covers?" I asked.

He shook his head again, so I slid in on my side and kept my back to him. The bathroom light was on, spreading a small dusting of light through my room, but other than that, it was dark. Vincent lasted all of thirty seconds before he got under the covers. I scooted my bottom towards him and he gripped my body. He pulled me tightly against him and possessively wrapped his arms and legs over me. I felt his erection pressing into me, and I moaned, turning my head exposing my neck to him. He held me tighter, and I felt like I could barely breathe.

"Fuck. I don't think I can stay. It may be better if I miss a night's sleep than staying here being tortured by you and your prefect body."

I moved my neck again, asking for him to give into me. His heart was pounding against my back, and I moved my foot to rub his calf.

"Please, don't. I'm doing everything I can to control myself. Every fiber of my being wants to be inside of you right now. I know how your tight little pussy feels, and you playing with me like this, has it screaming for me. If you move one more inch or make another noise, I'll lose control. I will devour every piece of you and fuck you all night. Then neither of us will sleep because I'll be buried inside of you. Sleep is the only thing that will allow me to control the beast inside of me."

He was perfect in so many ways. I was so aroused by his words, not to mention, the possessive grip he had on my body. I bit my lip to stifle the moan held deep within my throat, but I was unable to stop it. A whimper escaped, unleashing Vincent's beast.

Instantly, he was on top of me, and I was helpless beneath him. He took both of my hands and moved them above my head, holding them in a vise with one of his hands. My legs instinctively parted and wrapped around his body. He pressed his lips to my throat, and I tilted my head to let him kiss me. The attention he showed my body with his mouth was such a turn on. He released my hands and my fingers reached for the hem of his shirt. As I tugged it over his head, my nails scraped his back.

Once I had his shirt off, I looked for friction to calm the flame between my legs. I pushed my pelvis against him, and his fingers found my hair. He threaded them into the long strands and gently tugged on the roots. I sat up in his grip, kissing him, and he easily fell back, allowing me to take control. I kissed his jaw and neck and then worked my way down to his perfectly sculpted chest. He moved his hands and began working my nipples as they strained the fabric of my cami. I pulled it over my head and led one of my breasts to his mouth. I cried in pleasure as he teased the hardened peak with his tongue. He rolled the other nipple in between his fingers and then gave it the same attention with his mouth.

Persistently, I rubbed my pelvis against his shaft. The moment he released my nipples, I left a trail of kisses down his perfect body. When I reached his stomach, I licked along the hemline of his shorts before reaching in. His beautiful cock was waiting for me. I licked the cum that waited on the tip and then began swirling my tongue around him. I stroked him as I kissed and sucked the tip with my mouth. Taking my free hand, I tickled his balls.

"Fuck babe. Stop teasing me."

I had played long enough and couldn't wait to have

him all the way in my mouth. I slid him in my throat as deep as I could take him. On my way up, I swirled my tongue and gripped him aggressively. I continued this over and over, enjoying the pleasure I could feel building within him. He thrust his hips into my mouth and slid his hand inside of my shorts, cupping my sex. He started to caress my wet clit. The feeling of him finally touching me after twenty-four hours was incredible. I sucked him hard and fast, feeling him tighten. I knew he was close to coming, and I wanted him, every last drop of him. He was mine, and I wanted to show him that.

"Babe, if you don't stop, I'm…I'm gonna come." I couldn't help the gratification I felt as he exploded in my mouth, cursing and calling my name. I swallowed, savoring the taste of his sweetness. I slowed my movements, but I didn't stop as I continued to slowly suck him. When he couldn't take it any longer, he pulled away and pinned me underneath him

"God damn, you're quite talented with your mouth," he said.

When I cupped my hand over his cheek, he leaned into my touch, closing his eyes.

"I feel the same way about you."

He kissed me, and didn't waste a minute removing my shorts and then sliding his large cock inside of my throbbing core. Since I was used to his size, pleasure immediately spread through me. He moved from kissing my mouth to my neck, and slowly rocked his hips in and out of me. I moved my hips against him to meet him thrust for thrust, wanting more of him—needing more of him.

"Tell me what you want." he said.

"Harder, please. I want to feel you deeper."

He stopped his movements, pulling out of me, and met my gaze with carnal hunger. "Bend over and grab onto the headboard."

I did as he asked and wrapped my hands over the top of the wooden headboard. He spread my swollen lips with his soft fingers and nested the head of his cock inside of me. It didn't take him long 'til he was slamming into me. The pleasure was immediate, and I screamed into my pillow. He continued to pound me from behind. Holding my hips like a vice and pushing deep inside of me. It caused my body to shake and quiver in an unreal orgasm. Vincent came with me, gripping me tightly as he poured himself inside of me.

Chapter 12

Vivian

The week had progressed quickly. Vincent and I became good at hiding our relationship at work. We thoroughly enjoyed spending the nights cuddling and relaxing before we got tangled up in one another. If I wasn't at his house, he was at mine, Cara seemed to take a liking to him. They found it funny to gang up on me.

The three of us decided to go to the movies tonight, and Vincent had invited Abel. Cara said she was cool if he joined, and since she had sworn off tattooed men forever, he didn't have a chance.

It was Friday night after six, and I was finishing up what the guys needed for court next week. They had discovered new evidence in the Albertson case and were hoping to have a verdict by the end of the week. Vincent and I were the only two left in the office, and it was silent, minus him in his office on the phone.

He finally hung up, and yelled out to me, "Babe, can

you bring me the Albertson's bank account file?"

I hopped up and went into his office. He was typing away and didn't stop to acknowledge me when I walked in.

As I walked around his desk, he said, "Thanks, babe. I'm almost done and we can go."

I sat the file in front of him and hopped up on his desk. "Vincent, did you really just call me babe at work?"

He shrugged his shoulders. "Yeah, I did. It's just us here, so I don't see the big deal."

"What if someone else was still here?"

He ran his hands over his face. "Then they would've heard me. I don't see what the problem is. You're mine, and I don't care who knows. For some reason you're worried what everyone else will think, but it's okay for you to be sitting on my desk?"

I narrowed my eyes at him. "That's different."

"No, it's not. If people can't see the way we act around one another, then they must be blind. We could just tell everyone that we're dating so we don't have to have these conversations."

He was right, this wasn't the first conversation of this kind that we've had this week. "I still don't feel like we should drop this on anyone yet, not until the case is over. Plus it's only been a week, and we agreed on two."

"Fine. I'll give you another week, but if the case isn't settled, we're still telling everyone. It's hard enough to see the way some of the guys talk to you, not to mention the stupid shit they come to you for, just to stare at you and sit at your desk."

"Vince, that's ridiculous. No one here looks or treats me differently. I should be the one complaining about how Portia undresses you with her eyes. She drools when she sees you and then I have to hear about it."

He pulled me onto his lap. "I told her I have a girlfriend, and I wasn't interested. You haven't said a word to those douche bags."

I couldn't fight with him again, I didn't want to. I wrapped my arms around his neck and leaned in to kiss him. He held our lips together without moving his. He smelled of Vincent: clean and light. I exhaled, and a shiver moved threw my body.

"Are you cold?"

I shook my head. "No, I'm definitely not cold. It's your smell and your lips that do that to me. I can't control how my body responds to you."

"You have the same effect on me, beautiful. Come on, let's get going before Cara scares the shit out of Abel."

We had all planned on meeting at the movie theater. The one we were going to was new and unlike any theater I had heard of; you had your own private table with a server to bring your food and drinks while you watched the movie.

Thankfully, we arrived just as Cara was pulling up. She looked cute in a floral print, thin, strapless summer dress. She accessorized it with flats, a thin red belt, and of course her boobs spilling out of the top.

"Hey, girl. You look cute. I hope you brought a sweater," I said.

"Thanks, and no, I didn't. Why would I need a sweater in August?"

"Come on, you know how cold theaters get, and you're barely wearing any clothes."

"I'll keep her warm," Abel said as we approached him standing outside of the theater. He had been leaning up against a brick wall. He moved towards us, and I noticed that he carried himself with the same confidence as Vincent did. He looked different than the last time I had seen him. Tonight he wore a baseball cap, t-shirt, and jeans. His tattoos were visible, showing both of his arms were completely covered.

Cara laughed at him. "I'll be just fine, thank you very much."

"Are you sure? I'm happy to do the job," he said.

She rolled her eyes and Vincent interjected. "All right guys, let's not start the night off fighting. Cara, this is my brother, Abel. Abel, this is Cara, Alexa's roommate."

He grabbed her hand and kissed the top of it. "It's a pleasure to meet you, Cara."

She pulled her hand back and wiped it on his shoulder. We all laughed at her and went inside the theater.

The night had gone better than I expected, considering the rocky introduction between Cara and Abel. She definitely didn't take a liking to him, but it was fun to see the two of them bicker. They fought about everything, from what movie to see, to where we should sit, to how he chewed his food. I think it's safe to say she's no longer into tattooed guys, or at least she's not into this one.

Vincent pulled the Porsche into his garage and we went inside. I wanted to relax but didn't feel tired enough for bed yet.

"Do you want to soak in the hot tub or take a dip in the pool?" I asked.

"Whatever you prefer is fine with me."

I chuckled and glared at him. He never cared what we did, and he always made me deicide.

He wrapped me up in his arms. "I think you may need to be spanked first and then I'll throw you in the pool."

I wiggled out of his hold and sprinted off through the house. I didn't make it far before he caught me. "Now you're definitely getting spanked."

I looked innocently at him and pretended that I had done nothing wrong. It didn't take us long to make it outside and into the hot tub. We left the lights off so we could enjoy the night sky and soaked in the hot water.

I was twisted in Vincent's hold, my back to his front. I was enjoying the calmness I felt when I was in his arms and didn't speak much.

When I yawned and rested my cheek against his chest, he whispered in my ear, "Come on, baby. Let's get you to bed." I didn't want to move, but our skin had pruned, and it was late. Vincent helped me out and wrapped a fluffy towel around me. I started to walk towards the house, but he effortlessly lifted me in his arms. I rested my head against his chest, enjoying the sweet gesture.

He carried me inside and the swaying motion made me even sleepier. Vincent left me to stand on my own two feet as he turned the shower on. We got in together, and I felt exhausted. I didn't want to shower or do anything at that moment, but get into bed. Thankfully, he was more than willing to wash my hair and body. No one had ever done that for me, not even my mother when I was kid. As his strong hands massaged my head, I spoke to stay awake.

"You're really good at this."

"You think?"

"Yeah, it feels amazing."

"Good."

I wonder if he had ever done this for another woman. I'm sure he and Angela shared moments like this. The thought made me sick to my stomach, but I wasn't going to let the ugliness of my self-confidence issues get the best of me.

"What's wrong, babe?"

I shrugged my shoulders, trying to push away the thoughts racing through my mind.

"Talk to me. What's the matter?"

I took a deep breath, completely embarrassed at myself for getting jealous of his ex. I felt the tears prick the back of my eyes. He turned the shower off, wrapped me in his robe, and held me. I buried my face in him and let the tears take over.

Why was I crying over a mere thought? Was it the thought of him with someone else, or was it the thought of losing him to someone that scared me?

"Please don't cry. Talk to me."

I shook my head, too embarrassed to admit what had upset me. Vincent didn't push me; he just lifted me and carried me to his bed. He pulled the covers back and nestled us in the warmth. I stayed tucked in his arms, letting the tears flow. Vincent held onto me, stroking my hair.

"Please don't shut yourself off from me. You can talk to me."

"I'm scared," I whispered.

He turned me towards him and looked into my face.

"Baby, why?"

"I'm scared I'm going to lose you."

"Don't say that. You're not going to lose me."

"But I don't know how to do this, and I worry that you'll give up on me or leave me for someone else."

"Alexa, there is no one else for me. I only want you. I'm drawn to you in a way I've never been to anyone in my life. Don't ever question what we have."

He ran his thumbs under my eyes and brushed the tears off of my face.

"Do you understand what you mean to me? Together, you and I are everything."

I nodded my head and rested my face against his chest. Vincent squeezed me snugly holding me against his body. The sound of his heart beating and the words he had said to me made me feel secure. *Do you understand what you mean to me? Together, you and I are everything.*

"Baby, wake up."

I groaned and pulled the covers over my head.

"I'm sorry, sweetheart. I know it's early, but your phone keeps going off."

I peeked out from underneath the covers, and in front of me, sprawled across the bed, was a bright eyed, messy-haired Vincent. He handed me my phone, and I groaned again.

"You're definitely not a morning person, but you're cute when you hide under the covers."

I peered at him again and rolled my eyes.

"Keep that up and see what happens."

He laughed at me and said, "Clearly you're not up for verbal communication yet. So handle your phone while I run to Starbucks. It's been going off all morning."

I smiled and he kissed me swiftly before strolling out of the room.

I threw my phone down and stretched my body in his comfortable bed. I didn't want to get up but nature called. I padded quickly into the restroom and as I passed the shower it brought up last night's memories. I'd forgotten that I told Vincent I was scared. I had never opened up to anyone about my feelings before. I always avoided talking about what bothered me. When I went back into the bedroom, I grabbed my phone off the bed. I headed downstairs and went outside to the back patio.

Sitting down on one of the lounge chairs, I slid the unlock button on my iPhone. I had six text message, eleven calls, and three voice mails. I checked my voicemail first. My stomach dropped when I heard the first message. I went to the next message it was the same, and the final one broke my heart as I heard the pain in Bridgette's voice.

Fuck.

The first two were from University Hospital and the last from Bridgette. She was upset and crying. I could barely understand her when she spoke. I read the texts; all of them were from Bridgette except one that was from

Cara. They asked me to call, saying Vivian was ill and in the hospital.

I really was a shitty sister. I was never there for her when she needed me. I dialed her number, and she answered on the first ring.

"Hey, what's going on?" I asked.

"They just took her back for more tests. She got really sick last night and called 911. They brought her in, and she had them call me. She's not doing well."

"I'm sorry. Do they know what's wrong?"

"They are still running tests. They think it may be cancer, Lex."

Shit. Cancer? I may not be close with Vivian, but she was still my mother. I would never wish cancer upon anyone, not after watching my grandfather pass away from it. I talked to Bridge and calmed her down the best I could, then Vincent came out back with Starbucks in hand. He sat behind me and pulled my back against his chest.

"I'm so sorry, I'll be there soon. Do you need me to bring you anything?"

"No. I'm fine. Just get here."

"Okay, doll. I'm on my way. I love you."

"Love you too."

I hung up the phone and put my face in my hands.

"What's wrong, baby?"

"It's Vivian, my mother, she's in the hospital. They don't know what's wrong with her, it may be cancer.

Bridgette said she's really sick. She's been with her all night and was trying to get a hold of me. I feel horrible that I didn't check my phone last night."

He squeezed me tightly. "You were exhausted. Sleeping shouldn't make you feel bad. This is all out of your control anyways. There's nothing that you could've done. Your sister needs you now, so we'll go and find out what's going on."

I didn't want to drag him into my family drama. "I'll go by myself. You don't need to see how messed up Vivian is. She and I haven't spoken for three years, and we didn't end things on good terms."

"What happened?"

"It's a long story, basically I had taken all of the abuse I could from her, so I cut her out of my life."

"Well you're not going through this by yourself. You're going to be there for Bridgette, and I'm going to be there for you. If you think I'm just going to stay home and let you go alone, then you don't know me very well. I'll protect you and support you any way I can. Don't argue because I won't take no for an answer. Let's get dressed and go."

I nodded my head as Vincent kissed my temple. We changed our clothes and were out the door in less than five minutes. I was quiet on the drive to the hospital. My mind was trying to process what I was about to walk into. I didn't know if I was ready to face my mother after three years of not speaking. How does someone prepare themselves for a moment like this?

The hospital was busy, and people were bustling all around. Thankfully, Vincent was with me and led the way. He held my hand tightly as we approached the front desk. Behind the counter was an elderly woman with a beehive for hair and thin wire glasses.

"Excuse me, ma'am. Can you tell me how to get to Vivian Schaefer's room?" he asked.

She spoke quickly, and the instructions sounded confusing. I knew that without Vincent I would have gotten lost. Once we were in the elevator, he clasped my shoulders and turned me to look him straight in the eyes.

"Are you okay?"

I nodded my head and felt a lump form in the back of my throat.

"I'll be right outside the room if you need anything at all. Take your time and follow your heart, it won't steer you wrong."

He gently brushed his lips against mine, holding my gaze. I fought back the tears and found the strength I needed within him. I knew that no matter what happened, he would be waiting for me.

The elevator doors opened and we quickly found her room. Vincent gave me a kiss on the nose and went to the waiting area. I loved that he was there for me, but also gave me my space at the same time. I was hesitant to go in, so I stood there with my hand on the door handle for what seemed to be minutes. I looked behind me and caught Vincent smiling. He sat with his elbows on his knees, and looked concerned.

I entered the room, to find a frail woman in a bed that was too large for her. She was hooked up to every machine imaginable with tubes and wires throughout. She wasn't breathing on her own, which surprised me.

Bridgette jumped up and wrapped her arms around me, I hugged her back. She was crying, so I just held her. There was nothing I could say or do. I stared at Vivian and watched as the machine made her chest move up and down. She didn't resemble the woman I once knew.

Bridgette pulled away and walked back to the bedside chair. I followed her and we both sat holding hands in silence. Time moved slowly before either of us spoke. We stayed in the moment, processing what had become of the woman before us.

"Do they know what's wrong with her yet?"

She shook her head and let go of my hand. Pulling her legs up to her chest, she wrapped her arms around them and rested her cheek on her knees.

"When I got here last night, she was awake. This morning, when they took her to run tests, she went into cardiac arrest and they had to intervene in order to save her. That's why she is on the ventilator. She was fine one minute and like this the next."

"I'm so sorry. I wish I had gotten your calls sooner. I would've been here for you. You know that, right?"

She smiled at me and nodded her head. A single tear

escaped her eye landing on her pants. "Why didn't you get my calls? I called Cara, and she said you weren't home. Where were you?"

Now wasn't the time to gloat about my relationship with Vincent. I also couldn't keep him a secret, not with him sitting in the waiting room.

"I'm seeing someone. I was at his house. I left my phone in my purse, and I didn't check it until this morning."

She looked at me surprised. "Oh, I didn't know you were seeing anyone."

"It's new. Not many people know. He's here if you want to meet him?"

Was it wrong of me to be introducing Vincent, to my sister while my mother was so sick?

"I would love to meet him. I've never seen you with anyone. If he's here, then he has to be pretty special to you."

"Yeah. He is."

A middle-aged nurse bustled into the room. "Hi ladies, I'm Jane. I assume you're Vivian's daughters?"

We nodded our heads.

"Good. Well, I'm glad to see you're both here to keep her company. It's important to talk to her during this time. She can hear what's going on around her, so keep her included. I do need to switch her IV fluids and change her positioning. Would you mind stepping out for a bit? I'll come get you when I'm done."

We stood and Bridgette kissed Vivian's hand. "We'll be right outside the room Mom," she said.

We both left, and as soon as we exited, Vincent was on his feet coming towards us. A grin spread across my face. I was glad that he was here with me. All the anxiety and worry diminished when I saw him.

"Bridgette, this is my boyfriend, Vincent."

He took her hand in his, and with his most charming smile, kissed the top of it. "It's a pleasure to meet you, Bridgette. I've heard a lot of great things about you."

She blushed crimson and turned her head to hide the embarrassment. He released her hand and wrapped his arm around me as he kissed the top of my head.

"How is she, babe?"

I shrugged my shoulders as we walked to the waiting room. "She's not well. They don't know what's wrong with her yet. This morning she went into cardiac arrest. Now she isn't breathing on her own and is sedated."

"Damn. I'm sorry. I can't believe she took a turn for the worse so quickly. Do they have an idea of when a doctor will be in to check on her and give another update?"

"No. I'm not sure when we will know more. I'm assuming it won't be until later or tomorrow," Bridgette said.

"Bridgette, have you eaten today?" he asked.

"No, but I'm fine. Thanks for asking. I'll eat later."

"How do you expect to be healthy for your mom if

you're not taking care of yourself?"

She looked shocked by his statement. He was a no nonsense kind of guy. He kissed me on the forehead and stood.

"I'll go get you both something to eat. I'll be right back."

He didn't wait for us to confirm that we even wanted anything. I loved how he took charge. I watched him stroll to the elevator; he pressed the button and put his hands in his jeans pocket waiting for the car to arrive. He looked delicious today in light jeans and a navy blue t-shirt. His hair was messy, and I could tell he had been running his fingers through it.

Bridgette elbowed me. "Holy cow. Where did you find him? He's a keeper."

I couldn't help but smile at her comment. She was right. He was a keeper.

"We met on your birthday at 9th Door. Now he happens to work with me. What a small world, huh?"

"No way. Is he an attorney?"

"Yeah, and he is also a partner at the firm. I've broken about every rule to be with him, but so far, he's worth it."

She smiled at me. "I'm so happy for you. You deserve it."

"Thanks. I feel lucky."

"You should. Did you see the way that he looked at you? He's really into you. I'm always here if you ever need relationship advice."

"Thanks," I said.

Bridgette had never offered me support, and quite frankly, I was so new to this dating thing that I might even take her up on it.

Chapter 13

The Past

"Babe, will you please eat something?"

I shook my head. I didn't feel like eating. I had been a ball of anxiety all weekend. What had started out with so much potential soon turned out to be so hard. Vivian was still sedated, and they planned to keep her that way until she was strong enough for surgery. She needed a stint placed in one of her arteries. All of the tests had confirmed that she had stage four lung cancer, thus complicating the entire process.

"Please baby, you've barely eaten anything for two days. I don't want you getting sick because you're famished."

I knew Vincent was only trying to help. I pushed my spoon around my wonton soup and took a small sip of the broth. It tasted bland and I just didn't have an appetite.

"I won't get sick from lack of food, or famished, as

you like to call it. If you force me to eat this, then yes, I might get sick."

The guilt I felt for Vivian was horrible. I had turned my back on her three years ago, and now stood in limbo waiting for her to improve. Worst of all, there was nothing that I could do to control the situation and that was a hard pill for me to swallow. Normally, I would take charge and handle things, but in this case, all anyone could do was sit back and wait. Vivian needed time for her body to get strong and that's what we gave her.

"Fine. If you won't eat your soup, is there anything else that sounds appealing?"

"I'm fine really."

"Come on. If you could have anything, what would it be?"

"I guess I could go for some ice cream."

"See, that wasn't so hard. Ice cream is better than nothing. Do you want to get out and walk? Some fresh air may do you well and help to clear your mind."

"Yeah, that sounds nice. I feel like we've been sitting in the hospital all weekend."

I was currently on the floor nestled next to the coffee table leaning against the couch. I much preferred to sit down here. It was more comfortable to eat here than in the formal dining room. Poor Vincent couldn't fold his legs up enough to get comfortable on the floor. I guess when you're over six feet tall you have to think about those things. He reached for my hand, linking our fingers together and helped me up.

We walked outside, and there wasn't a cloud in the sky. The sun was hot on my skin, warming me instantly. We cut through the street and onto a gravel path that led us towards the entrance of his neighborhood. Down a block from there, was a small strip mall with an ice cream shop.

Vincent had been overly supportive these last two days and spent every moment with me at the hospital. He was patient and made sure Bridgette and I had whatever we needed. He was a huge help in keeping up to date with the nurses and doctors on Vivian's progress.

"Thank you for spending the weekend with me at the hospital. I know it's not what you had in mind, but I couldn't have made it through the last few days had you not been there with me."

He lifted our linked hands and kissed the inside of my wrist, "Of course. I'll always want to be where you are. You're right, it isn't what I had in mind, but as long as I'm with you, I'm happy."

The walk was nice. When we arrived, the place was crowded. I ordered some chocolate ice cream in a waffle bowl, and Vincent settled on a cone with mint chocolate chip. We got our treats and took them outside to enjoy in the sun.

"I need to talk to you about something," he said. "I know you have a lot going on with your mother, but Charlie revamped the menu at Lazio's, and he's having a grand re-opening this Friday. He asked if you and I would go."

"I have plans with Cara on Friday night."

He licked his cone, and I watched his mouth suck on the ice cream.

God, that's hot.

We hadn't had sex in almost two days. By the time we would get home from the hospital, the exhaustion took over, and I would already be asleep in the car. Vincent had to carry me inside both nights and was out cold as soon as he hit the mattress next to me.

"Bring Cara. The more the merrier. I think Abel will be there, so at least she'll know someone besides us."

"Okay. I'll talk to her about it tomorrow. I'm sure it will work out fine."

He kissed my nose and left a cold feeling lingering from his lips.

"Really? That's all I get?"

"What else do you want, beautiful?"

I wiggled my eyebrows at him and he laughed.

He cocked his head to the side and hunger burned in his eyes. "How about we go in the bathroom?"

I didn't doubt that he would actually take me in the bathroom here. I shook my head at him as I stood and he scooped me up in his arms.

"What are you doing? I can walk home."

He playfully swatted my backside and set me down on my feet. We linked our hands together, and I grinned, thinking about what we were about to do to one another when we got back to his place.

"I like you calling it home."

My phone rang, interrupting him, and I swatted *his* backside as I answered it.

"Hey, Bridge. What's up, doll?"

"Mom's awake. She was getting really restless, so they weaned her off of the sedation."

"Oh, that's great news. We'll head down there now."

"No, Lex, don't. I called to make sure you weren't on your way. She didn't wake up too happy and has been saying some really mean things. I told her that you've been here all weekend and also about Vincent. I didn't want you to come down here and get yourself upset. Stay with Vincent, and I'll keep you guys updated. They said she is strong enough to not be sedated until the surgery as long as she stays calm. I'm so sorry, Lex."

"It's okay."

"I love you."

"Love you too. Bye."

Fucking Vivian. I knew she wouldn't change. I was done with her. I wrapped my arm around Vincent's waist and leaned into him. He held me tight while we walked in silence. He knew me so well, he knew when I needed space and when to let me just *be*.

We approached the house and walked up the front stairs in sync. When he opened the door, I couldn't control myself. I threw myself at him like I did the first night we met. He caught me with one arm and kicked the door closed.

Our mouths touched and his lips pulsed electricity though my system. He kissed me with tenderness, and I enjoyed indulging in his sweetness. He squeezed my body when he did that, and it made me want him even more.

We stumbled backwards towards the living room. Once we reached the couch, I fell onto it. The soft fabric was cool on my hot skin. He lowered his body on top of mine and cupped my sex. I was in a summer dress with no underwear on, making it easy for Vincent to touch me. He separated my pussy lips and rubbed my clit up and down with two fingers. I bit his lip because I couldn't keep kissing him, the pleasure was too intense. He slid two fingers inside of my wet core and slowly circled them while his thumb rubbed my clit.

I reached down and massaged his erection through his pants. His mouth moved to my neck and across my chest. He left a trail of kisses on my delicate skin. Taking his free hand, he pulled down the top of my dress over one of my breasts. His other hand was still inside of me, moving in and out slowly. I was enjoying his touch, but I also needed to feel him, so I reached into his pants and aggressively squeezed his cock. He latched onto my nipple with his mouth. I jerked his shaft and imagined him inside of me. Suddenly, he stopped and looked in to my eyes.

"Stop, Lex. You're going to make me come."

I smiled at him, not realizing how carried away I'd gotten. He kissed my neck, and I lost all consciousness. I laid there enjoying the attention. I heard his zipper go down and looked up to see him guide his cock into my pussy.

Once he was all of the way inside of me, he removed his t-shirt. Vincent grabbed my leg, resting it up against his body with my foot next to his head. He held me tightly and started to move. I had never had sex with a man while my leg was stretched up the length of their body. It was hot as hell watching him grip my skin as he slid in and out of me. I had to close my eyes because the pleasure was so much to handle. This angle was intense and pushed me close to coming.

"Fuck, baby," I whimpered as he started to pound me.

"You like that? You like it when I fuck you hard?"

I whimpered again and nodded my head. I couldn't hold back any longer. His words pushed me over, and I came hard. My orgasm exploded around his cock as my muscles tightened and flinched. He came with me, moaning loudly and pumping himself inside of me in long, slow stokes.

Vincent lowered my leg and laid on top of me. With his cock still nestled inside of me, I wrapped my arms around him.

"What did Bridgette say about your mom?" he finally asked.

"Just that she woke up and was in a shitty mood. She's back to her normal self and doesn't want me there."

"Why wouldn't she want to see you? Doesn't she realize that you've spent all weekend there worried sick about her?"

"Bridgette said she told her that both you and I had been there, so she knows."

He looked into my eyes. "Then why don't we go see her? I'm sure once you're there she'll be happy."

"I don't know. You don't know how she can be."

"Come on, baby. I'll be right there with you. I wish I could have one more time with my mom. Don't have regrets."

I nodded my head. Vincent gave me the strength to do things I normally wouldn't.

He stood and eased out of me, I hated not having him inside of me. He reached for my hand and helped me up. I was amazed that he was still hard as I looked down as his impressive erection, but he was insatiable.

We dressed and went into the garage. We drove the Range Rover, which was nice and comfortable. It was roomy on the inside and had the darkest tint on the windows. It almost made it hard to see outside.

We parked in the nearly empty garage and took the elevator down to the main entrance. Vincent grabbed my hand and guided me along the way to Vivian's room.

As we stood outside of the room, I felt sick to my stomach. I was staring at the floor and nervous as ever.

Vincent lifted my head.

"Hey, you can do this. Don't be scared. Remember, I'm right outside the room if you need anything."

I nodded my head, and he kissed my nose. I turned and opened the door; Bridgette was talking to Vivian. They both looked at me, and I could see the surprise on their faces.

I turned to close the door and I saw Vincent standing right there.

"Hey, what are you doing here, Lex?" Bridgette asked.

"I wanted to stop by and see how you both were holding up. I couldn't just stay home after you called."

I looked over at Vivian, and she was staring at the wall. She wouldn't even look at me.

"Has she been like this since she woke up?" I asked Bridgette.

Before she could answer, Vivian turned to me, and anger burned in her eyes.

"No, Alexa, I have not been like this since I woke up. It's just been since you walked into my room uninvited. Your sister told you that I didn't want you here. What in the world would make you think that I wanted to see you or have anything to do with you? You're the one who, three years ago, abandoned me. Did your dumb-as-shit brain forget that too, like it has everything else?"

Her words were venom, and they hurt. I went to

open my mouth, and before I could speak, Vincent was behind me, his hand touching my wrist. Tears filled my eyes, and I thought twice before I stooped to her level and tried to hurt her the way she'd hurt me. Vincent had a hold of me and I chose him. I turned my back, wrapping my hand tightly in his and walked out of the room.

"Get me out of here, Vincent. Now."

"I got you, baby."

Tears rolled down my cheeks, and I wiped them away with the back of my free hand. When we reached the Range Rover, Vincent opened the passenger door and moved the seat all the way back.

He lifted me in his arms and moved us into the car. He shut the door, and I clung onto him. I wrapped my arms around his neck and cried into him. I let everything out, every bit of anger I felt towards Vivian that I wanted to tell her in person. The tears seemed to be never-ending.

Vincent tightened his hold on me. "I'm so sorry, baby. We shouldn't have come here."

I shook my head and tried to calm myself so I could speak.

"It's okay. That's how she always is. I tried and that's all I can do."

"I can't believe the way she spoke to you. You're her daughter."

"That's the way she has been my whole life; ever

since I can remember."

"Why? I don't get it?"

"I've always been the black sheep. She blamed it on her depression and bipolar disorder. But she never took her pills consistently and it literally made her crazy. My childhood was a battle of survival. As the years progressed and I grew up, she got worse. For myself, I found it was better to cut ties. I told her to call me when she was ready to make a change and take care of herself. The call never came, and it's been three years."

"I couldn't imagine having a mother like that and growing up in those conditions. I'm so sorry, baby."

"It's okay, there's nothing anyone can do. I know I will never have a relationship with my mother and tonight just proves that."

Chapter 14

My Love

"Damn it, Vincent. If you let me oversleep one more time, I'm not going to have sex with you for a week."

He wrapped his big arms around my waist from behind. "Oh come on, love. What did you do before me? Surely you made it through life waking up on your own."

"For one, I wasn't having all this mind-blowing sex that kept me up late and exhausted all of my energy. Then, there's the fact that I sleep with goliath the grizzly bear. You're like an electric blanket, and when I'm warm and comfy, it puts me into a comatose state."

He laughed out loud and I got out of bed to start dressing. "Goliath the grizzly bear, really?" he said, and I narrowed my eyes at him. "Fine. Point taken. You're mighty feisty this morning," he said.

"What can I say? I overslept again, and here you are, getting dressed in another one of your three-piece suits. What is it with you and suits? Do you always have to wear them?" I tried to keep a straight face while I was having fun picking on him.

He kissed my nose. "Yes, babe, I do. We have court today, remember? We want a verdict so we can finally tell everyone at the office about us dating. Plus, don't act like it's just the suits. You act the same way when I'm in basketball shorts, a t-shirt, and a hat. I should be the one complaining about you wearing those damn stockings and no underwear every day. You know I can see your legs perfectly from my desk and that shit keeps me hard all day?"

He was right, it didn't really matter what he was wearing; I was turned on regardless. He was gorgeous and that was putting it lightly. Now that I knew he could see my legs from his desk, I planned on playing with him a bit.

"Point taken. I'll be sure to not cross my legs when you're in your office."

"Fuck," he grumbled, running his hands over his face.

It was quarter 'til noon, and I was starving. I grabbed my purse and headed to the elevator. I was going down to the lobby to get a salad and eat out by the lake. Vincent had been in court all morning, and I missed him. I checked my cell phone, but there were no new calls or texts.

A new message chimed in from Bridgette:

Mom's the same. I miss you. Maybe we could have dinner this week?

My poor sister had not left Vivian's side while she was in the hospital. It angered me that she felt obligated to spend so much time there.

I texted her back as I waited for the elevator. When it finally arrived, I froze in my tracks. Vincent was staring at me, a mischievous grin spread across his face.

"Vince, what are you doing here?" I whispered.

He grabbed my arm pulling me along with him. He walked with purpose, taking long strides. "Come with me, and I'll tell you."

I pulled my arm away, afraid someone would see us. He didn't skip a beat and continued walking as I followed quietly. Once we were in his office, I closed the door behind me and turned towards him. His back was to me, and he was staring out the windows.

"Vince, what's going on?"

He turned, pinning me with his gaze. I was unable to move, my breathing became rapid.

"Baby, we won our case! I came here to surprise you."

I was elated. I knew how much this case meant to

not only Vincent, but to Liam and C.J. as well. They had spent so much time preparing, and with the new evidence, they had pushed hard for a verdict. It came faster than I would have thought, but I never doubted them.

"I'm so happy for you. I knew you would win. You've never lost a case. Tell me all about it. How did you get a verdict so quickly?"

He brushed the loose strands of hair off of my face and said, "I'll tell you later, baby. I have been waiting to do this all day."

Leaning down he possessively, as only Vincent could do, placed his mouth over mine. He walked us backwards towards his desk. When my legs touched the wood, I leaned against it and instinctively wrapped my arms around his neck. Pushing my tongue into his mouth, we explored each other like it was the first time. Maybe it was the excitement of the verdict, or the fact that I had missed him all morning.

He lifted my skirt and slid two fingers inside of me. "Mine," he murmured. I moaned in response, unable to speak. He gently pulled his fingers out and separated my wet lips by running them in between the slickness. I reached for his belt, unbuckling it as fast as I could while he shrugged his coat off, and threw it aside.

I unzipped his pants, freeing his erection. Gripping his length with both hands, I stroked it incessantly. Vincent continued to torture my clit, rubbing it with his fingers in a perfect circular motion before he slowly slid his fingers back inside of me. All the while, never taking the pressure off my clit with his thumb.

"Fuck, babe. You're so wet. Did your little cunt miss me?" I whimpered and pulled him towards my opening. He gladly exchanged his two fingers for his rock hard cock.

"Oh, fuck. Yes it did." He gripped my hips, and I wrapped my legs around his waist. He filled me and stared down at my body stretched across his desk, my arms rested above me on the cool cherry wood. He slid in and out of me at an aggressive pace. I reached up for his glorious hair, pulling him to me in search of his mouth. He kissed me again, moving with precision and pushed my body closer to coming. I was all sensation, as he was on top of me fucking me and kissing me in unison.

"Come with me, love." His words were all I needed, and in that moment, all of my fears washed away. The word love didn't scare me, it ignited me. I ran my fingers through his hair and linked my hands at his neck. Staring into each other's eyes, I knew he felt it too. We didn't speak it, with Vincent we didn't have to.

My eyelids were heavy, and I was nestled on the couch, wrapped in my favorite throw, enjoying some TV with

Cara. We shared a tub of Ben and Jerry's. Tomorrow was the open house at Charlie's restaurant, and surprisingly, Cara seemed excited to be going with us. Although she had been giving me a hard time all week about spending so much time with Vincent, I think deep down, she was just looking out for me and didn't want me to get hurt. She made me agree to spend the night away from him tonight and it was killing me.

"What time do you want to get our nails done tomorrow?" she asked.

I shrugged my shoulders and snatched the ice cream back from her. "It doesn't matter to me, I can take my lunch whenever."

"Do you think you could leave a little early so we could get the works? I mean, make up, hair, and nails? It would probably only take an extra few hours?"

"I'm not sure. Let me ask my boss real quick."

She laughed at me, and I handed her back the ice cream.

My fingers deftly flew over the touchscreen of my iPhone.

Would you mind if I left work a little early tomorrow to get pampered for your dad's re-opening?

He responded right back.

Hmm, I'm not sure you deserve to leave early. You've been quite naughty this week. It also depends on what 'getting pampered' entails?

Hey there mister, I've paid for my naughty tendencies with plenty of spankings. Pampering will entail hair, nails, and make-up. Oh yeah, and a good waxing.

Cara leaned over my shoulder. "So, what did he say?"

I pressed the phone against my chest, hiding it from her. It vibrated and I glared at her. "Let me check it, and I'll tell you. Stop being so damn nosey." She rolled her eyes at me and flipped though the channels on the TV.

Ooh, a waxing. I like that. Then YES, you can definitely take off a little early.

Thank you. I can't wait to see you, I miss you.

I miss you too. Sleep well, my love.

Since the morning, when he first called me 'love,' he had been saying it more often. Neither of us had spoken the words to one another, but I knew how he felt about me, and I felt the same for him.

"All right, we are good for tomorrow. Will you make the appointments since you're off all day, and can you find somewhere for us to get waxed?"

Her eyes bugged out of her head. "Waxed? Really? Since when do you get waxed?"

I shrugged my shoulders and acted like it was no big deal.

"I cannot believe the things you are willing to do for him."

I threw a pillow at her face, and she tossed it right back at me.

"Stop giving me a hard time about him. I mean it, Cara. I'm already staying the night away from him tonight so we can have some girl time."

"Okay, I'm sorry. I just don't want you to get hurt."

"I won't, okay? Plus what does staying a night apart have to do with getting hurt?"

"You guys just met and have been spending every waking minute together. I think a little space would be good."

I rolled my eyes and blew out a deep breath. "Cara, you can think whatever you want, but I'm tired so I'm going to bed."

"I'm sorry, Lex."

I turned around. "It's fine, Cara. I'm just tired. I need to sleep, and my mood will be better tomorrow."

I went to my room and crawled into my bed. I couldn't sleep. I laid there and thought of Cara and how she had no right to tell me that Vincent and I had been spending too much time together. She was the one that fell hard and fast. She always got her heart broken and was the last person that should be giving relationship advice. For once in my life, I had a good thing, and I wasn't going to let her interfere.

After laying there for far too long, I checked the clock. It was almost midnight, and I had yet to fall asleep. I grabbed my phone to text Vincent, but I didn't want to wake him up. I decided to head out front and watch the stars for a while. They always seemed to make me sleepy. It was warm and dark, the sky was clear, and moon was bright. I sat on the front stairs and pulled my knees up against my body.

As I looked up into the desolate night sky, I wished that Vincent was sitting with me. I missed him so much. I couldn't sleep without him. Dammit, I was twenty-eight years old, and I was not going to have anyone tell me what I could and couldn't do.

I got up and went inside the condo. I grabbed my phone off of my bed, and I went to the front door, grabbing my purse on the way. I fumbled for my keys in the dark and locked the door. I slid into my car and searched for the ignition key. On the ring was an unfamiliar key. Normally, I only had my car and house key on there, but now there was a third key that was long and silver. It looked like my house key, but I didn't put it on there. Vincent would've been the only one to have added it.

Thoughts of him being so sweet and caring made me want to get to him even faster. I wanted to crawl into his arms and then we could just sleep for the night. I pulled out of my driveway and thought about calling him, but I decided against it. Hopefully the key on my ring was to his house. *What else could it go to?*

As I turned downed his street, it was dark and still. I parked in his driveway and got out of my car, quietly closing the door. I walked up to his front door and found the new key on my ring. Slowly, I slid it into the lock, and it fit like a glove. I turned it effortlessly, and I felt the lock move with it.

I couldn't believe he gave me an extra key to his house and told me nothing about it. I walked into the dark house and closed the door behind me. I took my shoes off and set my purse on the table next to the door. As I moved through the house, it was silent.

I reached the top of the stairs, and to my surprise, he wasn't sleeping. Before me, Vincent was sitting on my side of the bed with his head in his hands. His back was to me, and he was naked from the waist up, only wearing a pair of shorts. I quietly walked over to the bed as he ran his hands over his face. It was as if he was in pain.

I crawled across the bed and my movements caused him to turn. Before he moved his body, I clung onto him. Kneeling behind him, I slid my arms underneath his, and gripped his chest. He moved his hands over mine and

187

leaned his head into me. I rested my cheek against his shoulder.

"What are you doing here?" he asked.

"I couldn't sleep. I needed to be with you."

"Why didn't you call me?"

"I was going to, but I didn't want to wake you. Why are you up?"

"I told you, Lex, I have insomnia. I can't sleep without you."

I removed myself from the tight hold I had on his body. He turned to look at me, and his eyes were red. It looked as though he'd been crying. I pulled the covers back and patted for him to climb in. He did and I followed. Vincent turned me so that my back was to him. He pulled my body tightly against his, taking a deep breath, once he had me securely in place.

"Vince, is this what you do every night? Do you just sit here?"

He squeezed me tighter and kissed behind my ear. "Yeah, it is. For the past five years this has been what my nights consist of."

"Why for five years?"

He took another deep breath and pressed his lips to my shoulder. "That's when my mom passed away. I don't know how to get over it."

"What happened?"

"We were driving, and our car was struck by a drunk driver. I was behind the wheel, but there was nothing I could do in that moment. The car lost control and slid off an embankment. The next thing I knew, we were airborne, and all I heard was her screaming. When the car finally came to a halt, she was silent. There was blood all over her face. I screamed and yelled for her, but she was gone. Her eyes were open, but behind them was nothing; they were blank. I tried to get out of the car, but I couldn't. The door was jammed and I was injured. So, while I sat there and waited for help, I just looked into her eyes. I wanted her back more than anything. All I could hear were her screams over and over in my head. Since that day, every time I close my eyes, minus when I'm with you, I hear her screams and see her eyes. Not the eyes I grew up loving and trusting, her eyes when she'd passed. "

I rolled over and faced him. Tears were in my eyes as well as in his. I tightly hugged him and pressed my wet cheek against his chest.

"Baby, I had no idea that's how you lost your mom. I'm so sorry."

"It was horrible, and I miss her every day, but I feel like she is looking down on me, and is proud of the man I've become."

I pulled away and looked at him. He cupped my neck and ran his thumb over my cheek. In that moment, I knew that I needed him as well.

"Thank you for trusting me to tell me about your mom. I need you just as much as you need me. I'm not letting Cara tell me what I can and cannot do, so we will spend every night together."

"Do you have any idea how happy you just made me? Being sleep-deprived makes me crazy and knowing you'll be here calms me. I've not talked about my mom's passing to anyone since it happened. It feels good to get it off my chest. I really don't know how I have lived my life as long as I have, without you."

I couldn't help myself from kissing him. It felt so good to firmly press my lips against his and instantly be calmed by our connection.

"Baby, you make me happy every day. I'm glad that I was the one you opened up to. I'll always be here for you. I'm not going anywhere, I promise."

He smiled at me and reached for my wrist. Taking it in his hand, he kissed the inside of it. "Good, because you're everything I've ever wanted and needed."

Chapter 15

Lies

I woke, cool and restless. Not my usual morning. I reached for Vincent, but he was gone. I looked over to his pillow, and in his place, there was a single white rose. I reached for it pressing it against my nose. It smelled sweet like only a rose could. Nothing compared, but it would do.

I reached for my cell phone to text him and thank him for the rose. On my nightstand was an envelope. I opened it to find a handwritten note, a single car key, and his black Amex card.

Baby,

Take today off of work. Go shopping and buy whatever you and Cara want, along with something to wear tonight. The card has no limit and the key is to the Bugatti. I won't take NO for an answer. Thank you for making me the happiest man alive.

Enjoy your day.

Until later, only yours, XOXO Vincent

Holy shit. Was he for real? Screw texting; I grabbed my phone and called him. I should tell him how much I loved him, but that would have to wait 'til we were in person. I needed to hear his voice; Jesus he was pure perfection. Unfortunately, he didn't answer, so I left him a voice message.

I couldn't wait to tell Cara what he'd done. I'm sure she would let go of protecting me, once she found out what he did for us today. I got out of his bed, taking my rose into the kitchen to put into a vase. I placed it on the kitchen island and collected my things before going into the garage. Tucked away in the corner was the black and red beauty I'd come to love. I slid into the sleek red interior and got situated. Pulling out of the garage, my stomach was in knots from excitement. Driving home I was responsible, but I really wanted to see how far I could push this car. It took all of my control to not floor it.

I pulled into our driveway and went inside yelling for Cara. She didn't answer, so I went upstairs, but her room was empty. I came back down and into my room to take a shower. Just as I set my purse on the bed, Cara burst into the room. She was wearing her full running gear, earphones, sports bra, tennis shoes, and yoga pants. "Where is he, Lex? His fucking car is in the driveway."

"Whoa slow down there crazy." I dangled the key at her and shook my head, "It's our car today."

Her jaw fell open. "No way. Why?" I handed her the note, and she read it in a way only Cara could do and fell onto my bed in the most dramatic fashion. Her arm rested on her forehead as if she had fainted.

I smacked her playfully. "You know, you should have been an actress, not a nurse."

She rolled her eyes at me. "Sure, and you, my friend, should've been a singer."

I threw a pillow at her and stormed into the bathroom. She yelled something back at me, but I couldn't understand her. She knew I couldn't sing to save my life. I turned the shower on and steam quickly filled the room. I took my time lathering, washing, and shaving.

I wanted to be perfect for Vincent tonight, to repay him for giving me not only this special day, but everything else. I hopped out of the shower refreshed and ready to venture out with my best friend. I dressed in a pink terry cloth sweat suit. It was supposed to rain today, making it a bit cooler than normal. This allowed me to pull out some of my fall clothes. I slid on a pair of flip-flops to ensure my pedicure stayed pristine. I left my room to grab a fresh cup of coffee from the kitchen. When I walked into the living room, Cara was signing for a delivery, and the man set two vases of white roses on the counter.

I grabbed the card that was tucked inside of them, knowing they were for me.

Thank you for last night.
Only yours, XOXO Vincent

The doorbell rang, interrupting my train of thought. I set the card down and opened the door, allowing the delivery guy to leave before I could see who was outside. A cute Asian girl was standing there with two Starbucks cups and a bag in her hands.

"Alexa Schaefer?" she asked.

"That's me."

She smiled and handed me the items she was carrying. "These are for you. Enjoy."

I took the Starbucks and turned towards Cara. When I turned around to thank the girl, she was gone.

"Oh my God. This is so over the top," Cara said.

I walked to the couch and set the coffees on the table. Over the top was an understatement, but that was Vincent. Everything about him was over the top, and he was all mine.

"I don't even know what to say, Cara."

She laughed and took one of the drinks out of the carrier. "Well, you need to think of a way thank him, but first we have to get going, or we're going to miss our appointments. I just called and moved them up."

I grabbed my coffee and peaked into the Starbucks

bag. It had two croissants in it, my favorite. I didn't want to eat in the Bugatti, but I knew what Vincent would say if I told him I worried about the crumbs and had not eaten again.

I turned out of the driveway and noticed the neighbors staring. The noise the engine made as I peeled out onto First Avenue, maneuvering about, was sexy as hell. It was hard to believe that Vincent trusted me with this car, out of all the cars he could've lent me.

Thankfully, Cherry Creek Mall had valet. I didn't even want to think about where to park this thing. When I turned into the mall, I followed the signs and I think every person around us turned their head. We acted like this was our everyday car, but climbing out, I was a little shy in my sweat suit. I felt like I should be wearing something designer. Vincent was comfortable driving this in his basketball shorts, so I shouldn't worry about my outfit.

Our first appointment was to get waxed. I was nervous and didn't know what to expect, but it went over without a setback. I was only doing it for Vincent; I knew how much he was going to like it. Thinking of his expression when he saw my freshly waxed sex had my heart racing. Next we got our hair done, then make-up and nails. We ended the day with a little shopping. Being with Cara was always so fun. She was a confident free spirit and never cared who was looking at her.

After an exhausting morning of pampering, we were

in the dressing room at Nieman Marcus. The poor sales woman must have thought we were crazy with the number of dresses we had taken in to try on. I came out in, what had to have been, the tenth dress.

"Oh my God. That's it. That's the one," Cara said.

I had on a gold satin floor-length dress. It had one strap on the left shoulder decorated in black Swarovski crystals, leaving the other shoulder open. The right leg had a long slit going up the front, exposing my thigh, and it hugged my waist and hips flawlessly.

"You think so?"

"Yeah. Vincent is going to die when he sees you wearing this."

I scanned over the dress and turned to look at the nonexistent back. This was the one. It was definitely the one.

We checked out with our dresses. I had paid for everything else myself today. I didn't want to take advantage of him, regardless of what he'd told me to do. On the way out, I saw a black pair of Christian Louboutin heels. I halted at how beautiful they were. Cara picked one up and was just as amazed as I.

A sales woman approached us and asked, "Would you like to try those on?"

I shook my head and Cara said, "Yes, in an eight please."

I scowled at her. Eight was my size. What was she doing? I couldn't afford these shoes and I was *not* going to put them on Vincent's card. The woman came out and gestured for us to have a seat in two leather chairs. I set my stuff down behind me, still in shock. The woman went to Cara and kneeled down in front of her.

"Oh…they're not for me. They're for her," Cara said.

"My apologies ma'am." The sales woman unwrapped the black patent leather heel with its signature red bottom. Instinctively, I removed my flip-flop, and she slid the shoe on. It fit like a glove. I stood and looked in the full-length mirror. Gaping at my reflection, I saw Cara smile at me through it.

"What do you think?" the sales woman asked.

"They're gorgeous," I said.

"We'll take them," Cara told her.

I spun around and saw Cara digging in my purse. She pulled a card out and handed it to the sales woman.

"Cara, do you know how much these cost? I cannot buy them."

"Good thing you're not. Vincent is."

Vincent had been more than gracious. I couldn't buy these shoes on his card, not after how much my dress cost. Thinking of buying them made me sick to my stomach. I looked to Cara and she glared at me. "Cara, please," I pleaded.

"It's done Lex. Vincent would want you to get them." I just shook my head. She was crazy. We took our new items and left the mall to head home. We stopped by

Vincent's on the way and picked up my car, since we had the extra time. The day had truly passed in the blink of an eye. We were primped, groomed, gussied, waxed, polished, and ready for the evening. All we needed to do was put on our dresses and for me, my new shoes.

As I pulled the Bugatti in the driveway, we had about thirty minutes before it was time to leave. I texted Vincent earlier and told him I was going to drop it off. He demanded I keep it, since the day wasn't over. I had butterflies in the pit of my stomach. I couldn't wait for him to see me in this dress. Cara pulled in ahead of me and parked my car in the garage.

When she hopped out I asked, "Do you think it's going to start raining again?"

"God, I hope not."

We gathered our bags from the trunk, which was in the front of the car. As we went inside, we immediately went into our own rooms to dress. Normally, we would've gotten ready together, but since we were just dressing, we opted for a little privacy. I took my gorgeous gown out of the bag the sales woman had placed it in. It was the prettiest dress I'd ever laid eyes on.

I pulled the gold satin up my body and put the finishing touches on my outfit for the evening, sliding on my new black Christian Louboutin heels. I'd never owned a pair before, and they were fabulous. I put a few of my make-up items in one of my black clutches, then gave myself one last look in the mirror, checking my hair and complexion. I was more than satisfied with the results.

When I went out into the living room, Cara was dressed and waiting for me. She went with a red strapless mini dress. It hugged her body perfectly with a thin silver belt and silver heels. We both wore our hair up, and Mac outdid themselves with our make-up.

"Wow, you look stunning," I said and she spun around.

"Thanks. You look beautiful. You're going to blow Vincent away."

The doorbell rang, making my heart race. With Vincent, I often got butterflies, but tonight it seemed different. I was on a whole other level of excitement. I wanted to take his breath away, not just physically, but emotionally. Tonight, I would not just show him how much he meant to me, I'd tell him.

I opened the door, and standing in front of me was a very dapper Vincent dressed in a black tux. His eyes scanned my body, and he shook his head, taking me in his arms. He kissed me with so much power it caught me off guard. I wrapped my arms around his neck, threading my fingers into the back of his hair.

"Come on you two. Get a fucking room," Abel, *so* rudely, said. I hadn't even noticed him at the door with Vincent. I was too focused on how mouthwatering Vincent looked. The comment from Abel didn't affect Vincent. He slightly pulled away, but continued to nibble my lips.

He looked deep into my eyes. "You are absolutely breathtaking. You're the most beautiful woman I've ever laid eyes on."

I smiled at him and noticed there was a bit of anxiety hidden deep within his eyes. "Thanks. You look mouthwatering in that tux."

"Seriously guys, I mean it. Get a fucking room."

Vincent growled, and for once, I heard Cara laugh at something Abel had said. We walked inside, and Abel pushed past us in a hurry to get to Cara.

"Wow, you look fucking gorgeous, and you're wearing my favorite color," Abel said.

Cara blushed a bit, but rebounded quickly, putting a sober expression on her face. "Don't try to flatter me or flirt with me. I didn't wear this for you. Where's your date anyways?"

He laughed at her and popped the bottle of Chrystal he had in his hand. "Sweetheart, *you* are my date."

She rolled her eyes. "The fuck I am. Have you lost your mind?"

He chuckled at her. The sound reminded me of Vincent.

"All right you two. You have all night to fight. Can we please enjoy a toast and get on the road?" Vincent asked.

Vincent ignored them as they glared at each other and handed me a sleek blue Tiffany box. "Here, beautiful. I got this for you."

He had already gotten me so much. Another gift was too much. He placed it in my hands, and I knew I couldn't argue with him. I opened the top, and nestled in the fabric was a chain with a single pear-shaped diamond.

"Oh, Vince. It's beautiful."

He smiled, looking into my eyes. "You like it?"

"I love it." I said, wrapping my arms around his neck.

"When I saw it, I knew it was perfect for you."

I kissed him with everything I had. When I pulled away, I could still see the anxiety. Maybe we just needed to get on the road, and he would relax.

Vincent put the necklace on my neck and then Abel said a toast. "Here's to the best double date, I've ever been on." We all laughed and clinked glasses, sipping our champagne.

"Are you guys ready?" Vincent asked.

"Absolutely, let's get this party started," Abel said, wrapping his arm around Cara's waist. A limo was waiting for us when we went outside. An older gentleman held the door open, and we all climbed in.

The limo ride was entertaining, to say the least. We joked and made fun of Cara's apparent dislike for Abel. The atmosphere was fun and light, and I couldn't keep my hands off of my necklace. It felt foreign around my neck. I never wore jewelry, but this was a piece I didn't want to take off.

Vincent grabbed my hand, removing it from the

chain. Leaning down he kissed the diamond and then placed our hands in his lap. Our hands lie intertwined, and I felt his erection present through his pants.

I listened as Cara and Abel debated about real sugar versus fake sugar and if they would rather get diabetes or cancer. Who knew how they got on the subject, but watching them banter back and forth was funny. I turned to Vincent and wanted to ease his worry, so I pressed my lips against his, watching as he closed his eyes.

"Thank you for everything today and my necklace, I love it."

He looked at me and nodded his head without speaking. Leaning down, he kissed me again, and we got lost in each other in that moment. I enjoyed the sweet taste of his lips and how he loved me with his mouth. My lips instantly parted inviting his tongue in, but then he stopped.

"I need to tell you something," he said.

No, not now. This was not the place to say the words, especially with his brother and my best friend sitting next to us.

I placed two fingers on his soft lips. "Not now, love. Later, okay?"

He stared at me confused and unsure how to respond. The car slowed, and my door opened. The driver reached for my hand to help me out. As the four of us entered the newly revamped Lazio's, I noticed Charlie had gone all out. The restaurant was completely transformed. Not only had he re-done the menu, but the inside had been completely redecorated. Previously, it was dark and dim with old world charm. Now it had a light and airy feel. I liked the change. The colors were cream and lime green with tons of greenery throughout. He also had the patio remodeled for outside seating and added a bar as well.

Looking around, the men all wore tuxedos and the women were in elegant gowns.

Charlie approached us as we found a table. "Alexa, Vincent, Abel, I'm so glad you made it. Forgive me, but I haven't had the pleasure of meeting this lovely young lady."

Abel went to speak, I'm assuming to introduce Cara, but she stepped in front of him and shook Charlie's hand.

"I'm Cara, Alexa's friend. It's a pleasure to meet you, thank you for having me tonight. I've heard a lot of great things about you from Lex and Vincent."

Charlie looked confused and Abel threw his arms in the air and walked away to the bar.

"Cara, it's a pleasure to meet you. I hope I'm not overstepping my boundaries, but I assumed you were here with Abel," Charlie said.

"Not at all. But no, I'm not. I came with Lex and Vincent."

Charlie chuckled. "Ahh, then would you like to have a drink with me?"

"Absolutely. I love free drinks," she teased.

He laughed and said, "I like you, Cara."

She smiled and took his arm as he held it out to her.

"Well, that was unexpected. Who knew that Cara would get along better with Charlie than with Abel." I said.

Vincent pulled me close to him. "My dad is a charmer. What can I say?"

I shook my head at Vincent. I was glad to see Charlie enjoying himself, even if it pissed Abel off. I was also happy that Charlie wasn't working. He was a guest here just like everyone else. I watched Abel stare at the two of them as they approached the bar. He took a swig of his beer, but didn't take his eyes off of Cara.

"Would you like a drink, babe?" Vincent asked.

I shook my head. I was too nervous to drink. I felt awkward next to Vincent. He had already caught the eye of everyone around us. Although I looked the part tonight, I was far from it. I scanned the room at all of the prim and proper rich couples around us; this seemed like a typical Friday night to them. I felt misplaced and unsure of what I was supposed to do.

"Dance with me," he said.

Vincent had already walked us halfway to the dance floor before I could respond. I was not a dancer and was self-conscious about being in front of people I didn't know. I cringed on the inside and felt like I was losing control of the situation, but I wasn't going to turn my back on Vincent. He sensed my anxiety and saw the uncertainty in my eyes as we stopped just short of the glistening dance floor.

"Don't worry, love. Just follow my lead and look in my eyes."

Vincent was an amazing dancer, he moved with precision and grace. I looked into his eyes and found the clarity I'd been searching for. There was my man; he was calm, confident, and loving.

When the song ended, Charlie cut in. "May I have the next dance with Alexa?"

Vincent didn't question him as he handed me over to his father. There was a clear bond of trust that couldn't be broken. I watched Vincent walk over to Cara and Abel standing at one of the small tables. Charlie started to move, and I tripped a little on his feet, we both laughed at the little miss-hap.

"Sorry. I have two left feet. I'm nothing like my son when it comes to dancing. He and Judith were the dancers of the family."

"Was Judith your wife?"

He smiled, and I could see his mind drift back to the memory of her.

"Yeah, she was. She and Vincent were so close. I never thought he would come around after we lost her. It's taken him years to smile again, especially with the recent betrayal he endured. I'm assuming he told you about both?"

"He did. It's one of the things I love about Vince. He's always so open with me."

He smiled from ear to ear. "So, you love him then?"

"Yes, I do."

"Good, because I know he feels the way same about you."

I looked at Vincent as he was watching me, with love and devotion. We exchanged a smile, and he turned to see who was behind him when Liam and C.J. approached.

Shit!

What were they doing here? We hadn't told anyone at work about us and this was neither the time nor the place. Tonight was about Charlie and Lazio's.

As the song ended, I said, "Charlie, thanks so much for the dance and telling me about Vincent and Judith."

"Oh, it was my pleasure. Thank you for making my son so happy."

I smiled at him and gave him a hug before I excused myself to the ladies room. I needed a little time to process what I had just seen. As I rushed off of the dance floor, Cara saw me and immediately followed. I walked as fast as my legs would carry me in my heels. Entering the restroom Cara was right behind me. I walked to the sink and braced myself by holding onto the edge of the counter.

"What's going on?" Cara asked.

Lifting my head, I looked at her in the reflection of

the mirror. "Liam and C.J. are here."

"Did you not know they were gonna be here?"

I turned around to face Cara and said, "Of course not. We haven't told anyone at the office we're dating."

"Oh," she whispered, and when I saw the concern in her eyes, I knew there was something she wasn't telling me.

"Why are you looking at me like that?" I asked nervously.

"Umm... I think Vincent invited them."

"Why would you say that?" I questioned her. My stomach tightened in disbelief. Why would he do that without telling me?

"Because I was standing there when they walked up, and they both thanked him for inviting them."

I shook my head as tears filled my eyes. Why would he go behind my back?

"Maybe you should go talk to him," Cara said.

But I didn't want to talk to him, not here. It hurt that he would do something like this without talking to me first. I thought that I could trust him.

The tears began to fall down my cheeks. "I don't know what to say."

"Just be honest."

I turned my head when the bathroom door opened. Quickly wiping my tears away, I watched as a beautiful brunette woman slowly walked into the restroom.

Her eyes locked with mine when she said, "You

must be Alexa."

I don't know how she knew me because I was pretty sure I'd never seen her before.

"I'm sorry, do I know you?"

She leaned over the sink and grabbed a tissue. I felt a little foolish crying in front of a stranger when she handed it to me.

"Here, sweetie. You may want to clean yourself up. You look a mess."

By the tone of her voice, I knew she wasn't being polite.

"I'm Angela, Vincent's fiancée," she said.

Her eyes never left mine when Cara asked, "Excuse me, who are you?"

I hardly heard Cara's words, as my body suddenly grew cold. I was frozen, in complete and utter shock. I didn't think this night could've gotten worse. *She was Vincent's fiancée?* I was unable to grasp the thoughts that were flooding through my mind.

With a shaky voice I asked, "What are you doing here?"

"I should be asking you that. This is a family event, and I'm practically family."

"What are you talking about? He told me you cheated on him." I shook my head. "He told me he left you." *He left her didn't he?* I no longer knew what to believe.

"Come on, let's go," Cara said as she grabbed my

hand. I jerked it back. I had to stay. I had to know the truth.

Angela tilted her head to the side and said, "Sweetie, he tells the same story to all of them. You're not the only one. You haven't fallen for him already have you?"

"I am the only one. Vince wouldn't do that to me." *Would he?* I glanced down and got a glimpse of the huge ring on her left hand. How could I be so foolish to put my trust into somebody I barely even knew? I let my walls down and he completely took advantage of me.

"I'm sorry I had to be the one to tell you, but this is who he is. This is what he does. He tells them all the same thing: that I cheated on him, that I broke his heart. It's nothing but a game to him."

"Why would he do that?"

"Because he doesn't know how to be faithful. But we love each other, so I accept him for who he is."

"I can't stand here and listen to this shit any longer," Cara said.

As I peeled my eyes away from Angela, a new sheen of tears washed down my face. Emotions took over. The one time I allowed myself to open up to someone, it was just a sick game.

My breathing increased and I looked at Cara. "I don't know what to do."

"We will figure it out, Lex. Let's just go." She reached down and tightly held my hand in hers. She walked me back out into the restaurant. Stepping out into the crowds of people, I was overwhelmed by embarrassment. I tucked my head down in shame, and I tightened my grip on Cara's hand. I couldn't control the tears. My body trembled with anxiety, and with every step I took, I felt pieces of my heart breaking away. I was humiliated. It was like every person in that room knew what Vincent had done to me.

"Cara, go! Just get me out of here," I said.

Cara wrapped her arm around me and rushed us as quickly as she could to the front doors. She pushed the doors open, and the cold rain stung my skin. It was pouring. Our limo driver saw us and ran to the car opening the door.

"Lex, wait!" I heard his voice calling from behind.

"Stay the fuck away from her, Vincent," Cara snapped over her shoulder.

When the driver opened the door, I turned to him. Vincent looked between the two of us, completely bewildered.

"Lex, what happened?" he asked, grabbing me.

I jerked away from him. "Don't fucking touch me."

"Baby, what's going on?"

"Leave her alone, Vincent. Just walk away."

"Cara, just give us a second," he yelled.

Cara reluctantly slid inside the car.

Vincent placed both of his hands on my shoulders and looked me in the face. "What happened? Is this about Liam and C.J.? I'm sorry I didn't—"

I cut him off and pulled out of his grip. "No it's not about them. How could you lie to me?" I asked wiping my tears away with the back of my hand.

"What are you talking about? I've never lied to you."

"Do you think I'm stupid? I'm not a fucking idiot!" I screamed.

With fear in his eyes, he stepped closer to me. "No, I don't, love. Please tell me what you're you talking about? What happened?"

"I never should've opened myself up to you. I knew I should have never trusted you. Angela told me everything. I saw her ring."

He grabbed me again, this time, tightly around my waist and held me to him. "Baby, I never lied. You're everything to me. I don't know what she said to you, but it's not the truth."

With both of my fists clenched, I slammed them on his chest as I cried through my words, "I don't know what to believe anymore, but I don't think I can believe you."

"What did she say to you?" he demanded.

"It doesn't matter, Vincent. We're done. I should've known better. There's a reason why I have my rules. I should've *never* broken them for you. Just tell me how many other girls there are?"

I stood, shaking, trying to catch my breathing as the cold rain pelted my skin.

"Baby, it's only you. It's only been you. There is no

one else in this world for me but *you*." He reached for my chin and turned my face to look up into his.

I shrugged out of his grip. "I'm not stupid. I met you at a club. How many other girls have you met at that place? You know what, just forget it. I don't want to know. Just stay the fuck away from me. You're nothing but a goddamn liar."

With a pleading tone, he said, "Baby, I can't stay away from you. Don't you get it? I love you."

I looked at his pain-filled face as tears rolled down his cheeks mixed with the rain. "You don't know how to love."

I got into the car and slammed the door. Cara yelled at the driver to go.

Looking into Vincent's eyes and seeing his tears killed me. My heart was crushed. It had been ripped out of my chest and was left bleeding on the rough pavement at his feet. I howled into Cara, and with every breath, the pain increased. I had never allowed myself to love anyone, and the one time that I did, he *used* me. He *lied* to me, and he *betrayed* me. Then he had the audacity to say that he loved me. He didn't know the first thing about love.

As the world I had once known shattered, I clung to Cara. She was my only constant in this fucked up world. Thinking back to Angela's words was like a knife to my gut. I was nothing to him, but another girl he could use and throw away when he was finished.

The tears flowed through me. I wished the pain I was experiencing would stop. It was unlike anything I'd ever felt before. In a short period of time, fate had brought me what I thought was my soul mate. I let my walls down and lost all control, allowing myself to fall in love. I was naïve enough to only see the good in him and never questioned anything else. The moment I said *yes*, I'd give us a chance, I had lost all of my logical thinking.

The driver pulled up to the condo and quickly opened our door. Cara and I ran through the pouring rain. When we entered the condo, I dropped my shoes, which I was holding, and immediately went into my bathroom to shower. I hoped the hot water could ease a little of my pain. Cara was right behind me as I struggled to get out of my dress. Due to the rain it stuck to my skin. She unzipped the back and peeled it down my body.

"Are you okay?" she asked as she turned on the water.

I didn't answer her. It took every ounce of my energy to not collapse to the floor as I stood there lifeless. She didn't speak again; she just continued to help me. First unclasping my bra and then she reached for my necklace. I grabbed it instinctively and pulled away, shaking my head. She nodded at me in understanding, and I stepped into the shower letting the hot water flow over my numb body. I don't think the water could've been hot enough to take away an ounce of my pain, but I turned it up anyway, trying to dull the ache within.

I was overcome with emotion, thinking about walking away from Vincent. I pictured his hazel eyes filled with tears when he finally said the words to me, he told me he loved me and it was all a lie. As hard as it was for me, I knew it was better to push through this now. He wasn't the man I thought he once was, and tonight proved that point.

This is what you have to do.

I got out of the shower without even washing myself. I grabbed my robe from the back of the bathroom door and slid it on. As I crawled into my bed, I curled up on Vincent's side. The pillow still held his scent. I inhaled into it deeply with everything I had, holding onto his smell, and wept into the pillow. Smelling him was too much for me to handle. I wished the blackness would take me over. That was the only way I could be free of this pain for a little while. Each minute felt like ten, and the darkness never came. It felt like hours had passed when I looked at the clock, but it was only nine o'clock.

Then I heard banging on the front door, and I knew it was him. Cara came down from her room and talked to him through the door. His voice was muffled, so I couldn't make out what he was saying. She was smart enough to not open the door. I knew if he had any way in, he would have barged in here and demanded that we speak. When the silence returned, and I lost the sound of his voice, the weeping took over again.

About an hour later, Cara came in to check on me. I was awake and scooted over for her to sit down.

"Hey. How are you?" she asked.

"I can't sleep. It hurts so bad."

"I'm sorry, sweetie. I'd hoped you were able to get some rest, that's why I've left you alone."

"It's not your fault. It's no one's fault, but Vincent's."

"I know. I hate to tell you this, but he's still outside. He hasn't left. I know you're angry with him, but he's not leaving until you talk to him. Maybe you should hear him out?"

"I can't talk to him. I have nothing to say."

As much as it pained me, I needed my space to regain some composure before I faced him.

"Tell him I'm sleeping, Give him the Bugatti key, and tell him to go home."

She rubbed my back and leaned down gently kissing my tear stained cheek.

"Okay."

She walked out of my room, leaving the door cracked. I heard her open the front door. Cara spoke softly as she repeated exactly what I had told her to say. As she spoke, I could hear him sob.

I heard him say with so much pain in his voice it was almost unrecognizable, "I'm not taking the fucking car. Please, Cara. Just let me see her. I need to talk to her. I'm losing my fucking mind. I need her to know that I didn't cheat on her. She's my everything."

Cara kept her cool and continued to speak to him in a soft even tone. She was good at handling angry patients, and I could tell she was taking the same tactic with him.

"I'm sorry. She's asleep and exhausted. I'm not going to let you wake her up. Go home and get some rest yourself. She just needs a little space. I'll have her call you tomorrow."

"Cara, please," he sobbed. She closed the door and he cursed, slamming what sounded like his fist, on it. Cara never came back into my room, and I hoped to God that he went home. When I woke from a little sleep with a headache from so much crying, I went in to the kitchen to get myself a drink and some Tylenol. To my surprise, the Bugatti key was still on the counter. I peeked out the kitchen window, and slumped on the front porch, was Vincent. He held his head in his hands and was frozen. Watching him sitting out there killed me. The man I loved, was so broken and hurt. A sob escaped my throat, and he turned to the door.

"Lex, are you there?"

I put my hand over my mouth to stifle the noise. My instincts moved me to the front door, and I placed my hand on it. I wanted to be as close to him as possible. As angry as I was, I loved him. I rested my head on the door and cried, trying my best to stay as quiet as I could. Vincent spoke again, his words immediately calming me. And for the first time in hours, I felt like I could breathe.

"Please baby, talk to me. I'm so sorry. You have to know that. I never meant to hurt you."

I couldn't stand any longer, and I yearned to be in his arms. My body slid to the floor. I know that he knew I was there, but if I stayed quiet, I could selfishly indulge in Vincent one last time.

"Baby, please let me in so we can talk. I can't stand being away from you."

I curled into a ball and left my hand resting on the door. Every so often he would speak to me; the sound of his voice calming everything within me. I was pressed against the cold tile floor, my hand gripping the door, as if I could feel Vincent. I dozed off, letting the darkness wash away my pain.

Chapter 16

Angela

"Sweetie, are you okay?" Cara woke me, and instantly, I wished she hadn't. The pain of being without Vincent hit me like a Mac truck. "Why are you on the floor?" Cara asked.

I stood up and went to the kitchen window. Vincent was gone. I walked to the couch and sat, pulling my body into a tight ball. Cara covered me up with my favorite throw and sat next to me.

"I came out here to get some Tylenol and Vincent was still here. He heard me cry through the door and I was drawn to him. I couldn't help myself from selfishly indulging in him one more time. His voice calmed me and I must've fallen asleep, on the floor."

"I'm sorry. I had no idea you were out here."

"It's okay. There's nothing that you could've done. Do you know what time he left?"

"I texted Abel after Vincent wouldn't take the key.

When I told him what had happened, he had no idea and said Vincent told them all you were feeling sick and went home. I told him Vincent was here and wouldn't leave, that he'd been on our front porch for almost an hour. He was working and said he would get someone to cover for him and come over as soon as he could. I don't know what time that was though, I'm sorry."

A tear rolled down my cheek as I thought of Vincent on my porch and having to be taken home by his older brother. Cara sat next to me, and I lifted my head to rest it in her lap. We sat in silence and she let me just be.

"What do you say we get out and walk to Starbucks? You need some coffee and fresh air."

I nodded my head. I didn't want to lie in my bed and stare as the spot Vincent normally occupied or smell his lingering scent. I knew I wouldn't be able to sleep so getting out was my only other option.

The sun was bright, and although the rain from the night before had dissipated, you could still smell it in the air. As we headed out I didn't look at his car still parked in my driveway. Thoughts of that car and us rolled through my mind. I let the tears run down my cheeks and focused on putting one foot in front of the other.

Cara walked alongside of me, not rushing my pace. She didn't talk or force me to relive the events from the night before.

Starbucks was packed as it normally was on the weekends. All of the locals needed their Saturday morning coffee. I didn't want to go in, so I sat outside on one of the benches, letting the sun warm my skin while Cara got our drinks. Looking up, I watched the rolling clouds move across the blue sky. It reminded me of waking up in Vincent's bed. I closed my eyes, and let the feeling of the warm sun remind me of his body wrapped around mine.

Cara came out, interrupting my daydream, and handed me my drink. "Are you okay?"

I shrugged my shoulders and got to my feet, walking away without answering her. I was unable to talk as the tears rolled down my face and ran off of my cheeks. I didn't bother to wipe them away. There was no point because they weren't going to stop. I'd never cried so much in all of my life. The pain was unbearable. It was like nothing I'd ever experienced. My insides felt as though they had been ripped out of my chest, leaving an enormous fissure in their place. I thought back to the day my grandfather had passed, remembering the pain I experienced when I lost him. I watched him take his last breaths, as the cancer slowly ate away the strong man he once was and it didn't even compare to what I was feeling right now.

"What are you going to do today? I have to work at two o'clock," Cara said.

What was I going to do? I sure as hell wasn't going to sit at home alone, and wallow in my self-pity. Since I couldn't go to work with Cara, I needed to figure out on my own how to handle talking to Vincent.

"I think I'll take a drive to clear my mind. I need to do something to keep my mind busy and figure out what to say to Vincent; I can't avoid him forever."

"That's a good idea. I do agree you need to figure out how to handle seeing and speaking to him again, especially before you go to work."

I really didn't know what else I could do. When we walked up to the condo, there was a note tucked in the front door. My heart broke; he was not going to make this easy.

Baby, please talk to me. You cannot believe a word that Angela said. Trust me. I love you, Vincent.

I figured I would text him and tell him that I would call him later. I didn't need him stopping by here again. I found my black clutch from last night. Tucked neatly inside was his black Amex card, my ID, cell phone, and Vincent's favorite lip-gloss. He said he liked the way it tasted and would always nibble it off my lips. I threw my clutch across the room and sat on one of the barstool chairs. Cara came down from her room, finding my items scattered about the living room.

"Lex, what happened?"

I didn't answer her, what could I say besides 'I childishly threw my clutch across the room, thinking about my ex-boyfriend nibbling lip-gloss off of my lips.' I couldn't believe he was my ex.

She collected my items and sat next to me. She had

my phone in her hand and set my clutch on the counter. When she slid it towards me, I pushed it back. She glanced at the screen when it flashed, and I saw the alarm on her face.

"What's wrong?" I asked, and she shrugged her shoulders. "Tell me, damn it. I can't look at it," I snapped.

She pressed the center button, illuminating the screen. "You have twenty-two missed phone calls and fifteen text messages."

Fuck.

I snatched my phone, unable to ignore the insane amount of missed calls and texts. As I scrolled through the call log, I saw they were all from Vincent. I went over the text messages and it was the same, minus one from Bridgette.

"I can't talk to him yet."

She nodded her head in understanding. "I know you can't. Why don't you take a shower and get dressed and we'll leave at the same time?"

I knew that was what I needed to do. Then the thought of his car blocking mine crossed my mind. I couldn't bring myself to move the Bugatti, and I didn't think Cara would be able to figure out how to start it, much less drive it.

"Cara, will you call Abel and ask him to pick up the car and take it to Vincent?"

I grabbed my clutch and opened it. Staring at me

was his Amex card. I placed it on the counter next to the key, and I walked off without waiting for her response. I knew that Cara would do anything I needed. She had always been there for me. Without her, I'm not sure what I would do.

As I stood under the scalding hot water, it didn't ease the agony. To complicate things, I wasn't looking forward to spending the entire day alone. My mind was racing and I already felt anxious.

As I washed myself, thoughts of Vincent doing it for me flashed through my mind. I rinsed, trying to erase the memories, and turned the water off. As I dried myself off I noticed the towel smelled like Vincent, and I immediately dropped it. All I wanted to do today was not think about him for one minute, but he was consuming me.

I dressed in long yoga pants, flip-flops, a tank top, and a zip-up hoodie. I grabbed my keys and when I picked up my cell phone, it vibrated with a text from Vincent:

Baby, please call me.

If I wanted a fighting chance at surviving work on Monday, I needed to clear my mind and put some distance between us. I texted him back.

I don't know what there is to talk to about.

Cara and I went outside and the Bugatti was gone. Having his car no longer there made me feel that much farther away from him. I was saddened by the memory of it, and now that it was gone, I felt like we were really over. I looked to Cara, and she saw the disbelief on my face.

"Abel had one of the guys from the station bring him here as soon as I texted him. He said Vince isn't doing well, and he really wishes you would talk to him."

I kept walking and opened the garage. Getting in my car, I avoided her insinuation that I should talk to him.

"I'm sorry, Cara. Thank you for everything," I said.

She gave me a half smile and walked to her car with her shoulders bowed. I knew she was only trying to help. We both pulled out of the driveway together and headed out of the neighborhood at the same time, except I had no destination in mind, I just drove.

I felt like a zombie; I was completely zoned out. I tried to think of what to say to Vincent when I saw him. Maybe it would be easier to just call him. He was so intense, I knew if I saw him in person, things would be so much harder to handle.

I had driven for over an hour and had not gone anywhere, or made a plan of how to handle things. I headed back home, feeling exhausted. I was desperate to clear my mind, if only for a minute. I turned up the music as loud as it would go when 'Sail' by Awolnation came on the radio. Prior to Vincent, music was my only release to the world around me, and the thoughts that would run rampant through my mind. I let the music absorb into me and thought of nothing but the lyrics, as I sang to them.

I pulled up to my house and he was there.

Fuck!

I wanted to keep driving, but he saw me, and I knew he would've gotten in his car and followed me if I didn't stop. I turned the music down and pulled into the driveway. I took off my sunglasses and placed them in their case, wasting as much time as I could before I got out of the car. I opened my door and mustered up as much strength as I could, slowly walking towards the porch. I tried to not look at him, but I was drawn to him like a horse to water. When my eyes connected with his, the expression across his face was that of anger.

"Wow. Looks like you're having a great day. I'm so glad to see that you're out and about, driving around with your top down and music blaring. You're really handling this well."

Was he fucking serious? Did he not know me at all?

"Vincent, knock it off. You know damn well I'm not handling this well. You broke my fucking heart. I was trying to clear my mind, so please tell me, to what do I owe the pleasure of this visit?"

"I want to know why you had my brother give me back the Bugatti. I told Cara I didn't want it. The least you could've done was face me yourself."

I walked past him and went to the front door. I sure

as hell was not going to be fighting on my front porch with him.

"That car is yours. You loaned it to me for a day. I gave you the opportunity to take it back last night, and you refused. It was blocking my car in, so I had Abel return it to you."

He was inches behind me, and the fucking door wouldn't open.

Damn lock!

"Why can't you keep it?"

I spun around, shocked, and glared at him. "I don't want the fucking car, Vincent. Don't you see what you did? You broke my trust and lied to me. Not only did you lie to me, but we had a deal, and you went behind my back."

"Fuck your deal. That's not what this is about. You were having second thoughts about us. I know you were."

What was he talking about? I was in love with him. I still am, and I for once in my life, I can honestly say that I never second-guessed a minute I spent with him. I opened the door and flew inside. I went to the couch and turned to see him heading towards me.

Vincent continued, "Just like Angela, you doubted me. Rather than speak to me about it, you brushed it off like it was nothing. Then you decide I have to agree to some bullshit deal while you figure out what the fuck you want. Well, news flash, babe. Welcome to the real world where people talk about their feelings. I wanted you, plain and simple, and I didn't care who knew. Clearly I wasn't enough for you, and you found your way out by saying I lied to you. Now you believe some bullshit my ex told you. Alexa, I never lied to you. Every word, every feeling, and every emotion I shared with you was from my heart and one hundred percent *true*. I fucking love you."

I placed my head in my hands, and I tried to collect my wits. When I looked up, he had walked out on me. I froze like a statue, unable to move. My breathing increased, and I gasped for air. I felt like my heart was being ripped out of my chest all over again. He'd left me. I knew now what he must've felt like the night I left. I realized then I was hyperventilating just as my vision blurred. The world around me spun, and I was panting for air. I grasped for my breath, but it was gone. There was nothing left for me grab onto; it had walked out the door.

Chapter 17

Letting Go

"Are you okay?"

I looked up and saw Cara standing above me. I realized I'd passed out on the couch. My memory clicked with the incidents that had taken place earlier in the day. I must have hyperventilated after Vincent left.

She grabbed my arm to help me stand. "Come on. Let's get you to bed."

I halted in my tracks and shook my head. I couldn't go in there and sleep in that bed. I couldn't lie there, where we had so many times and loved one another. I crawled back on the couch, and she covered me with my blanket. Cara moved the loose tendrils of hair out of my face.

"Do you need anything?" she asked.

"Water would be great."

She got up and went into the kitchen. "Did you know the front door was wide open?"

"He was here," I said.

She spun around and looked at me wide eyed. "What do you mean he was here? Did you call him?"

I kept my calm and gathered my thoughts before I spoke. "No. When I came home from my drive he was here waiting and pissed about the car. He walked out on me. It's really over between us," I said letting out a small cry.

"Oh, sweetie, I'm so sorry I wasn't home."

"It's okay. It had to be done. Maybe now we both can move on."

"You're a strong and brave girl, you know that?" she said.

I didn't feel strong or brave. Inside everything was broken, I was completely shattered. I may put on the façade that I was strong, but the truth be known, I was far from it.

It was Wednesday and Vincent had worked from home so far this week. It made things easier to not see him. I don't know how I'd survived three days straight at work, putting on a façade. It took all of my strength to act as though everything was normal, when I felt like I was going to lose it at a moment's notice. I only had two more days of this torture and then I could crawl into a ball and wallow in my self pity.

I hadn't made it back to the hospital since Vivian went off on me. Bridgette had been asking to have dinner with me, but I kept making up excuses, avoiding her. I didn't want to explain what had happened between Vincent and I. I knew if I saw her she would be asking questions about us, and I couldn't lie.

All I could do at this point was focus on getting through the minutes. I didn't know what the next minute would bring or where my emotions would take me. As I looked down at the clock on my computer, it was already four o'clock, and I was exhausted. I hadn't been taking lunches, so I gathered my things to head home and sulk.

Cara wasn't home tonight; she was working another swing shift. Walking into the quiet house was still something I didn't like. I went over and turned the TV on, along with a few lights. I popped a piece of toast into the toaster and headed into my room to change. Besides caffeine, toast had become my new meal of choice. It was all that tasted good and about the only thing I could keep down. I put on the rattiest sweats and t-shirt I had and went back to the kitchen. My toast popped up, and I added a little butter on it before making myself comfortable on the couch. I was trying my best to move forward and out of this slump, but something was holding me back.

I woke around four in the morning after only having an hour of sleep. I knew I wouldn't be able to go back to sleep. I'd tried every day this week and was unsuccessful, so why try to beat a dead horse today. I decided to go ahead and throw myself together.

The one good thing about these extremely early mornings was the lack of traffic and being the first one at the office. I was able to stay caught up on what I needed to do and was even helping Portia with some of her work.

Since it had been close to five days with little to no sleep, I knew my appearance looked like death. I stayed as busy as I could to keep from talking to others and kept my head down. I also spent a great deal of time in the file room, alone. My skin was pale, and I had black circles under my eyes. It didn't help that I couldn't keep much food down.

I was surviving solely on caffeine and toast when my body would accept it. It was time for my second latte of the morning as my stomach growled to remind me. I took the elevator down and walked across the street to the Starbucks. When I walked in, I was the only customer. The employees had gotten to know me well and knew my order, so I paid and was on my way back to work in no time. The weather outside was nice today. It was finally starting to cool down since we were in September.

I texted Cara as I walked back, just like I did every day to say 'good morning' and to let her know I was well. As I exited the elevator and rounded the corner to my desk, my heart stopped when I saw Vincent in his office.

Shit, he's here!

I kept my head down and went straight to my desk. I knew he had a perfect view of me as I did of him. I didn't dare let him see me looking at him, especially in the condition I was in. Quite frankly, I looked pathetic.

I grabbed my purse and went to the bathroom. When I walked in, I rested myself against the sink and turned on the water, splashing it on my face. I focused solely on my breathing to keep it under control. The last thing I needed was another panic attack and to pass out at work. The cold water calmed me, and I felt a little better. I dried my face and put on as much powder as I could to hide the dark circles under my eyes. I added a thick layer of lips gloss in hopes that it would draw any attention away from my eyes and to my mouth. I took a few more calming breaths before I left the bathroom. I wanted to make sure that I was in complete and total control. *I needed control.*

Vincent was talking to C.J. when I left the bathroom. I was surprised to see him looking so well. He seemed to be rested and didn't have any dark circles under his eyes like I did. Apparently, he no longer needed me to help with his insomnia. Maybe that was another lie as well, or since Angela was here, he now had her. I heard him apologize to C.J. for working from home this week. He told him he wasn't feeling well and didn't want to get anyone else in the office sick. *Fucking liar.* I guess I shouldn't be surprised.

I walked past them without looking in their direction. I could feel both of their eyes on me as I passed, but I kept my head held high and went back to my desk. I didn't realize how hard it was going to be to see him again, much less working together. This was going to be impossible. I don't think I would be able to come in here every day and look at him.

As I sat at my desk, I searched online for paralegal jobs in the Denver area. I had to find something else, plain and simple. Vincent was a partner here, so there was no way he was going to leave. I kept myself occupied with job searching for hours. It was four o'clock when I checked the time, and as usual since I hadn't taken a lunch, I left. I grabbed my stuff and started to walk towards the elevator without looking in the direction of his office. As much as I wanted to glance in there, I didn't. I put my head down and focused on getting out of there as fast as I could.

It didn't happen. Vincent caught me as I waited for the elevator. "Hey, how are you?" he asked with concern etched across his face.

What kind of question was that? Was I okay? I was at a loss for words and didn't want to break down. I swallowed hard and nodded my head. He stepped closer to me and ran the back of his hand down my cheek. Instinctively, I closed my eyes and leaned into his touch. When the elevator arrived, I forced myself to walk in. I wanted nothing more than to collapse in his arms, but I couldn't.

As I stood in the elevator, I looked into his eyes and pressed the lobby button.

"I'll see you tomorrow?" he asked.

I gave him a half smile and nodded my head as tears started rolling down my cheeks. Unable to take my eyes off of him as the doors closed, I watched him until he was gone.

On my drive home I called Bridgette. I had been blowing her off for days and wanted to apologize.

"Hey, Bridge. How are you, doll?"

"Hey, I'm good. Mom's doing really well. All her blood work came back normal. So they scheduled her surgery for tomorrow morning."

"Oh, good, sweetie, I'm glad to hear that."

"Do you want to have dinner tonight? I really miss you."

I knew I should be there for Bridgette, but I felt so tired, and seeing Vincent today had taken all of my energy.

"I wish I could, I really do, but I have to work late."

"Okay. I understand. How are you?"

"I...I'm okay. Just busy with work, like always."

"Well, that's good. I'm glad to hear work is busy. Tell Vincent I said hi."

"Thanks, and I will."

"I love you."

"Love you too, doll. Bye."

After I hung up, traffic came to a halt on the freeway. Great. This was just what I didn't need tonight. As I rolled through the slow traffic, I pictured Vincent's face as the elevator doors closed. He looked genuinely concerned, although well rested. Maybe he was relieved that we were broken up and took a few days to give me space. I knew I needed to come to terms with the fact there was no future for us, but that was easier said than done.

I felt bad for lying to Bridgette about working late, but my mind had been too preoccupied with Vincent. I wouldn't have been good company.

Chapter 18

Goodbye

I slept for a total of two hours, which was the most sleep I've had in almost a week. It was six o'clock, and thankfully Starbucks was open. I slipped on a pair of leggings and a hoodie and quietly went outside. The weather was crisp, but a nice change from the heat I had become accustomed to.

The walk to Starbucks was short. It took me all of five minutes to get there, and at this time of the morning, there were few customers. I forced myself to order a yogurt and a croissant. I knew I needed to start eating better. Normally, I would devour the croissant, so I knew if there was anything I was going to keep down other than toast, it would be this. Vincent was taking care of himself, so why shouldn't I?

I sat down with my latte and breakfast to eat what I could. The croissant tasted great, but watching my spoon poke around in the yogurt made with the fresh berries unsettled my stomach. When I left, the sun was rising, and the birds were chirping, it was a surreal feeling being out this early in the morning. As I headed back home, I managed to eat the rest of my croissant and sipped on my latte.

The house was still dark and quiet when I got home. I took my time checking my emails. By the time I looked at the clock, I was running late. We had our usual morning eight am staff meeting, and I was in charge of filling everyone in on a new case.

I hopped in the shower and washed myself as quickly as I could. When I got out, I wrapped myself in a towel and started my normal process with as much speed as I was capable of. After my hair was done, I applied a little make up and ran into my closet. I picked out my simple grey dress slacks with a baby pink silk top. When I laid the clothes on my bed, I noticed a missed call from Bridgette on my cell phone. As I called her back, I walked into the bathroom to put some lotion on before I got dressed.

"Hey, sorry I missed you. I was drying my hair."

She was sobbing uncontrollably, and I knew something was wrong.

"Bridgette, what's the matter?"

"Fuck, Lex. I…I can't believe it. She… she's gone."

"What? What are you talking about?"

"Mom. She died."

I fell to the floor. The weight of what she just said

hit me like a ton of bricks. Fuck, I couldn't breath. My insides spasmed like I'd taken a swift blow to the stomach.

"I don't understand. How did this happen?" I asked far too quickly.

She continued to cry, trying to speak through the tears and I knew I had to get to her.

"It's okay, you don't need to explain. Just stay where you are. I'll be right there."

I hung up and chucked my phone across the room in rage. I heard it hit the wall, then the floor. How the fuck did this happen? My mother was dead. No, it couldn't be true. She was fine last night. I tried to get up. I had to get to Bridgette, but the emotions took over. Dammit, I should've seen her again. I should've tried to mend our relationship.

I got on all fours in an attempt to get up. My sister, I have to do this for my sister, but I couldn't. Regret consumed me and I screamed into the ground, resting my head against the cold tile floor. I never imagined losing her would feel like this. Tears ran down my cheeks, as everything within me ached. My world was fucked up, everything was *so* wrong. I knew when I reached the point of hyperventilating, all I could do was wail and let everything out.

During my entire life I never had anything go my way. Vivian had never been there for me, and now she was gone. Damn it hurt. In that moment all I wanted was

Vincent, he would make everything better, but he was gone too. This was too much for me to handle. My life was one shit storm after another. I must've been cursed because, the one time I had something good going, that felt so right, it was taken away. I didn't have Vincent anymore, and now I'd lost my only parent. Although she at times made my life hell, she was still my mother.

Cara must have heard me and came downstairs. I looked at her through the tears and she sat on the floor with me, wrapping me in her arms. I cried into my best friend's shoulder for God only knows how long. She rocked us back and forth, while I released every last bit of energy I had.

Suddenly nausea took over, and I pushed off of her, barely making it to the toilet. Instantly my breakfast came up. Through the sounds of my gagging, I heard the doorbell repeatedly ring and then there was banging. Cara hopped up and ran out of the room. I wondered if it was Bridgette. I didn't know how long I had been in the bathroom. She probably came here. Thoughts of Vivian being dead flooded my mind and the hyperventilating took over. The room started to spin. I leaned my head on the wall behind me to keep from fading into the darkness and tried to control my breathing.

Something caught my peripheral vision. I had to do a double take and turned to see what it was. *It was him.* Vincent was standing in the doorway with despair in his eyes. He raced over to me and scooped me in him arms sitting on the floor with me. I embraced him tightly; surely this wasn't for real. He held me tighter than he ever had, and then pulled away placing his large hands on either side of my face staring into my eyes. Without speaking we just stared at one another. Looking at him caused me to cry harder. He folded me securely in his arms. Mixed emotions flowed through me, not only over the loss of my mother, but because I was in the arms of the man I loved, whom I'd recently lost as well. Sitting together, he held me tightly against his body. He smelled of Vincent, clean and light. My towel fell off but I didn't care. I clung to him and he rocked us back and forth in silence. My tears soaked through his black shirt, it was now stained white with my make-up.

He finally spoke. "Baby, what's wrong?"

I shook my head and buried it in the crook of his neck. I nestled my naked body as close to him as I could get. I saw Cara come in, and she grabbed the blanket off my bed. She came over to us and draped it over me. Vincent didn't move his arms; he kept me tucked tightly in his hold.

"Vincent, Vivian passed away this morning. We just found out before you got here," Cara said.

He kissed the top of my head and laid his cheek against my hair.

"I'm so sorry, my love."

"Lex, do you want me to go to the hospital and get Bridge? I don't want her there alone," Cara asked.

I nodded my head, unable to speak. I knew I needed to be there for my sister, but I couldn't bear the thought of leaving Vincent's arms.

Cara kneeled down and rubbed my back. "I'll be right back, sweetie. Just take deep breaths and stay calm. You got her, Vincent?"

"Yeah. We'll be fine," he said.

I didn't want to move. I was afraid if I did, I would wake up from the comfort of Vincent's arms and he would be gone. Cara left and my sobs eventually slowed.

"I'm sorry I wasn't here sooner," he said.

I looked into his eyes. They had so much care and compassion in them. "Don't be sorry. You're here now. How did you know something was wrong?"

"You told me I would see you this morning, and when you didn't show up for our staff meeting, I panicked. It's not like you to no call, no show. I tried to call you, but your phone went straight to voicemail. I knew something was wrong, so I came here to check on you. Lex, I can't stay away from you anymore. This last week has been a fucking nightmare. You and I are meant for each other, and I'm not going to let you give up on us. I fucked up. I should've talked to you before I told Liam and C.J., but dammit Alexa, you're mine, and I want the whole world to know that. There is no one else for me. As for Angela, she's a fucking psycho. She called me when I moved out here, and said her boyfriend left her. She wanted to get back together. I told her that she and I were done. I said I'd met someone else, and that you're the only one in the world meant for me. I haven't spoken to Angela since that call. I swear on my mother's grave."

"I don't know how to respond to all of that. When I saw you yesterday, you…you looked so great. You seemed happy and well rested. How could you have been in pain? If you really cared, what kept you away from me for those three days? It killed me to not see you."

"Baby, the only reason I'm rested is because Abel and my dad forced me to go to the doctor on Monday. I was put on a ton of medication including something for my insomnia, and between him and my dad, they've been babysitting me, ensuring I take what the doctors prescribed. I literally slept for three days straight, and when I woke up, I had to see you. It killed me to be away from you. You have to know that."

"God, Vince it killed me just as bad. What's happening between us it isn't natural. The connection is so strong. It scares the shit out of me, what happens the next time we fight?"

"I know. I feel the same way and we'll figure it out. We need to talk through our problems next time and not run from them. It's not a bad thing to have a connection like we do. Please just give me another chance. I promise I won't let you down. I know I said it once, but no matter what happens, we'll make it through together. I love you Alexa, more than anything in this world. I cannot live or breathe without you."

As much as my brain told me I needed to push him away to keep from ever hurting again, I couldn't. Being with him for half a millisecond was worth the risk of my heart being ripped out of my chest every day for the rest of my life.

"Vince, I love you too, more than you'll ever know. I've been dying to say those words to you. To be honest, I've loved you since the night I fell into your arms—"

He cut me off and sealed his lips around mine. Jesus it felt so right to mold our mouths together. With Vincent it was as is there hadn't been a lapse in time. Kissing him was indescribable. I missed it more than I'd even known possible. Vincent kept the kiss sweet and tender, never forcing anything, just allowing our lips to do as they pleased while we stayed pressed together. When he stopped, I looked deep into his hazel eyes. I knew in that moment, that I would fight against the world to make things work.

He smiled at me. "God I love you. You have the same look in your eyes as you did the night I met you. I've missed seeing that sparkle."

I gave him a small smile. Butterflies raced through my insides and I didn't want to get out of his arms.

"Don't get shy with me, Lex. You're sitting naked in my arms. Speaking of which, we should get you dressed before Bridgette and Cara get here."

I went to stand, but he gripped me tighter and stood with me in his arms. He sat me on my bed and went to my dresser, pulling out my favorite sweats and one of his t-shirts.

As I dressed myself, he watched me intently and said, "I love you so fucking much."

I smiled at him as my heart began to race. "I love you more."

The front door opened, and I heard Bridgette crying. This was my turn to be the big sister I was meant to be. I needed to be strong for her. She, unlike me, didn't have anyone to turn to. I thankfully now had Vincent, and I was grateful, more than ever, for that.

We went into the living room, and my little sister was a mess. She looked awful. Her hair was a stringy mess, her make-up was smeared, and she had dark circles under her glazed over, puffy, swollen, and red eyes. I ran to her and wrapped her in my arms as we both cried. It killed me to see my sister in so much pain. I know I didn't have a good relationship with my mother, but she on the other hand was extremely close with her. She loved her unconditionally, even with her quirks and all.

I walked us over to the couch, and we rested against the plush fabric. Vincent and Cara went out front together, I assume to give us some time alone.

"Bridgette, I'm so sorry I wasn't there for you."

"It's okay. There's nothing you or anyone else could've done. She was strong enough for the surgery, even the doctors didn't see this coming. Thinking back on things, deep down I think she knew something was going to happen."

A cry escaped my throat as I thought of my last interaction with her. I could vividly see the hatred in her eyes. Little did I know that would be that last time I would ever see her. I didn't think losing her would hurt like this, but dammit it did.

Chapter 19

Connections

The weekend was arduous. I was drained not just physically, but emotionally. Although I'd managed to take a few naps and finally started to sleep through the night, I was still exhausted. Having Vincent cuddle me as I fell asleep was unreal. He'd been amazing, taking care of us girls and making sure we all had what we needed.

He called the funeral home and arranged for them to pick up Vivian as well as discussed what Bridgette's wishes where for the service.

Cara and Bridgette were asleep upstairs as I sat on the front porch, enjoying one of the last warm nights of the summer. I looked up at the stars and took in a breath of fresh air. Vincent came outside and sat behind me, wrapping his large body around mine. He rested his chin on my shoulder, and his feet were on the stairs next to mine.

"What are you thinking about, baby?" he asked.

"About Vivian and how horrible I feel for not really mourning her death. It hurt at first, but now it's like that pain is gone and I feel bad. Am I a bad person?"

"No, you're not and you shouldn't feel bad. That woman was nasty your entire life. She not only mistreated you, but she verbally abused you until the day she died. You can't help how you feel; she made you feel this way."

"You always know what to say. Thank you for making me feel better."

I turned to kiss him, as he cupped my face with one of his hands. Gingerly he pressed his soft lips against mine and I closed my eyes getting lost in our kiss.

Fuck. I overslept again. How could I not? Vincent's whole body was draped over mine. He was sound asleep, which I knew was something that didn't come easily to him. His head rested in the crook of my neck with his arm and leg thrown over me. God he looked as peaceful as ever. I didn't want to wake him, but I needed to, we had to get to work. I turned my head to get a better glimpse of his face. His lips were parted as tiny breaths escaped them. I ran my fingers over his mouth, and he began to stir, moving slightly, but ultimately just holding onto me tighter.

"Good Morning," I said in a hushed voice while

gently kissing him.

He blinked a few times and closed his eyes stringently. I couldn't help but giggle at him. Who was the grumpy one now? I stroked his hair and wrapped my free arm around him. He slid completely on top of me, finally looking at me with those alluring eyes.

"Good morning, beautiful."

"We over slept again. I'm not mad, but we have to get to going to work."

He pressed his lips against mine and then got comfy, cuddling on top of me.

"No, we don't. We're not going anywhere. You're taking the week off for bereavement, and I'm taking it with you. So unless you have somewhere else to be, I'm perfectly happy right here in your arms."

My heart scrambled, racing faster that was normal, he was incredible. I couldn't believe he gave me the week off and was taking the time with me.

I shook my head. "No, there is nowhere else I would rather be. Can we stay in bed all day?"

He took my face in his hands, bracing his weight on his elbows at either side of my shoulders. Leaning down, so slowly, he pinned me with his gaze. A flame inside of me burst, and I needed him. Now. It'd been too long and I missed him. Before I could get lost in a kiss with him, I wrapped my legs around his waist and grabbed his ass guiding him into my slick folds. Thankfully we were both naked, because had we been clothed and needed to take the time to get undressed, I may have perished. I moaned as he obliged and buried himself deep inside of me. I clenched my muscles tightly around his cock.

"Fuck, baby. You're so tight. I've missed you so much."

I didn't speak, but squeezed him again.

He groaned, "It's been too long. Don't do that again, or I'll come."

I felt the same way and as I tightened my pussy around him I couldn't stop, I rocked my hips and we both exploded. It'd been too long for us. He threw his head back, biting his bottom lip and pumped long, slow strokes of himself into me. I leaned up and sucked on his neck to muffle my cries of passion.

Vincent didn't stop moving after the trembles of our orgasms stopped. He continued, rubbing the inside of my pussy with a need and urgency that I missed. As we indulged, he kissed me, and I was lost in him. We didn't stop. Neither of us slowed our movements, as we loved one another. Our bodies worked together as they knew how to do so well.

"I've missed your body," he whispered in between kisses.

"I've missed you too babe. Let me on top and I'll show you?"

A warm smile spread across his face. "By all means."

He suddenly flipped us over. I loved when he let me take the lead and how comfortable he was relinquishing over to me. I stayed bent down so I was close to him. I didn't want to be any further away than needed.

I kissed his face, jaw, neck, ears, and chest. I ensured my lips touched every inch of him I could reach. As I slowed my movements and stopped kissing him, he leaned up and kissed my necklace.

"I'm so happy you're still wearing this."

"I'll never take it off," I said breathlessly.

I couldn't stay still for long and as I moved Vincent gripped my ass, slowly guiding me up and down. The feeling pushed so hard inside of me, the pleasure literally took my breath away. We picked up speed and moved like animals as our bodies loved one another. I was close to coming again and he knew it.

"Vince," I whispered.

"Come with me, my love."

I let go and crashed my lips into his to quiet my sounds. My hands fisted his hair. We both tried to stay quiet, but it was hard to silence the whimpering and groaning. As we slowed, I stayed on top of him. Like always, he didn't force me to move. I rested my head in his neck and relished in the feeling of being so connected to him. For the first time in over a week, I felt calm. I was where I was supposed to be. No matter what challenges we faced, we would face them together.

"Can we *please* stay in bed like this for the entire week?" I begged.

"You have no idea how much I want to do that, but

we can't. I'm sure Bridgette and Cara are awake, and we have a lot to do for the service tomorrow. But I promise, we won't spend a moment apart. I might even consider hiring a driver so I can have sex with you anytime I please."

I laughed at him, even though deep down I knew he was serious. "I think I remember you saying that if anyone ever saw me naked you would, and I quote, 'go ape shit on them.'"

"You're right. I did say that. But if I buy a limo and a driver, I could bury myself inside of you any time I pleased. It really is a good idea. Don't tempt me."

"Trust me, Vince, I don't doubt that you would do just that, but isn't human trafficking illegal?" I teased.

"You know what I meant; hire one. I'm glad to see your attitude is back and in full swing this morning. I've really missed that mouth of yours."

"Good to know, and in that case, I'm going to suggest that you make yourself useful and go get us Starbucks."

He kissed my nose. "It would be my pleasure, love."

I got out of bed and looked at Vincent sprawled out. He looked sexy as hell. His right arm was above his head, and the sheet was just across his waist. He watched me move around the room naked. I rummaged through my dresser for something to wear, finally deciding on a pair of navy blue cotton capris and a tan tank top. I blew him a kiss and headed into the living room.

When I saw Bridgette and Cara, I felt like I was making the walk of shame. They were on the couch, and I wondered if they had heard us having sex.

Brushing aside my worry I said, "Good morning, girls. How did you guys sleep?"

"Good. How about you?" Cara asked.

Before I could answer, Vincent came out of my room wearing only a pair of basketball shorts and a panty-dropping smile. His shorts hung low on his hips. He ran his hand through his hair as he walked over to me. When he reached me, he leaned down and gave me a kiss on the nose.

"Morning, ladies." The girls said hi back then he continued, "Do you mind if I shower? Then I'll run to Starbucks."

I nodded my head, unable to speak. I was mesmerized by his beauty.

"Are you okay?" he asked.

I nodded my head again, and he laughed. Leaning over me with his large frame, he rested his hands on my thighs and kissed me again. Without another word, he turned and walked back into my room. I stared at his back muscles as they mimicked his movements as he strolled away. My eyes traveled farther down to his ass. He was so yummy.

"I'm sorry, girl, but that man is fucking gorgeous. I don't care what he does, you're not breaking up with him again," Cara said.

I laughed although I knew it was true. "Well, good thing for you, he has a brother that is just as delicious and very single."

"He's all yours, Bridgette. There is no way I would ever get involved with that douche waffle."

We all laughed at Cara's blunt comment. "Douche waffle? Cara, really?" Bridgette asked.

She shrugged her shoulders and said, "What? That's how he acts."

"Stop, he's a good guy. She's just judging him because of his tattoos, and he's really outgoing."

Cara's phone rang, and she glared at me. She answered it and went out front.

"I'm going to get in the shower real quick," Bridgette said.

"Okay, take your time."

I walked back into my room. Vincent had his back to me and was in the bathroom drying off from his shower. *Damn.* He looked absolutely edible. I sprawled across my bed laying on my stomach and stared at him as he towel dried his hair and then his body. He turned around, naked, and I had a grin on my face. I motioned with one finger for him to come towards me, and he did, dropping the towel on the floor. He walked with his usual confidence. His cock was already hard and ready for me.

He stopped at the side of my bed, looking down at me. I stayed laying and I took him in my mouth without using my hands. Slowly I sucked him, swirling my tongue over the tip as I pulled him out of my mouth each time. He moaned as I worked and I pushed him as far back in my throat as I could. He reached his hand into my hair, threading his fingers into it. Although he helped me, he didn't control my movements or push into me. He allowed me to love him with my mouth at my own pace, and I was enjoying every second of it. As I picked up speed, I felt his fingers twist in my hair. I moved fast and hard causing him to come in my mouth. I swallowed quickly and continued to suck, lapping up every last drop I could. I looked up into his eyes, still holding him in my mouth and he smiled down at me. I released him and sat up on my knees. He sat next to me and pulled me onto his lap. He kissed me on the forehead and rested his cheek against my hair.

I took a deep breath enjoying the comfort of his arms. "I love you, Vince."

"I love you too, beautiful. I hate to tell you this, but I have to run home and grab a few things and then stop by the office."

"Do you have to go? I whined. "You promised we wouldn't be apart." I leaned into him and looked into his gorgeous eyes. I felt sick at the thought of him leaving. For some reason, it felt like he was never going to come back.

"As much as I would love to make you beg for me to stay, yes, I have to go. But you should know that your pouty face does things to me. I'll only be a few hours.

Enjoy some quality time with your sister. You guys should go out, but whatever you decide, just enjoy being together."

He grabbed his wallet off of the nightstand and handed me his black Amex card.

"I can't take your card again and keep spending your money."

"You can't or you won't? Baby, let me take care of you. I want to. Take your sister out: eat, shop, or do what girls do. I don't care what that is, but the card is there for you."

"But Vince—"

He cut me off. "No 'but Vince.' This isn't up for discussion."

When I rolled my eyes, he kissed my nose and placed the card in my hand.

"Why do you always get your way?" I asked.

"Stop it. Don't act like you're not a little excited."

He was right; I was excited. Between my outrageous car payment, credit card debt, and the up keep on this town home, I was maxed out each month.

I rolled my eyes again, and he pinned me down climbing on top of me. "Keep that up and see what happens next time." I nipped at his nose and he shook his head at me. "Behave while I'm gone. I'll be back soon, okay?"

He kissed me again and I clung tightly to him, I don't know how I ever survived without him. There's no one more perfect in this world for me.

Bridgette was reading on the front porch when I walked Vincent out. I watched him climb into his sleek Porsche. I loved that car, and him in it, was a sight to be seen.

I sat next to Bridgette and she put her book down.

"How are you holding up?" I asked.

She took a deep breath before speaking. "I'm okay. I know I've said this before but, I feel like mom knew it was her time to go, and she'd accepted it might happen."

I looked at Bridgette and admired her strength. Although she was younger that I was, she was truly the rock of our little family.

"What do you say we do something fun together today, just you and I? Anything you want, we can do," I said.

"Really? We can do whatever I want?"

"Yes. You're my sister, and I love you. I know that we haven't had the closest relationship lately, but I want that to change. I want to hang out like we used to. I want to know you like a sister and not someone that I always have to protect."

"I would love that."

"Great. What should we do?"

"I have the perfect thing in mind, but you have to be open-minded and trust me. Can you do that?"

"Yeah, of course I can."

"Great. Let's get going then. Can I drive your car?"

"Sure, but on one condition; you have to be really safe."

She smiled at me and my stomach turned. My car was my pride and joy, but I promised Bridgette I would be open-minded.

As she turned the Mercedes into an unfamiliar lot and pulled into a parking spot, I tried to figure out where we were. On the building in front of us, was a huge wall of graffiti. We hopped out of the car and walked around the building. Right away, I noticed the sign on the door which read, 'Tattoo.'

I whipped my head around and stared my sister in the face. "Are you serious right now?"

"Calm down. You said you would be open-minded."

She opened the door and let me walk in ahead of her. A short skinny guy, who was covered with tattoos and had gauged ears, greeted us.

"Holy shit, Bridgette. Is that you?" he said.

She ran up to him as he rounded the counter and they embraced in a hug.

"Yup, it's me. I told you I would come and get a tattoo from you one day. That day happens to be today, and I brought my sister along as well. Alexa, this is Jordan. He and I went to school together."

"I can see the resemblance. You guys look identical," he said.

"It's a pleasure to meet you, Jordan. Forgive me if I

seem a little nervous, but my sister just sprung this on me."

He laughed a little. "It's all good. We get a lot of first-timers in here."

"Well today you are dealing with two of them," I said.

He and Bridgette exchanged a look, and I knew I was missing out on something.

They both nodded their heads, and Jordan pulled out a few portfolios with sample drawings in them.

"Here, why don't you guys take a look at these, and I'll get the station set up."

We flipped through the pages and talked about every possible option. We wanted to do something as sisters. We decided that each of us would get an orchid with half of a butterfly perched on it. I would have one wing and she would have the other, resembling each of us. We decided to place them on our rib cages. Bridgette went first, and when she pulled up her baby blue tank top, I was shocked to see the script scrolling down her other side. She had a full length quote on her body.

"When did you get that?" I asked.

"I got it for my eighteenth birthday. I actually have five tattoos. This will be my sixth."

My eyes bugged out of my head. "Why didn't I know you have five tattoos?"

"I never show anyone. They're part of who I am and private. I like to keep it that way."

"What does this one say?" I asked, pointing to the script.

"It's the lyrics to the song you used to sing to me when we were kids and hid in the closet while mom was having one of her episodes."

I couldn't believe that Bridgette had a tattoo resembling something that I used to do. I didn't think she remembered those times. I've pushed those memories so far they're a blur between a dream and reality. When Vivian was off of her medication, and in a crazy fit of rage, I would hide Bridgette in the closet with me. We would cuddle and I would sing softy to drown out the noises trying to keep her calm. Sadly, Vivian never even noticed we were missing.

"I'm sorry that you have to remember those times. I tried to protect you to ensure you never had to relive them again."

"It's okay. I'm glad I had you with me to get through it. That's why I got the tattoo. Like I said, my tattoos are sort of who I am. They all have a story to be told. I'll show you the rest later and tell you about them, okay?"

"Okay," I said, staring at my sister a bit shocked.

"You ready to do this for us?" she asked.

I nodded my head as she jumped up on the table. Bridgette took her tattoo like a champ. She laid on her side and allowed Jordan to do his work. The colors and detail were amazing. As I watched him, I thought of what

Vincent would say about my tattoo and if he would like it or not. He didn't have any tattoos himself, so he might have something against them.

With the way he worshipped my body, I think he would love any addition I added to it. I did wonder how he would feel if I got something for him. I was in love with him, and we had determined that we couldn't live without one another. Why not give him something to show him that every time we were intimate?

"All right sis, you're up," Bridgette said.

I snapped out of my daydream and went to get worked on. The pain wasn't as bad as I had imagined it would be. It was no worse than what I had recently endured. Plus, I was doing it for my sister.

Jordan finished mine, in what felt like record speed. As I stood I felt a bit sore, I guess from being so tense during the process. As I checked my new tattoo out in the mirror, Bridgette and I stood back-to-back, looking at the two wings of the butterfly now becoming one. It was beautiful. I saw the smile on her face through the mirror. It felt good knowing I had a part in making her so happy.

"What do you girls think? You like them?" Jordan asked.

"I love it," Bridgette said.

"I love mine as well. Thank you."

"Of course. Let me grab the aftercare instructions, and I'll ring you up so you can both enjoy the rest of your day," he said.

"Actually, I want to get another one, something small. Do you have time to do that today?" I asked.

"Yeah, of course. What were you thinking?"

Bridgette looked at me surprised, but gave me a smile. I knew she would support my decision, and it was nice knowing I had her on my side.

"I want to get a tiny V inside of a heart."

"That would be dope. I can do that, for sure. Where do you want it?"

I pointed to the outside of my upper right thigh.

"That's perfect. Can I free-hand draw it on you and add some detail?" he asked.

"Yeah, that would be awesome."

Chapter 20

Moving On

After our tattoos, we had lunch and when we got back home, Vincent was there. I was so nervous to show him my tattoos.

When we walked inside, he was working at the dining room table on his laptop. "Hey. You guys are back early. I thought you'd be out all day," he said.

I walked over to him, and he pulled me onto his lap. I yelped in pain as his hand crashed against my side.

"What's wrong? Did I hurt you?" he asked.

Bridgette grabbed a bottle of water from the fridge and laughed to herself.

"No, you didn't hurt me. Bridgette did."

She swung around with a smirk on her face. "So now this is *my* fault?"

"You took me there."

"Will one of you please tell me what's going?" Vincent asked, sounding worried.

Bridgette lifted her shirt and showed him her tattoo. His eyes darted to me, and he lifted the hem of mine. I stayed frozen in his arms, scared of his reaction. He rubbed his thumb around the swollen skin and met my eyes.

"Do you like it?" I asked.

"Yeah. It's beautiful. Tell me about them. What do they mean?"

Bridgette rambled on and then proceeded to show us her collection of art. She has some amazing tattoos. I was still in shock that I was unaware she had so many tattoos.

Cara got home early from work and cooked us dinner. It was nice that we all ate together. Not long after, we retired to our rooms in preparation for tomorrow. I was grateful to not have to go through this alone. I would also be able to get a full night's sleep with Vincent by my side. As he closed the door behind him, he pinned me with those hazel eyes.

"Jesus Christ, do you have any idea how fucking gorgeous you are? I've been imagining the things I want to do to you all day."

I was excited and also nervous to show him my other tattoo. I swallowed hard and pulled my pants downs. He sauntered over to me, and before he could touch me I turned to my side. His eyes scanned down my body as I removed my shirt. As soon as he saw my thigh, he dropped to the floor.

He didn't say a word he just stared at it. My heart pounded so hard against my chest, I swore he could hear it. His expression was unreadable. He was motionless, kneeling next to me, just blinking. Finally he moved, brushing his lips just below the sensitive skin; his touch sent a tingle through my body.

"Is this for me?" he asked.

"Uh huh. Do you like it?"

"Do I like it? I fucking love it. You put a tattoo on your body for me in my favorite place, and it looks sexy as hell on your pink skin. It's swollen and angry. Jesus, I can't imagine the pain you went through for me. I'm so lucky you're mine."

He lifted me onto the bed and covered my body with his.

"Alexa?"

"Yeah?"

He shook his head as he searched for the right words. "I want to fuck you hard."

"I want that too, but my sister and Cara are upstairs so we have to be quiet."

"I don't want us to have to be quiet. I want you to be able to let go, let your body release how it's feeling. Move in with me."

"What? Vince, we just got back together."

"I know, but it makes sense to live together."

"I know it does. Just give me a little time to think about it, okay?"

"Just a little, okay? But first, I need to pay attention to my new favorite piece of art."

He kissed and tickled the skin around my tattoo. It melted my heart to see him so elated over it. I was worried that he wouldn't like it. As he grazed my entire body with his mouth, he left a trail of sweet kisses everywhere.

My mind drifted. I wanted to move in with him, I really did, but I was also scared. Things with us had moved so quickly. I wanted to make sure that when I did move in, it was forever. I'm not saying I needed a ring, but I needed to know that we were strong enough to survive anything. I couldn't bear to lose him again and I feared rushing things could do just that.

I hadn't been to a funeral since my grandfather passed away. I could never bring myself to attend them when those around me passed. In this case, I didn't have the luxury of not going and sending my condolences. This was my mother.

The church had been transformed into a beautiful layout all in remembrance of Vivian. Vincent had gone above and beyond to ensure that every last detail of what Bridgette said she wanted was fulfilled.

There were more people here than I thought there would be, but I recently found out that Vivian was heavily involved in the church. We had her cremated, and as I sat in the front row nestled in Vincent's hold, I stared at the gleaming silver urn that held her remains. It was all that was left of her, minus the memories. There were a dozen or so flower arrangements all around her urn and a large poster-sized picture.

As the service began and the pastor spoke, his words told me she'd traveled to the other side and that she was okay. Bridgette took the podium and spoke about her. Watching my baby sister up there, speaking of the mother she loved, killed me. It was almost unbearable to watch, but Bridgette was strong. As she fought through the tears, I wished I could take away the pain she was feeling. The service ended with one of Vivian's favorite Bob Marley songs.

As we stood to head out of the church, a line formed, and people from all different walks of life expressed their condolences and sorrow. Vincent stayed by my side and shook the hands of those who greeted us. I was in a daze, as people kept coming up to me over and over and over again.

Finally, there came a break, and I saw Vincent speaking to a middle-aged man. As they shook hands, the man made eye contact with me, and I froze. Immediately I recognized him. It was my father. I hadn't seen him since the morning he left us when I was eight. He smiled kindly at me and walked away. I watched his back as he left the church and then the procession continued. In between trying to figure out why he didn't speak to me, and the constant amount of people, I felt my anxiety level spike. Quickly I lost my breath and began to panic. I grabbed Vincent by the lapels of his jacket and as he looked into my eyes the darkness took over.

"Lex, baby. Can you hear me?" Vincent spoke in a worried tone.

A cold hand touched my wrist. "Her pulse is strong," Cara said.

I forced my eyes open and Bridgette was standing over me holding a cold, damp cloth on my forehead. "There you are. You scared the shit out of us. What happened?" she said.

I looked around me to find the three people that I absolutely and unconditionally loved most in this world.

"I don't know. I must've hyperventilated again. I lost my breath when I started thinking about seeing him, and... the next thing I knew I was gone."

"Saw who?" Bridgette asked.

"No one that either of you would know," Vincent interrupted.

My eyes darted to him, and he leaned down to kiss me cheek. I was in his arms, and he whispered in my ear, "Trust me, love. I'll tell you everything."

I looked at him and gave a small nod. I had nothing but faith and trust in this man. If he said to trust him, I would do just that. I learned my lesson to never doubt him.

"I don't know what I'm talking about guys. Can we just go home now?"

"No. You need to see a doctor," Cara snapped.

"You said yourself that my pulse was strong. I'm sure I just need to eat something. Let's go home and eat, and I promise I'll go to the doctor if I don't feel well tomorrow."

"You promise?"

"Yes."

Vincent didn't set me down or give me the chance to walk on my own two feet; he carried me outside to the waiting limo. We all got in, and as we pulled away, I stayed on his lap, resting my head against his chest. The car ride was quiet and the silence made my mind go crazy. I couldn't stop thinking about my father and why he'd come to Vivian's funeral. What did he want after all these years? I was also curious as to why he felt comfortable speaking to Vincent and not to me or Bridgette.

The limo pulled up to the condo and we all went inside. I headed straight into my room, and Vince followed. As soon as he shut the door, I wanted answers.

"What the hell happened? Do you have any idea who that was?" I questioned.

"Yes. It was your father."

"Why was he there? What did he say? Why didn't he speak to me?"

"Slow down, babe. I don't want you to get upset again. Please take a seat, and then we'll talk."

I sat on the bed and crossed my arms. He sat next to me and wrapped me in his arms.

"Please don't act like that. Let me explain, okay?"

I draped my arms around him and stared into his beautiful face.

"Obviously, I didn't know who he was at first, but when he approached me, he acted as if he knew me. He called me Lincoln, and I was confused, so I corrected him. He said he was sorry that he thought I was Vivian's son, Lincoln."

"Oh my God. Are you serious?"

My mother has a son?

"Yes, I'm one hundred percent serious. When we cleared up who I was, he asked how you and Bridgette were doing. I said that you both were doing as well as could be expected. He asked if I would take care of the both of you, and I promised I would. That's when you saw him and he left."

I ran my hands over my face trying to process what I had just heard. *Bridgette and I had a brother.*

"What am I supposed to tell Bridgette?"

"That's why I didn't want you to tell her at the church. I wanted you to have time to process this and then we could figure out what to do with the information. Maybe we should figure out if Lincoln really exists, and if he is in fact your brother. Then we will tell her about him, but if this isn't true, it may be better that she doesn't know."

He was right.

"Okay. But how do we search for him? Do we just start with the internet?"

"No, beautiful. You don't start with the internet, you're not doing anything. I'll hire someone, and they'll take care of everything. For now, try and enjoy your last day with your sister before she has to go back to school."

I nodded my head and leaned up to kiss him. He cupped my face with both of his hands and asked, "Are you sure you're feeling okay?"

"I'm fine. I promise. I'll make a doctor's appointment if it happens again."

He kissed me, and I didn't waste a minute taking it further. I slid my tongue in his mouth and twisted my body so I was straddling him. His hands moved to my hips and slid down my thighs as our mouths worked together. His fingers brushed my tattoo under my dress, and he lifted it, stopping the kiss to look at it.

"This is so beautiful. I love it," he said as he traced his finger over the V.

"I'm glad you like it."

"I do. Have you thought any more about moving in with me?"

"I haven't had a chance, but I will."

I felt horrible for lying to him. I had plenty of time to think about it and over-analyze the consequences. I needed to tell him that I was scared. I was worried that we were rushing things. I couldn't bear to lose him again, and moving in with someone full time and working with them was *a lot* to put on a relationship.

Vincent's phone rang and he had to take the call. I climbed off of his lap and went to join the girls while Vincent stayed in my room.

"Wow, it smells amazing. What are you cooking?" I asked Cara.

"BLTs and pasta salad. Does that sound good to you?" Cara asked.

"Yes. I'm starving, and I finally have my appetite back."

"Where's Vincent?" Bridgette asked.

"He's on the phone, I'm sure he'll be right out."

I set the table and couldn't help, but think that I might have a brother out there. I wondered how it was even possible. Why hadn't Vivian told us about him?

As the four of us sat down for lunch, I devoured my food. It was the first full meal I'd eaten in weeks. After we ate, I was full and tired. I laid on the couch, trying to fight through my heavy eyelids. I had my feet rested in Vincent's lap, and he softly rubbed them while they all visited.

"Do you want to go to bed?" he finally asked.

I nodded my head. "As long as no one minds. I think I need a nap."

He scooped me up and carried me to my room. He didn't even wait for the girls to answer. Swiftly, he pulled back the covers, nestled me in, and sat next to me running his fingers through my hair. I wanted to talk with him, to ask more about Lincoln, and if my dad had said anything else about him, but I fell asleep.

When I woke, it felt like it was morning. I checked the clock on my nightstand and it read 5:37pm. I'd only slept for a few hours, but God it was a nap. Vincent wasn't in the room, and his side of the bed was untouched. I went into the living room and the girls were there, but he wasn't. Bridgette was putting the last of her things in her suitcase.

"Did you have a nice nap?" she asked.

"Yeah. It felt great. Are you heading home already?"

She walked over to me and slung her arm across my shoulder. "Yup. I have to get back to school if I want to graduate on time. Thank you for everything. It was great to reconnect, even if it was under these circumstances."

"I've missed you. I'm happy you stayed with us. You know you're always welcome."

"Don't say that because I might be needing a place to live after I graduate, and your couch might have to tolerate me for a while."

"Wherever I am is your home."

Cara and I both hugged Bridgette and said 'goodbye' to her as we walked her outside to her car. We loaded her suitcase and waved as she drove off. Watching her car turn out of the neighborhood made me sad and I missed her already.

Cara and I sat on the porch, and I noticed Vincent's car was gone. I knew he'd left, but I found it strange for him to leave and not tell me.

"Did Vincent tell you where he was going?"

"He said he was going home. He left a note on the counter for you. Do you want me to grab it?"

"Yeah that would be great, thanks." I said as I pulled my knees up into my chest and wrapped my arms around them.

She came out and handed me the note. The outside of it was in his handwriting, and it simply read, 'Beautiful.'

I unfolded the paper and read his heartfelt words.

My love, I'm sorry to have left you sleeping, but I wanted to do something special for you tonight. Please meet me at my house at six o'clock. Only yours, XOXO, Vincent

"What does it say?"

"It says that I have to be at his house at six o'clock."

We hopped up and ran inside. Cara grabbed my purse and gave me a hug. I tightly hugged her back, ran to my car, and peeled out of the driveway. I called Vincent on the way, but he didn't answer. He always answered.

Crap, Crap, Crap.

I took the back roads because I knew the highway

would be busy with rush hour traffic. I made it in record time and pulled into his round driveway only eighteen minutes late.

I raced up to his house and ran through the front door. I could hear music playing and the place smelled divine. Vincent wasn't in the front room, so I ran into the kitchen. He was out back, I could see him through the glass wall; he was sitting on our favorite lounge chair. He sat leaning forward, resting his elbows on his knees, and ran his hands over his face.

I went to the door and opened it. He heard me and stood, turning around. I saw the agony on his face, and ran to him. I jumped into his arms and clung to him. He caught me like he always did, as if I weighed nothing. I looked into his eyes and watched as the pain diminished. I was so thankful to be in his arms.

"You're late," he said.

"I tried to call you."

"You did?" he asked, surprised, and reached his hand into his pocket for his phone. He came up empty handed.

"I must have left my phone inside. If you would just move in with me, we wouldn't have these problems."

I took a deep breath. I didn't know how to express what I was feeling.

"Talk to me."

"I don't know how else to say this — I'm scared. I'm worried that things with us are moving too quickly. If

I move in and we add working together, then you'll get tired of me."

He squeezed me tighter and shook his head. "Why would you think that? I've told you there is no one else in this world for me but you. That's why I want you to move in, so we *can* be together all the time. Alexa, I love you. I love you more than anything in this world, and those are not even the right words to describe how I feel for you. You take my breath away every time I see you. What I feel for you, It's more than love, you are my one and only, and I want to live together so I can share my world with you."

I was moved by his words. I crashed my lips to his, and he walked us to the lounge chair, setting me down first and then covering me with his substantial frame. Our mouths worked together, and our bodies molded like the last few pieces of a puzzle clicking in place. I reached my hands up and ran my fingers through his soft strands. He pressed his erection into me, and I wanted him inside me. I pulled away and stopped kissing him.

"I want you," I said.

"I know."

Chapter 21

Lincoln

Dinner was amazing. Vincent had prepared a three-course meal and my favorite dessert, s'mores. After we ate, we relaxed in the hot tub and gazed at the stars. This was the happiest I'd ever been. I really never knew love could be like this until now.

"Baby, that tickles," I said.

"I know."

"Then why do you keep doing it?"

Vincent kept running his hand up and down my side.

"Because I can't get enough of your body and how your skin feels under my touch."

I climbed on top of him and straddled his lap. I started tickling him back. Granted, I used more force than he did with me, but I was trying to make a point. He squirmed underneath my touch and laughed.

"Okay, okay. I get your point."

I stopped tickling him and held his face in my hands. "I love you."

He started to tickle me again, and I bolted off him and out of the hot tub. I dove into the pool and just before I hit the water I heard him say. "I love you too."

When I came up for air I looked in the hot tub, but he was gone. I searched around the pool and couldn't see him either. Then he pulled me under by my leg and wrapped his body around mine as we floated to the surface.

"You can run baby, but you won't get far. You're mine."

"And you're mine," I said.

"Damn straight."

"You know, you're really light considering you're over six feet tall. I like carrying you, I could get used to this. I also like it when you let me take control. That's one of the things I love about you. Thank you for not taking my control away."

"You can control me anytime. How about we go inside, and I'll let you do anything you want to me?" he said.

"Really?" I asked.

He reached for my hand and helped me out of the pool. We grabbed our towels and I led him inside. When I looked back at him, he was so cute. His hair needed a cut and hung on his forehead. With his free hand he clutched the towel around his waist and hunger burned in his eyes. I loved that I could do that to him.

As we walked into the bathroom, I turned the shower on.

"We have rules tonight, Vincent. You're not allowed to do anything unless I tell you. Do you understand me?"

He nodded his head.

"Good. Drop your towel."

He did, immediately, and I let mine fall as well. He stood before me, naked, and sexy as hell. I pushed him back against the wall and dropped to my knees. Aggressively, I took his cock and kissed it up and down. He tipped his head back when my lips met his velvet skin, and moaned with pleasure. I squeezed him hard, and was rewarded with a small drop of cum. I licked it off and slid his dick into my mouth, sucking as hard as I could. I went as far down on him as I was capable and then moved back up again. Since Vincent was so big, there was no easy way to fit him all the way in my mouth. I took my left hand and cupped his balls, massaging them as I continued to suck. Vincent made a low moan as he thrust into my mouth. I pulled him out and stood up.

"Did I say you could move?"

He smiled shyly at me and said, "No, you didn't, but your mouth felt amazing."

I pressed my index finger to his lips. "Did I ask you how it felt?"

He shook his head, looking so cute. It was fun playing this game with him.

"Mr. Mileski, are you going to have a hard time obeying my rules?"

"I can follow your rules. I promise."

"Good." I turned his body around and walked him into the shower, while holding onto his hips. The water felt amazing cascading over our bodies. I could tell he wanted to touch me, but he knew better.

"Sit," I commanded, pointing to the built-in tile seat. He did as I asked, and I grabbed the soap, pouring a little into my palms. I started at my neck and worked it into a lather, running my hands down my body. I pressed hard over my nipples while caressing them slowly. His eyes burned with avidity when I touched myself like this. I turned around, facing away from him, and continued to stroke each leg, one at a time, over and over. I bent slowly, pushing my ass in his face. I stood up and slipped falling back onto his lap. He caught me, and then removed his hands. I reached for them placing them back on my hips.

"They can stay," I said in a hushed voice.

Touching between us, I took my hand and caressed it over my sex and down to his dick. I fondled both of us, moving up on him and over my clit. I lifted my legs and rested my feet on either side of his knees, spreading my legs open far and wide. I took his hand and moved it over my pussy, working it in just the right tension.

"Fuck, baby. That's so hot," he said.

When I stopped moving his hand, he didn't falter.

He continued to work my pussy. I squeezed my breasts with both of my hands. As I did so, my body went into an intense rage from us working together. I twisted my solid nipples in between my fingers, and Vincent lifted me guiding his cock inside of me. I moved my body up and down, and he worked my clit with his deft fingers. He was rubbing it to the point of almost making me come undone. I loved him being inside of me, there was nothing I enjoyed more than the euphoric feeling I had when we made love. I balanced myself with my hands on his knees and slowed my movements. He stopped the assault on my clit and held my hips tightly, guiding my body as I devoured him. I pushed myself back against him, as the pleasure inside of me jumped like a wild fire moving from tree to tree.

I was close, but I wanted more and moved as fast and as hard as I could, indulging in my greatest addiction. I wanted to come hard, and give him the same feeling.

"Kiss me," I commanded.

Instantly his lips were on my neck kissing and sucking,

"Touch me," I said.

He knew just what I wanted and took his hand off of my hip and rubbed my clit again. The feeling of his hands on my body and sucking on my neck sent me over. I came long and hard, slamming down onto him. He groaned loudly as he poured himself inside of me. With each thrust, his body spasmed under my control.

Once I slowed my movements and rested back against him, he wrapped me in his arms and delicately kissed my neck.

"I love you," he whispered.

"I love you too. Thank you for that."

"Baby, you can control me anytime. You're so fucking hot when you do it."

"Really? Well you give me the confidence to do it."

"You don't need confidence from me. You're perfect, Lex."

"Will you please make your phone stop ringing?" I moaned into my pillow.

Vince leaned over me to grab it off of the nightstand. "There. It's on silent. Are you happy, crabby ass?"

I pulled the covers over my head.

"I'm not going to have you living here acting like this every morning. You're like an angry grizzly bear coming out of hibernation."

"Fine! Then I won't move in," I snapped.

"Oh, you're moving in, and there are no ifs, ands, or buts about it."

I contemplated on when I *was* going to move in. I hoped that Cara would be cool with it. Wait, who was I kidding, she would be elated.

"I know I am, but my morning attitude isn't going to change. I've been this way my entire life. Get used to it."

He laughed and hopped on top of me, pinning me against the mattress. I loved the way he looked at me. He looked into me, not at me. He saw what was on the inside.

His phone rang again, vibrating on the nightstand, and I threw my arm over my face. He kissed my nose and answered it.

I tried to make out who he was talking to and what they were saying, but Vincent didn't speak much. I ran my hands up and down his body, feeling every curve and contour. He said 'okay' and 'yes' a few times and then hung up. His eyes never left mine the entire time he spoke.

"That was the investigator I hired. He found Lincoln. He lives about an hour outside of Denver."

"Wow, are you serious? That was fast. What else did he say?"

"He's going to email me the file in a little bit."

I took my eyes off of Vincent's and looked up at the skylights; the sky was grey, and it looked like it would rain. He ran his fingers through my hair, and I could sense he was still staring at me.

"You're staring," I said.

He laughed and nuzzled my neck, still running his fingers through my hair. "Can you blame me? I'm worried about you; tell me what you're thinking."

"I don't know. Part of me is excited and the other part is scared. I really don't know what to do."

"I think that's natural. Baby, you just had a bomb dropped on you. You might have a brother. That's not easy news for anyone to handle. What do you say we look at the e-mail and then decide how to proceed? You may not even be related, don't get ahead of yourself, okay?"

Knowing that he was going through this with me made things easier. In my entire life, I never felt like I had anyone to depend on. It was only myself. Decisions were always made on my own, regardless of how hard they were. With Vincent, it was easy to let that all go and allow him to guide me, to guide us.

"Okay, let's check the email, but can we do it at breakfast?"

"Sure, where do you want to go?"

"I don't care, you choose, as long as they have eggs and coffee, I'm sold."

"You're so easy to please."

"You act like that news. I'm simple."

He lifted his head, and looked so relaxed. I loved to see him like that. He leaned his head back down and kissed my neck, slowly sucking on the tender skin. Gently he moved his mouth along my throat and down my sternum. He leaned on his side and pulled the sheet down, exposing my breasts. His mouth wrapped around one of my swollen peaks while his hand traveled down my body until he reached my sex. He touched in between my wet folds and indulged in the smoothness with two of his fingers. Slowly he slid them inside of me, moving in and out. Each time he pressed his fingers deep inside of me his palm grazed my clit.

"God, that feels so good," I murmured.

"Mmm, You like my fingers, baby?"

I bit my bottom lip and nodded my head.

"Don't be quiet. Not now that we're alone. I wanna hear you. Let go, especially when you come."

I whimpered and then squeezed my eyes shut as pleasure coursed through me. I spread my legs wide and pushed against Vincent's hand. His mouth was back to loving my body. He drenched me with kisses as if he couldn't control himself. Slowly he sucked on my nipple, tugging on it hard, and I cried with pleasure.

"Let me hear you, baby. You sound so fucking sexy."

I was lost in that moment, about to come. I was being greedy and enjoying the pleasure holding onto my orgasm as long as I could. I imagined Vincent fucking me with his big cock, and when he sucked on my hard nipple again, I exploded, throwing my head back into the pillow and screaming his name. His two fingers worked inside of me, leaving me senseless. He held my nipple in his mouth and then flicked it back and forth. I whimpered again and finally had to pull away from the pleasure. I stared at him with heavy lids. I was speechless.

"Are you ready for breakfast?" he asked.

"Of course, but I wanna make you come."

"And you will, later. This was for you, baby." He kissed my sex and jumped off of me, naked and hot as hell.

It wasn't long before we were dressed and out of the house. It was still cloudy, but so far, no rain. We pulled up to a huge restaurant that sat nestled on a hill. There were expansive windows and a large staircase leading up to the entrance from where we parked. I grabbed Vincent's hand as we headed up the stairs.

As we entered, we were greeted immediately, and the hostess sat us by one of the large windows, in the corner. The tables all had white linen table cloths and were spread far apart.

The waitress approached our table and said, "Welcome to Simms, my name is Meredith. What can I get the two of you to drink this morning?"

"I'll take a coffee," I said.

"The same for me as well."

"Great, I'll go grab those while you two look over the menu." She left us with the most endearing smile.

We scanned the menus, and I quickly decided, closing mine and staring outside to enjoy the view.

"What are you going to get, babe?" he asked.

"Biscuits and gravy. What about you?"

"Really?" he questioned laughing at me. "You said you wanted to go somewhere that served eggs. Here we are, they're world renowned for the best eggs benedict and you decide on biscuits and gravy."

I nodded my head and leaned over to him, reaching under the table to stroke his thigh. It's a good thing Vincent always sat next to me, rather than across from me as my hand quickly traveled to his awaiting cock. I rubbed slowly and watched his expression change. He twitched under my hand and hardened. I knew he was putty after that moment.

Abruptly I stopped and sat back in my chair. "You were saying?"

"Nothing. I wasn't saying a thing. You can eat whatever you want as long as you do it quickly, so I can get you home."

"Why do we need to go home? This is a nice place," I said, raising my eyebrows at him.

I was dead serious, and he knew it. With him, I was no longer scared. I didn't second-guess my decisions or choices. I followed my heart and did what I felt was right. In that moment, I wanted him, and I didn't want to have to wait.

"Here are your coffees. Have you decided on what you're going to order?" Meredith asked, setting down our overly large cups of deliciousness.

I nodded my head while adding the cream and sugar to our coffees.

"She's going to have the biscuits and gravy, and I'll take the French toast."

"I'll get that in right away," she replied.

I loved how much of a team we'd become: I made his coffee, and he ordered for me. Plain and simple, we worked well together.

"Are you ready to look at this email, beautiful?"

I grabbed his iPad and turned the cover over. Vincent scooted his chair a little closer and draped his arm over the back of mine as he opened the email icon.

Reading through the email, I was given a plethora of information. His name was Lincoln Alex Sanders. He was born April 12, 1992 and was adopted, never knowing his birth parents. It also stated he was in and out of foster care until he was twelve-years-old and was adopted by Mark and Shelly Sanders of Buena Vista, Colorado.

Vincent clicked on another attachment, and it opened up his photo. He had the same green eyes as I did but light, wavy hair. It was a family photo of him and his adoptive family. They were hiking and had two brown labs with them.

"He has your eyes, Lex."

"I know. It's crazy. I don't think we have the same father though. My dad has dark hair and so did Vivian."

"Yeah, you're probably right. What do you wanna do?"

"I don't know. We can't just show up at his front door. I guess I need to decide if I'm going to call him, and if so, what should I say to him? 'Hi, I'm your long lost sister and our mom just died?'"

I rubbed my neck in frustration, and Vincent pulled me into his chest. I nuzzled him and enjoyed the comfort. I didn't want to think about this anymore today. I only wanted to enjoy the day with my man.

"I have the biscuits and gravy for you, my dear and the French toast for you, sir." Meredith said, setting our plates down. "How does everything look?"

"It's perfect," I said, grabbing my fork and digging in. Vincent laughed and Meredith walked off. We ate and kept a little small talk going in between bites. We both enjoyed the beautiful city view as we ate and poked at each other's food.

Neither of us brought Lincoln back up, and I was fine with pushing that to the back of my head for another day.

"What else do you want to do today?" he asked.

I looked deep in thought, and he caught right on to my game.

"You know, I hear they have nice restroom's here. Wanna check 'em out?" I said.

Quickly he yanked his wallet out, opened it, and threw a hundred dollar bill on the table. There was no way our meal cost that much, even at this place. With the fire brewing in his eyes, I knew he couldn't wait another minute.

We both rose out of our chairs, and I snatched the iPad because he would've left it. Taking my free hand, he practically dragged me into the restroom. The rooms were private, and he locked the door as he pressed me up against it. His right hand rested on my hip while his other hand braced his weight on the wall.

"Are you sure you want to do this here?" he asked.

I reached for the button on his jeans and popped it open. "Yes," I said, as I slid the zipper down and rubbed his erection as it strained through his underwear.

He did the same to my jeans but pulled them all the way down. I stepped out of them, and stood there, pressed against the door, naked from the waist down. He dropped to his knees and lifted my left leg, draping it over his shoulder.

He left a trail of kisses along the inside of my thigh and all around my sex. Finally he ended, licking down the center of my wet slit. Slowly he began flicking my clit with his tongue. I pressed my body against the door and tightened my leg over his body. As he sucked and worked his expert lips on me, I twisted my fingers into his hair.

"Oh God. That feels good."

"Mmm. You like that?" he asked, as he stopped to look up at me. I nodded my head, and he sank two fingers inside of me. I clenched my pussy tightly around them, and watched his face as he pleasured me. Seeing him concentrate so hard made me want to come. He bit his bottom lip and tilted his head to the side. He looked so hot on his knees, moving his fingers in and out of me.

"Fuck, baby," he said slowly pulling his fingers all the way out of me. "That's a tight little cunt you have."

He said and sucked on his wet fingers.

I was panting watching him lick his own fingers. I was so close to coming, and when he sank his adept fingers back inside of me and sucked on my clit, it pushed me over the edge. I came hard, convulsing around him. I gripped his hair and hoped my knees wouldn't buckle. Vincent slowed his movements and detached his mouth, but he started rubbing large circles around my wet core.

I squirmed as the pleasure became too much. He stood and walked me over to the sink.

"Bend over and hold on baby. Whatever you do, don't let go."

I did as he asked and watched what he was doing in the reflection of the mirror. I could tell he was fumbling with his pants and next I was rewarded with the head of his cock. He nestled it against my sex, slowly rubbing himself in between my wet slit, while his free hand gripped my hip.

"God, I love teasing you," he said.

I bit my lip to keep quiet, but I wanted to moan as he rubbed himself on me.

"Don't let go of the sink. Okay, baby?"

I nodded my head as he penetrated me. Once he filled me, he circled his hips pushing and expanding, touching every inch inside of me. It was so much to handle and keeping quiet had become almost unbearable. I dropped my head and closed my eyes tightly as he began moving, slowly thrusting himself inside of me. He kept his hands tightly clenched around my hips pulling and pushing my body with his.

"Look at me, baby," he demanded.

Right away my head snapped up. His hair was a mess and the small amount of facial hair I saw in his reflection was hot as hell. His brows were creased as he loved my body with his. "Oh fuck, Lex," he grunted, picking up speed 'til he was pounding me. I whined as he showed me no mercy; he was being rough and I loved it. I loved when he fucked me like that. I think I might have loved it even more seeing how much he enjoyed himself. A thin sheen of sweat covered his forehead as he worked so hard to pleasure both of us. I clung to the sink with everything I had. Realizing then why he'd told me to not let go. The pressure from Vincent's weight, gripping, and slamming into me would have been impossible for me to take had the sink not been there.

My breathing was erratic, and I couldn't help but tip my head back. As I did so, I made sure I kept my eyes locked with his. Watching me in the mirror, he grunted in a low tone and came inside of me. Seeing him come so violently sent me over. I relished with him and bit my lip so hard I thought it might bleed. I didn't dare close my eyes, which made my orgasm that much stronger. As my body came violently, I writhed back and forth. Settling down took a few moments and we both breathed heavily, still gazing at each other.

With his cock still tucked inside of me, I pushed

myself up and stood in front of him. He wrapped his arms around my body and lifted my wrist to his lips kissing it tenderly.

"I love you, Alexa."

"I love you too, Vincent."

Chapter 22

Surprise

"Do you have to go into the office today? You promised me we would have the whole week together," I whined.

"I'm sorry, babe, but I have to go in for the staff meeting. We have a lot coming up next week and one of us needs to be there to stay up to speed on things. Then I just have a few things to take care of, and I'll be home by this afternoon. I promise."

"Well if you do have to go, don't you have anything else you can wear?"

He looked down at himself, dressed yet again in another delicious three-piece suit. This one was navy with pinstripes, which he'd paired with a checkered shirt and that damn purple tie.

"Babe, I always wear suits to work."

"Well, I don't like it when I'm not there. Plus that suit's different. What's it even made out of?"

"It's polyester and it cost me over a grand, so I'm wearing it."

"Isn't Friday supposed to be casual day?"

"At some offices, yes. But not ours, love. What do you have planned today?"

"I don't know, maybe lay around naked and touch myself."

He came over to the bed and laid his full body on top of mine. I was face down and this pushed me into the mattress. "You better put some clothes on this sexy little body of mine, and *do not* touch yourself unless I'm here. That's my job."

"Fine. Maybe I'll go joy riding in the Bugatti." I rested my cheek on my forearm looking up at as much of his profile as I could.

"That sounds fun. Just stay out of trouble, okay?

"I'll try. I miss you already."

"I know. So do I," he said and kissed me quickly, hopping off of me in his sexy suit. When he left the room, I got up and slid on his discarded shirt from the night before. I hated being apart from him and was grateful we worked together. I kissed him good-bye and took my time adoring his lips. Then I watched him drive off until I couldn't see him any more.

I closed the front door and grabbed my cell phone, heading out back to the pool. As I sat on the ledge and dipped my feet in the warm water, I thought about what I was really going to do today. Cara was off, so I'm sure she would want to hang out. Then it hit me; I knew exactly what I had to do. I needed to do this for Vincent. After everything he'd given me it was my turn to return the favor.

Today I was going to move my stuff into his house. Well, as much of it as Cara and I could handle. I headed back inside and got dressed, pulling on a pair of leggings and a hot pink tank top. I struggled with my hair and got it into a messy bun on the top of my head. Then I grabbed the keys to the Range Rover and called Cara, as I pulled out of the driveway.

"Good Morning, doll. Time to wakey-wakey," I joked.

"Holy hell, what has you in such a good mood this morning? Did prince charming bang you already?"

"Suck it, snot! I need your help today."

"What is it? Don't you think I have other plans today?"

"No! I know you don't have other plans. Vince just left for work, and I want to surprise him. I'm gonna move as much of my stuff into his place as I can today."

"Hallelujah! You're finally making the right decision. Hell yeah, I'll help as long as I can keep living here rent free."

"Of course you can. We're never getting rid of that place. I'm on my way now. Can you start throwing some of my clothes into our luggage?"

"Sure thing. See you soon."

I hung up and called C.J., I also needed his help, but he didn't answer. They must be in their staff meeting. Screw it. I wanted to handle this now so I could focus on packing and moving.

I called him again. This time he answered. "Hey, is everything okay?"

"Yeah, I'm fine. Please don't tell Vince it's me calling, okay?"

"Okay."

"I need your help."

"Can you hold on a moment?"

Crap. Maybe I should've waited or sent him a text.

"Sorry I had to step out of the staff meeting. So, I see you're now calling Kane, 'Vince?'" he teased me.

I laughed a little. "Come on, C.J., don't give me a hard time. You know we're dating. I need your help today, please."

"Fine."

"I need you to keep Vince at work as long as you can and then text me when he leaves."

"That's it? You called me twice and interrupted our meeting to have me keep him at work? What are you up to?"

"It's a secret. I have a lot to do today. Are you going to help me, or not?"

"Yes, of course I'll help you. And just so you know, Alexa, I'm really happy for you two."

"Thanks C.J. I appreciate that and I really owe you for this, I gotta run."

"No problem. I'll text you later."

I hung up, just as I pulled up to the condo and backed the Range Rover into the driveway. When I got inside, my room already looked like a tornado had torn through it. Cara had almost emptied my entire closet into our suitcases.

"You're amazing," I said, giving her a hug as she walked out of my closet with an armful of clothes.

"You're really going to owe me for this. You do realize this is my one day off before I start three swing shifts?"

"You know I'll pay you back. Thank you, thank you, thank you." I said, hugging her.

I went into the bathroom and started to pack my toiletries. Cara and I worked for hours, and by the time I checked the clock after we'd crammed the last of the bags into the Rover and her Audi, it was already noon. Vincent would be calling soon to tell me he wouldn't be able to make it home until later. I wanted to get on the road to start unpacking. We locked up the condo and both hit the highway.

It didn't take long until we pulled up to Vincent's house — our house. I backed the SUV into the garage, and Cara pulled into the circular drive way.

"Holy shit, Lex! This is his house?"

I stood next to Cara and admired the beautiful

home. "Yup, this is it. Come on, I'll show you around before we unload the cars."

Cara was just as amazed with the house as I was the first time I saw it. I never in a million years imagined I would be calling this my home.

After a quick tour, we got to work unloading the cars – it was exhausting. We brought everything into the bedroom, as that was where most of my stuff would be going.

Thankfully the closet was made for two people, so there was plenty of room for my stuff. As Cara unpacked the suitcases, she handed me my clothes. I went through them and hung them where I wanted each item to go. After the addition of all of my clothes, shoes, and purses, it looked like a department store had vomited in his closet.

We decided to take a break and headed into the kitchen for some lunch. That's were we made a final game plan and decided how I would reveal everything to him.

"You know, you could always send him a text and say, 'just thought I'd tell ya I moved in today. Make sure you keep the seat down.'"

I laughed and almost spit my sandwich out. "Cara that's the dumbest thing you've ever said."

"Whatever. It was funny. Tell me what better ideas you have?"

"I don't know, maybe I should've asked him first?"

"Are you kidding me? He's going to be ecstatic; I can only imagine his expression when you tell him. I know what you can do. Instead of telling him, you can show him."

"What do you mean?" I asked.

"When he gets home, you can take him upstairs. As soon as he sees the bedroom, he'll know something's up. Once he sees the closet he'll figure it out for sure."

"Thank God, for once you have a terrific idea."

"Shut up you snot, I have a lot of great ideas. Now let's finish before prince charming comes home."

"Will you stop calling him that?"

"Why, he is your prince charming, right?"

She was right, but rather than argue I rolled my eyes at her and walked back upstairs. I didn't realize how many items I'd truly brought with me.

My phone buzzed, and I checked the text from C.J.

Vince, as you call him, is on his way. I kept him as long as I could, but he was anxious to get out of here. I wonder why?

I texted back:

Thanks so much. I owe you!

"That was C.J., Vince is on his way." We scrambled to collect the suitcases and get them loaded into Cara's car. My phone rang, and sure enough, it was Vince.

"Hey babe, I'm on my way home. I'm sorry I had to work all day."

"It's okay. I understand."

"How was your day?"

"It was good. I just hung out with Cara."

"Good. What did you guys do?"

"Nothing much. I'll tell you about it later."

"Okay, I'll see you soon. I love you."

"I love you, too."

I hung up and turned to Cara. Her jaw was practically on the floor.

"You might wanna pick up your jaw," I said.

"I'm sorry. Did you just say 'I love you, too?'"

"Yeah, so?"

"Why didn't you tell me you guys had said the L word? That's a huge deal."

"It just happened. I was going to tell you, I promise, but I got so preoccupied that it slipped my mind. Do you really think I would've moved in here had I not been in love with him?"

"Well, I'm really happy for you Lex. He's an amazing guy."

I threw my arm around her as we walked outside and crammed the last suitcase into her car, Vincent pulled up just as she slammed the trunk.

"I can't thank you enough for helping me today."

She hugged me tightly. "It was my pleasure. I'm so happy for you, Lex."

Vincent parked his car in the driveway, not bothering to open the garage. He got out and headed straight towards me, all confident, sexy, and mine.

"Hi, prince charming. You're looking fancy in that suit today," Cara teased him.

"Hello to you as well. What is it with everyone and this suit?" he asked.

She laughed. "Well, I better get going. Lex, thanks for a fun day. I'll talk to you later."

"What did you guys do today?" he asked.

Cara and I exchanged a nervous glance. "Nothing much. Boring girl stuff," I said.

Cara winked at me and walked to her car. We waved to her as she sped off. I turned and looked at Vincent; he was staring at me with pure love. I couldn't believe I was standing with him in front of *our* home.

I didn't feel nervous about showing him I'd moved in. I felt happy and excited.

"You look stunning today," he said.

I looked down at myself in a dirty tank top, leggings, and tennis shoes. That's why I loved him. It was the little things, just like that, which meant the world to me. He saw my beauty from the inside, and wasn't just saying the words.

I knew he truly believed I looked stunning.

"Thanks, baby. You don't look too bad yourself."

He laughed and wrapped his arms around me, kissing my neck. "Why are you all sweaty? What were you girls doing?"

"Nothing. Come on, let's get out of the front yard before I rip that suit off of you right here."

I grabbed his hand and walked up to the front door. I led him up the stairs to *our* bedroom. When we stepped inside, he froze. He looked at my favorite blanket laid across the end of the bed, then at my nightstand where I added my iPad charger, my favorite lotion, and a photo of us. He turned to me with elation in his eyes.

I wanted to show him the closet, so he would know for sure. "I think it's time we get you out of that suit don't you?" I asked.

He nodded his head, and when I walked into the closet, he followed me in. What was once a bare space with empty shelves and nothing but bars was now packed full. This was my time to re-pay him for all of the kindness and love he'd always shown me. I walked over to him and wrapped my arms around his waist, looking up into his hazel eyes. He went to speak, and I pressed my finger against his lips.

When he kissed my finger, I said, "Baby, I want to give you what you've given me. You've shown me how to love, and have loved me in a way I never knew was possible. You make me feel confident and beautiful every minute of every day. You are my love and fulfill every little piece of me. I wanted to surprise you. I couldn't think of a better way to repay you than by moving in. Vincent, I love you and have since the moment I laid eyes on you. I'm giving you my heart, and I trust that you'll forever protect it."

A small tear escaped the inside corner of my eye. Vincent leaned in and kissed it away before it reached my lips.

"Alexa, you have no idea how happy you've made me. I never thought in a million years I would have found someone as special as you. And here I am, looking into your amazing green eyes, with the sweet taste of your joyous tear on my lips. And now we're living together, where I get to love you every minute of every day. You're the most amazing woman in this world, and you're all mine. I love you so much, beautiful."

Tears glossed over his eyes, and I wrapped my arms tightly around his neck, pulling him to me. Tenderly, I kissed each of his eyes, tasting his salty tears. I moved my mouth to his and he opened his mouth caressing his tongue with mine while our hands gripped each other's bodies.

He lifted the hem of my tank top and pulled it over my head. I undid my bra and let it fall to the floor as we continued to kiss. Pushing his coat off of his shoulders, I quickly unbuttoned his vest and then unknotted his tie. His hand slid into my pants while I tried to undress him and it caused me to stop. The control he had over my body was like nothing else. His touch incapacitated me. I was frozen, bracing myself on the large built-in dresser behind me.

His skilled hand spread me open, and he circled my tender clit. I let my head fall back and moaned, enjoying the tingles that sparked throughout my body. He leaned into me, kissing my neck and began sucking as his fingers entered my core.

Once he began pleasuring me, I tried to keep undressing him, but he began sucking on my breasts. All I could do in that moment was hold onto the dresser behind me and focus on standing.

"I love how you tighten your pussy around my fingers like that."

I whimpered and accepted his tongue as he plunged it into my mouth. His hand moved faster and pushed my body into a frenzy. We kissed and sucked on each other's tongues.

Suddenly, he slowed his movements, but didn't stop kissing me. His fingers were still inside of me as he stopped. He was almost on top of me. We examined one another's eyes. With his thumb resting on my clit he asked, "Do you really live here now, or am I dreaming?"

"Look around you at all my bags and shoes, I definitely live here now."

"Good, because we're not leaving here all weekend. I plan to stay buried deep inside of you christening every room of our home."

"Closet first?" I asked.

"That it is."

He removed my leggings and his pants. When he

started to unbutton his shirt, I couldn't stop myself. I sauntered over to him, naked, and tore it open. The buttons flew across the room, and he looked at me with hunger in his eyes. I walked him backwards to the large ottoman in the corner. Pushing him into it, he grabbed me and I flew on top of him.

I kneeled next to him and grabbed his cock. Leaning down, I descended my mouth around his throbbing shaft, swirling my tongue over the tip as I sucked. He grabbed my body, moving me so I was straddling his face. We were in the perfect sixty-nine position. He spread my ass and latched onto my clit. As soon as his mouth touched me, I went into overdrive. Sucking hard and jerking him even harder. Our bodies were hot, and his hands were digging into my ass.

I was close to coming, but wanted him inside of me. I stopped sucking and looked back at him. He stopped as well, and I moved to straddle him.

"Turn around," he commanded.

I did so and he lifted me by my hips with my back to his front. I reached between us and placed his warm dick inside of me. As I sat there, his hands moved to my nipples and his mouth feverishly attacked my back with kisses. I braced my hands on his knees and started to move. The feeling was exquisite. I leaned forward and popped my ass up and down, making smooth movements to rub my G-spot.

"Oh God, Lex. Your ass is so hot," he said and

slapped it hard. I almost came from that one touch. I loved it when he spanked me, and he knew it. He helped me move my body. We worked together, pushing one another closer and closer to coming.

He spanked me again, and I cried out loud letting go. I came hard from his big cock and the firm slap he landed on my ass, had it still tingling. A long low moan came from Vincent as he came inside me.

Once we stopped moving, he stood us up and scooped me in his arms. This was the fastest he'd ever moved after sex. He carried me out of the closet and took us into the kitchen, sitting me on the cool granite counter top.

"Lie back," he ordered.

I did as he asked and watched him as he turned and opened the fridge. He had a bottle of chocolate syrup in his hand, and I cocked an eyebrow at him. "What are you planning on doing with that?"

"I worked all day and I'm hungry, plus you just fucked the shit out of me, so I'm famished. I'm going to eat my two favorite things for dinner: you and chocolate."

I shivered thinking of him licking chocolate off of my body. He popped open the top and drizzled the syrup from my collarbone to my left breast, around my nipple then right down and around my sex.

I looked at him as he licked his lips. The effect this man had on my body was like nothing else. I was so turned on I couldn't describe it. I surrendered my mind, body, and soul over to him.

"Lean back and close your eyes, beautiful."

I leaned all the way back, and spread my arms above my head. As I closed my eyes, it felt like I was dreaming. Then the reality of the situation hit me, as Vincent's mouth touched me and started licking the syrup off. I finally had what I'd been searching for my entire life. Although I lived behind a wall, and had been scared to ever love anyone. Vincent pulled me out of my shell, he showed me how to love, and loved me for me. I reached down and gripped his hair, watching him lick my body. He looked at me with those hazel eyes, and that panty-dropping smile. He licked my sex, and my head fell back. I held him closely to me, and couldn't wait for him to fuck me in every room of our home.

Epilogue

Vincent

I run my hands through the soft fur of my new pup, Blair. He's our new husky. I've always wanted one, and Alexa surprised me on Christmas morning with this ridiculously cute little guy. He's now eight months old, and no longer little. I, of course, went a little more extreme and bought her a Porsche Carrera Twin Turbo. She needed her own sports car, and loves the Carrera, so I got her one.

It's now March and the first seventy-degree day we've had all year. Alexa demanded we have an impromptu BBQ to enjoy the weather. I sit back, watching her sip her wine while she talks with Lincoln and Bridgette. She made the decision to call Lincoln shortly after she moved in, and their relationship has since blossomed. Telling Bridgette wasn't easy. Lex made herself sick for a week over it. When she finally got up enough courage to tell Bridgette, she was more than understanding and even excited to have a brother.

Watching the three of them together, it's like they have all grown up with one another. Lincoln is a genuine, down to earth guy, and I really like him. He has been through so much in his life and has prevailed. I love how caring he is, not to mention brutally honest.

A light gust of wind comes through the back yard, blowing Alexa's hair into her face. She's so delicate as she takes her fingers and sweeps it behind her ears. The breeze moves her short summer dress in just the right way so I can see the bottom of her ass cheek. I am fixated on her nipples as they strain against the thin material of her dress. My cock twitches as I imagine fucking her while she screams my name. Blair walks by her, and his tail moves her dress, this time I get a glimpse of her thigh with that tattoo she got for me. It's a simple V with an intricate heart and some added detail. That tattoo means the world to me. I'm going to repay the favor really soon.

Blair barks and runs towards the sliding door. I turn behind me and see my dad and Abel as they come out back. I get up to greet them, and the others join me. Alexa is by my side, and I can't help myself from pulling her against me and pressing her sweet lips to mine. She tastes like she always does, minty with a twist of coconut from that delicious lip-gloss she always wears. I should invest in stock in that company with how much I like it.

"Love you," she whispers in my ear.

"I love you more, babe."

Abel and I head inside to get the food to put on the grill.

"How are you holding up, bro?" he asks and pats my back.

"How do you think I'm holding up? I'm a nervous fucking wreck. What if she says 'no'?"

"Dude, there is no way she's going to say 'no.' You two are meant for each other, stop letting your head fuck with you. This is Alexa, okay?"

I know I shouldn't be nervous, but I plan on asking her to marry me tonight after everyone leaves and we're alone. I've waited as long as I can. She's my soul mate, fate brought us together and we promised each other forever. I guess I'm still a bit damaged from what Angela did to me, and that's what's causing me to doubt myself.

"Dude, it's going to fine," Abel says.

"I hope so. Help me take this food out to the grill."

When we walk outside, Alexa's laugh catches my attention. She glances at me out of the corner of her eye, and I can't help the warm smile that spreads across my face. When she sees me smile at her, she shyly looks away and continues to talk with her sister and brother. I love that look, the one she gives me when she acts shy. She's the sexiest woman I've ever seen, and she pushes my limits, not only sexually, but emotionally. Still to this day, I know I'll never get enough of her.

I throw an assortment of meats onto the grill and all I can think about is getting down on one knee in a few hours. What am I going to say? Is it too soon? Will she like the ring?

Just then, her tiny arms wrap around my waist, and she rests her face against my back. All of my uneasiness washes away the minute I feel her touch. She's my life, and without her, there is no me.

"Mmm, it smells good. I'm starving," she says.

"Good, baby. It's about done if you wanna get everyone seated and bring the sides out."

"Okay. I love you," she says and kisses my back. I don't think I'll ever hear her say those words enough. "Will you guys help me bring out the sides?" she asks my Dad and Abel.

They follow her inside, and shortly after Cara comes out the sliding door; she heads right towards me.

"Hey. I got everything set up for you. There's like a million white rose petals and even more candles. Is there anything else you need?"

"Nope, that's all. Cara, you have no idea how much your help means to me. Thank you so much."

"Are you kidding me? You are about to make my best friend the happiest woman in the world. It's the least I can do."

"Don't worry, I'll repay you. I promise. Whatever you want."

She laughs and says, "Oh my God. Really? Like a new car?"

"If she says 'yes,'" I whisper, "Then absolutely. I'll

buy you a new car."

Alexa, Abel, and my Dad come back with arms full of food.

"Hey when did you get here?" Alexa asks Cara.

"I just got here. I snuck around back. I rang the doorbell but no one answered."

"You could've just come in, Cara."

"It's fine, really. Let me help you set this down so we can eat. I'm starving."

We all sit down and take our time eating and visiting. I keep my hand on Lex's thigh. Thankfully no one can see my erection under the table.

I notice Abel being particularly quiet. I watch him as he sits back, sipping on his beer, observing Lincoln and Cara, who are laughing. I've never seen my brother show much interest in one girl. Until Cara. He is usually a one-time guy and that's it, but something about her has peaked his interest. I hate seeing him like this, and Cara is one of my friends so I need to be careful about how I proceed with giving him advice.

"Are you guys done?" Cara asks us.

Lex and I nod our heads and Cara starts collecting our plates with hers and takes them inside. Abel gets up as well and follows her inside. *Shit.* I told him to leave her alone, but he's a persistent little prick.

"Where is your brother?" my dad asks me.

I point inside where I see him talking to Cara in the kitchen. He's inches from her face, leaning against the counter with his hands on her hips.

"Well, we better get going son," he says, giving me a hug and whispering in my ear, "Good luck tonight, son. I really love Alexa. Your mother would be proud of you."

I hug him back and then release him so he can hug Alexa. She has come to love him like a father, and I am so grateful that we have him in our lives.

As they separate, he kisses her cheek and then walks inside, yelling at Abel, causing him to jerk away from Cara. The two of them walk off together, and I notice Cara's face is bright red as she runs her hands through her hair and shakes her head.

I grab Lex's hand and lead her inside. I'm anxious to get her upstairs.

"Everything okay with you and Abel?" I ask Cara as we walk inside.

She laughs. "I'm not even getting into that tonight. I'm beat. Do you guys mind if I run so I get home and to bed?"

"Of course. Are you sure you're okay?" Alexa asks.

"Yeah, I'm fine. Just tired." Cara pulls us both into a hug. "I love you both and am so happy that you found each other."

Alexa scrunches her eyebrows. "Boy, you must be tired. It's not like you to get all sappy. Time for you to get home and rest."

"I mean it," she says.

"We know you do. Thanks for helping clean up.

We'll see you later."

After she leaves, Alexa heads back into the kitchen and starts rinsing the dishes. I walk up behind her and turn the water off. Taking the dish out of her hand and turning her towards me, she looks at me confused, but I don't give her time to speak. I lift her in my arms and walk upstairs to our bedroom.

As we enter our room, I hear her breathing hitch. The room is completely covered in white rose petals. You can barely see the floor or the bed underneath them all. Cara was right; there are a ton of candles as well.

"What's all this for?" she asks.

I look deep into her green eyes, feeling her sweet breath on my skin. Taking a deep breath, I set her down on her feet.

"This is for you, my love."

I walk over to my nightstand and open the drawer, grabbing the blue Tiffany box. When I turn to her, she stands frozen and beautiful right where I set her down. Walking back to her, she looks at me with so much love and adoration. I know I'm the luckiest bastard in the world. I stand in front of her and kiss her nose.

With that kiss, I get down on one knee and profess my love.

Turn the page for an excerpt of *Determinism*, the story of Cara and Able, available now!

Prologue

- ABEL -

As I pull my Harley in the underground parking garage of my building, I cut the engine just as my cell phone rings. Still straddling my bike, I pull it out of my back pocket to see it's my brother calling.

I hit the answer button. "What's up, bro?"

"Hey, not much. How are you?"

"Dude, I'm fucking beat. We trained all week in a building that was hot as hell, and I carried more hose on my back than I knew was possible."

"Well, you are the new fire chief, so you gotta show those guys how to get shit done."

I laugh, "I guess. Anyways, what's up?"

"I'm sorry, I know this is last minute, but I told Lex that I invited you to the movies with us tonight, so she invited her friend, Cara. I don't want to look like an ass because I forgot to call you earlier. So, can you meet us there in an hour?"

Fuck, I hate the movies. I'm not a fan of crowds and this is the last thing I want to do tonight. But for my brother, I'll do anything. "Is Cara hot?"

"Yeah."

"Fine, text me where to meet you guys and I'll be there. She better be fucking smoking for me to see a movie at the theater."

"Don't worry, she is," he says and hangs up.

I get off my bike and walk to the elevator. I can't wait to get into the hot shower. My body is exhausted; every one of my muscles feels tense from work. I wish I could just chill tonight. But who knows? Maybe it won't be a waste, and I'll end up banging this chick. It's been weeks since I've gotten laid and I'm tired of the same bar flies that always flock to me because of my tattoos.

The elevator finally arrives and I press the button for the eighteenth floor. Living in the heart of downtown affords me a killer view. I just moved into this place and it's insane. Entering my spacious loft, the sun is bright and shining in all of the windows. Puss, my needy ass cat, runs up to me and winds in and out of my legs. She's a vocal, little bitch, but the only one I want.

I set my helmet on the counter, along with my keys, and grab a beer from the fridge. Cracking it open, I walk to the expansive wall of windows that is the back of my loft. I look out onto the city and take a pull of my beer.

Fuck, I'm tired.

Heading into the bathroom, I turn the shower on

and strip out of my clothes. As much as I love being a firefighter, the stench from the smoke is brutal. I take my time washing to ensure I'm clean. It's crazy how the faintest scent will drive you nuts. But who am I to complain? I'm doing my dream job and loving it. I've always had a passion for helping others. Plus the pay is awesome — fighting wildfires for twenty hours straight for a few months in the summer pays my bills for a year.

Stepping out of the shower, I wrap a towel around my waist and grab my toothbrush. My phone chimes while I brush my teeth. I walk back into the kitchen and grab it. It's Vincent, and of course we are meeting at a theater way across town. I dress quickly in jeans and a t-shirt, and grab a hat on my way out the door. I take my truck instead of my bike. The adrenaline rush I get from my bike can be a lot to handle, and I don't need any of that tonight.

I pull up to the theater right on time and park far away like I always do, taking my time as I walk up to the building. I approach and there are lots of people all around. I look for Alexa and Vincent, but don't spot them.

I lean up against the hard, brick wall and put my hands in my pockets. Looking down, I kick the loose gravel with my boots. Just two hours, and then I'll be home. If I weren't so tired it wouldn't be so bad. I check my phone noticing that those fuckers are late. I hate it when people aren't on time; I sure as hell can't show up late to a fire. Why does everyone else not give a shit about running on time?

When I take my eyes off of the ground, I look up and am immediately connected to a cute blonde. I watch her as she gets out of an Audi A4. Her red flats hit the pavement, and she slings a huge purse over her shoulder. She walks and I swear she is heading right towards me. I get a sense of déjà vu, like I've seen her before. My eyes scan down her perfectly built body — man, she's ridiculous. Her boobs are about to pop out of the top of her dress and those long, tan legs make my dick stir. *Fuck.*

My daydream is interrupted by my brother and Alexa as they approach her. Alexa hugs her and they continue towards me. Shit, this is the girl Vincent was telling me about. I fidget with the bill of my hat and then push myself off the wall.

"Come on, you know how cold theaters get, and you're barely wearing any clothes," Alexa says.

That's right, she is barely wearing any clothes, and I want to see her in even less. "I'll keep her warm," I say and can't help the smirk that's on my face.

She laughs at me. *Ouch.*

"I'll be just fine, thank you very much," she says in a mocking tone.

What the hell? I try again, giving her my best smile. "Are you sure? I'm happy to do the job."

She rolls her eyes at me and Vincent interjects. "All right, guys, let's not start the night off fighting. Cara, this is my brother, Abel. Abel, this is Cara, Alexa's best friend."

Suddenly I feel nervous reaching for her hand to kiss the top of it; this has to get her to warm up to me and stop being so cold. "It's a pleasure to meet you, Cara." I say and notice a small tattoo on the inside of her wrist. That's where I know her from — she's a nurse at University Hospital. I knew I had seen her before. I rode in with a patient once during transport while providing care. How could I forget her — not to mention how gorgeous she is — and those eyes? Yeah, this is definitely her. She has the most alluring aqua-colored eyes I've ever seen.

She pulls her hand back and wipes it on my shoulder. Everyone laughs at her gesture, and we head inside the theater. I tag along still in a fog; I could never forget the color of her eyes.

~ *Cara* ~

Why will my hair never cooperate? Not that it matters, but still, I don't want to look like garbage. I try again to pull my brush through my thick blond hair. I look over my shoulder at the clock on my nightstand. *Damn it.* I'm running late — again. I finish ripping the brush through my tangled strands. God, it needs a cut; it's almost to my ass. I slide on my red, patent leather flats and leave my room.

I have ten minutes to make it to the theater to meet my best friend, Alexa, and her new boyfriend, Vincent. Alexa said Vincent's brother is going to be there. She also told me he's covered in tattoos, which is my typical MO, but I've turned over a new leaf. I know it's going to be hard to resist, but that was the old Cara. The new Cara has sworn off tattooed bad boys.

Sliding behind the wheel of my Audi A4, I toss my purse on the passenger seat and fly out of the neighborhood. Of course traffic sucks; it's always bad in Denver this time of day. I roll along, wishing I could go faster, but I can't. You know what, who cares? It's not like I care what this guy thinks, and Alexa is always late.

I pull up to the theater and it takes forever to find a parking spot close to the entrance. Once I do, I'm out and heading towards the front. I look for Alexa and Vincent, but don't see them. Ahh, there they are.

"Hey, girl. You look cute. I hope you brought a sweater," Alexa says.

"Thanks, and no, I didn't. Why would I need a sweater in August?"

"Come on, you know how cold theaters get, and you're barely wearing any clothes."

Before I can answer I look up and see a tattooed god. *Shit.* Is that Vincent's brother? As we walk towards him, his eyes are glued to mine, and my heart starts to race. His hat is low, just how I like. He has his hands tucked into his pockets, making his forearms flex and his tattoos that much more visible. I look away from his hazel eyes. *Pull your shit together, Cara. You're done with guys like this.*

"I'll keep her warm," he says.

The hell you will.

It's time to be a bitch. I laugh at him, "I'll be just fine, thank you very much."

"Are you sure? I'm happy to do the job," he says looking deep into my eyes. His intensity makes me instantly wet between my legs. It takes all of my willpower to not play right into his game. Then he grabs my hand and kisses the top of it. My body tingles from his touch, and instantly I want more.

Fuck. I need more.

As I snap out of it, I pull my hand away from his and wipe it on his shoulder. I will *not* be hurt by another asshole with tattoos. Quickly I walk ahead of him and latch onto Alexa, leaving Abel behind and pushing away the emotions he has coursing through my body.

Acknowledgements

To have this book completed is a dream come true. To allow that dream to become a reality, is first and foremost, because of my husband, William. This book would not be possible if it wasn't for you. You sparked this idea within me and motivated me beyond belief. You dealt with many late nights and months of excessive laziness. I'm indebted to you, always and forever. I love you beyond words.

To my best friend Kate, you are the dirtiest snot I know, and I wouldn't have you any other way. Thank you for dealing with my obsessiveness and constant text messages. You had a dream I would write a book, and little did you know, I had just started writing. If that's not fate I don't know what is.

To my amazing editor, Mary Kelley, of Adept Edits. There are not enough words to describe how appreciative I am to have you in my life. You are extremely talented at what you do. Thank you for the countless hours of help, guidance, and yes, even yelling. You gave me the upmost amount of confidence within myself and helped me to mold this story into the perfect tale that it is today. I could *not* have completed this project without you. I enjoyed being tangled up with you in a war of words and look forward to many more.

To the best group of beta readers a girl could ask for. JC Emery, all I can say is, 'kiss on the mouth' because I owe you one. You spent more time than I even knew was humanly possible on this project. You made me laugh, cry, and most importantly, you made me become a better writer. Thank you from the bottom of my heart. RL Griffin, you neglected your family to indulge in the world I created and gave me nothing but kudos. Thank you. Katie Mac, thank you for taking the time to read my book while being beyond busy. I will forever be grateful for your open and honest feedback.

For my media team, whose countless hours of help and dealing with my incisiveness made this book a reality. Thank you all. Allie Brennan of B Design. I think we did three different covers, and you *never* complained. Third time's a charm, girl. You nailed it. Danielle Torella, you created a *true* masterpiece and captured exactly what I wanted in the photo trailer for Alexa and Vincent. I appreciate your patience and for making change after change while never complaining.

Then there are all of the amazing authors I have met along this journey. There are too many of you to name.

You all know who you are, and I appreciate the hours of conversations and help. What once was the unknown for me has now been discovered because of all of your help and guidance.

And last but certainly not least, to the readers and bloggers. I hope you all enjoyed Fatalism and becoming entangled in Alexa and Vincent's world as much as I enjoyed writing it.